COLE'S SAGA:

FEMA WARS

Book 2

By

AJ Newman

*

Acknowledgments

This book is dedicated to Patsy, my beautiful wife of thirty-four years, who assists with everything from Beta reading to censor duties. She enables me to write, golf, and enjoy my life with her and our mob of Shih Tzu's.

Thanks to Wes, David, Jeanette, and Mitchell who are Beta readers for this novel. They gave many suggestions that helped improve the cover and readability of my book.

Thanks to WMHCheryl at http://wmhcheryl.com/services-for-authors/ for the great proofreading.

The excellent cover design was by Mark / AKA Gig Freak at Fiverr   https://www.fiverr.com/gig_freak

Thanks to the folks I met in Kentucky at Calvert City, Paducah, and Graham for welcoming me into their cities. Cole's Saga Book 2 is based in those Western Kentucky cities and the area from there to Oregon.

AJ Newman

*

Published by Newalk LLC.

Owensboro, Kentucky

☆

Chapter 1

16 miles south of Dutchtown, Missouri

The road behind them was forlorn and desolate. The streets weren't used much now since the shit hit the fan so grass and weeds now choked the sides and crept into every crack in the backwoods road. Every highway and road they traveled on so far had been covered with leaves, twigs, and small limbs. Some even had large trees across them. It was now midsummer in the Missouri heat and humidity was stifling as it was typical in these parts of the country. They shied away from Highway 55 for fear of running into the FEMA troops and being recaptured.

Gemma sat beside her new husband, Cole, in the front seat of the old Ford Bronco with a smile on her face. Cole had his hand on her thigh, which made Gemma feel safe and comfortable. She had only known this wonderful man for a short time but had fallen deeply in love with him and knew that he would protect her forever. They had been through a lot the last few months from being captured by slavers in California to spending a couple of months working at a FEMA slave camp. Cole had brought this band of unlikely companions together and led them in a daring escape from

FEMA. Cole had saved her cousin Molly, her twin sister Jenny, and her from a horrible life of depravity in the FEMA camp.

Gemma turned her body and twisted her head to look back at her cousin and sister in the back seat of the SUV. The two women slept even though the truck bounced along avoiding stalled cars, breaks in the pavement, and downed trees. They had to take turns pulling guard duty every day and grabbed a few hours of shuteye anytime they could.

Gemma turned back to look at her husband and ran her hand across the stubble on his chin. She leaned over to him and laid her head on his shoulder. "Honey, I'm worried about Jack and Madison. Both were running a fever at the last stop, and Jack shouldn't be driving the truck. Normally, he is like a puppy when Carole gets after him to take care of himself, but he wouldn't even let her take his temperature. Honey, Madison was barely awake and has a raging fever. I hate to say it, but we could lose one of them."

Cole glanced down and saw the beautiful redheaded woman nuzzling on his neck. They had only been together for several weeks, but he had fallen for her at first sight, months ago on the day they were captured. "Damn you feel good against my neck. You might want to stop that or I may have to pull over and take you up into the bushes."

"Cole, I was talking about something serious. We have to do something about Jack and Madison."

"Babe I'm sorry, but it's hard to concentrate with you kissing on my neck. Yeah, I saw all of that myself. I tried to get Jack to take it easy for a while, but he wants to prove himself to the others and won't listen again."

Gemma took Cole's hand and squeezed it. "I don't know Babe, but my gut tells me that we need to stop long enough for them to recover from their wounds."

"Oh, shit that could take weeks, maybe months."

5

Jack was driving the lead vehicle in the small convoy. His wife Carole sat beside him, and Deacon and Madison sat in the back seat. Carole was trying to console her husband who was upset about a letter he'd read that night. His mother had written his son Joe and him a series of letters before she died. Her lawyer had presented them to Joe and Jack after the funeral. Both sets of letters contained Agnes Harp's wisdom and advice from the grave for her son, Jack, and grandson, Joe.

Joe had cherished and learned a great deal from his Grandma's letters; however, his father, Jack, didn't like the tone of his mother's letters to him. Jack never bought into the doomsday prepping that his mother kept pushing on him and Joe. She tried desperately over the years to get both to learn survival skills and stock up on food and weapons. Neither, had done an adequate job of preparing for the apocalypse, but at least Joe took his mother's letters to heart and was a quick learner. Jack felt that the letters put him down and made him feel like his mom thought he was a failure. Jack had done well running his business, but wouldn't listen to his mother's rants about an upcoming apocalypse.

Dear Jack:

I had a good day today, as I often do between the chemo treatments. I asked Alfred to take me over to the cabins and bunker east of Ashland. We took the company helicopter down to Ashland and rented an SUV for the trip up into the mountains. We visited the bunker but didn't make it over to the cabins because of a massive thunderstorm. I thought about you and Joe and how you two are unprepared for the apocalypse.

I deeply care for both of you, but I'd be lying if I didn't say that I'm very disappointed that you haven't taken being prepared more seriously. I know you put your heart and soul into your business, but when the shit hits the fan. Your business won't mean diddley.

You need to ditch that money-grubbing wife of yours, find a nice lady that cares for you more than your money and prepare for the apocalypse. Son, if you just paid attention to the news and current events, you would be scared. North Korea or Iran could launch a nuclear attack from ships off our coast and kill our grid. The EMP blasts would kill most electronics. If that doesn't scare you, I don't know what to tell you.

I know that you think I'm just an addled brained old broad harping on her pet peeve, but I really do care for you and want you to survive. Your dumbass sister and her family will probably die in the first few months of an apocalypse. I have much higher hopes for you and Joe.

Well, it's time to say goodbye. Alfred and I are taking the chopper over to Bandon for some seafood. Tell your miserable wife that your senile mother said hello.

Love Mom

Carole had read the letter that pissed her husband off and tried to console him. "Jack, Honey, you know your mom meant well, and she was right about your ex-wife. You take these letters too seriously. No one, well at least very few people prepared for this damned apocalypse. Don't be so harsh on yourself. I wish you would just take the advice from the letters, use the good stuff, and ignore her criticism. Remember you did take her advice and marry me and started some prepping before TSHTF. Your mom can't be all bad."

Jack reached across and held his wife's hand. "I know you're right that I should dwell on the good stuff. After all, mom did tell me to ditch that harpy and marry you. I think that's what eats me up, is that she always reminded me that I could've done better had I joined dad's company. Harp Enterprises meant everything to mom and dad. Hell, it made them millionaires. They offered me a job at least once a year for my entire adult life, but I wanted to make it on my own. The funny thing is that now, after the apocalypse, money doesn't mean shit. Hey, what's that up ahead?"

Jack saw the kids and hit the brakes as he saw an old truck around the bend just behind the kids. "Son of a bitch, it's an ambush, and the kids were the bait."

The Bronco slid to a stop. Carole saw several kids on the road. One was a baby. "Stop, there are babies in the road."

Before Jack could react, Carole jumped out to save the kids.

Cole saw the Bronco in front of him slide to a stop with tires squealing and smoke billowing. The smell of burning rubber permeated the early morning. Cole yelled, "What in the hell is Jack doing now? Babe, do you see anything?"

Gemma looked to the left and right of the stationary vehicle only to see Carole and Jack jump out and move ahead of their truck with reckless abandon. "Cole, I don't like this at all. They should have stopped and signaled for us to check the situation out before running into a possible... Oh, shit, look to the right about halfway up the hill. It's an ambush."

Cole saw the men behind the fallen tree and yelled, "Jack, it's an ambush. Retreat!"

Jack didn't reply, so Cole took action and barked orders. "Girls get out and take up a defensive position. Molly, take Jenny to the right and Gemma will go with me to the left."

Cole stayed low as he left his Bronco and ran into the thick brush and woods. The grass and bushes were still wet from the dew. The ground was mushy because of the rain for the past two days. Water ran six inches deep in the ditch beside the road.

Cole stopped and checked to see if Jack and Carole were okay. He saw Carole holding a bundle wrapped in a blue blanket with her good arm. She hid behind the Bronco as Jack tugged a small boy to safety behind the vehicle. Deacon huddled behind the vehicle and aimed his rifle at the men up in the woods. Madison lay in the floorboard of the Bronco due to her wounds from the last gunfight. Deacon was trying to protect her amid the confusion.

Cole waved at Gemma to follow him as he worked to get a clear view of the area in front of and to the left of the lead Bronco. Cole wondered why the men hadn't shot at Jack as he low crawled another fifty yards ahead of Jack's position in an attempt to flank the ambushers. The road curved to Cole's right and was covered in debris, leaves, and grass, which was growing through every crack in the pavement. He spotted an old truck parked in the weeds alongside the road, and the reason they hadn't attacked was now apparent to him. They wanted both of the Broncos and didn't want to take a chance on damaging them in a firefight.

Gemma saw Jack edging closer to the end of the Bronco and caught Cole's attention. "Cole, I think Jack is going to try to run with the kid in tow. Crap, Carole has joined him."

Cole knew he would draw attention to himself, but he still frantically waved and yelled at Jack to stay put. Shots rang out from the hillside at Cole and Jack as he tugged the boy toward the woods. Several bullets struck the road around Jack with bits of rock and bullet fragments spraying the boy and Jack. Carole drew back to the Bronco and hid with the baby. The boy fell to the ground as Jack retreated to the Bronco for cover. Jack had been wounded by several of the ricochets.

A bullet ricocheted off the pavement, and a small fragment hit Cole's right shoulder. There was a painful sting as the fragment struck his shoulder, and then blood trickled down his sleeve. Cole ignored the pain and returned fire at the men up on the hillside. Gemma, Molly, and Jenny joined in directing withering fire onto the men. Two died instantly as multiple shots struck their torsos.

Deacon yelled, "I got one." He then turned and shot another man trying to sneak up behind his position.

Gemma saw movement behind a bush, took aim, and fired. Gemma yelled at her husband. "Cole, there are two men behind the orange bush. I killed the third one. They're trying to escape."

Cole saw the bush and movement; he aimed and placed two shots into the left side of the bush. A body rolled down the hill, and a woman raised her hands to surrender. The fight was over as quickly as it started. Cole posted Molly and Deacon to guard them while they attended to their wounds and interrogated the young woman captive. Jenny tended to Jack's wounds while Cole and Gemma questioned the woman.

Gemma had her rifle trained on the short dark haired woman and made her squat down to sit on the pavement. Cole walked up and poked her on the side of the head with his rifle. "What kind of dumb shit were you and your friends trying to do? Was it worth the lives of the boy and your friends just to steal our trucks?"

The woman looked up and said, "We have to capture five people a day to sell to FEMA, or they will kill us."

Cole replied, "Take your kids and get your sorry ass out of my sight before I slit your damned throat."

They quickly regrouped and headed on to the next city. It was only a short trip to Dutchtown, where they thought they would just spend the night there, but the following day both Madison and Jack were running high fevers. Carole applied the antibiotic salve to the wounds as they had done in the past and placed cold, wet towels on their foreheads but nothing seemed to do the trick. Cole's injury from the ricochet was doing well and needed no attention.

While Carole and Jenny tended to the wounded, Cole took Gemma and Molly with him to scout the area. While they still had plenty of supplies and gasoline, Cole thought that it was best to use the downtime to scrounge the area to top off supplies and always be prepared. Deacon stayed back with the others to provide security and to check the Broncos to make sure everything was in running order.

Deacon caught Cole off to the side when he returned and said, "I am beginning to see what you tried to tell us about Jack. He's a great man, but he just doesn't think things through. I like him, but he's gonna get us killed if we don't do something about it. Cole, you're our leader, and I think the group needs to talk about it and figure out a plan to get Jack under control."

"Deacon, I just don't know if Jack gets it. As you mentioned, I was trying to think things through and always have a plan A and a plan B just in case the shit hits the fan. We should never go into a situation without scouting the area first. As my friend Earl used to say, I'm gonna sit down with Jack and tell him 'where the bear ate the buckwheat.' Either we get him under control, or he has to leave the group. No questions asked."

Deacon looked down at his feet. "I hate that it has come to that, but I have to think about myself and Madison. She's lying on that dirty bed and might die because of his rash behavior. You can count on Madison and me to back your play."

"Thanks, buddy I knew I could count on you in a pinch."

"Cole what will you do if Jack and Madison can't travel," Molly asked.

Cole looked in Gemma's face as he answered. "Molly I just don't know. Jack's stupidity has put us all in trouble, and now we're paying for his rash action. If I had to guess, we're faced with a possible delay of a month or two and even the death of Jack or Madison."

Gemma gasped, "Surely they won't die from those wounds. The wounds weren't that serious."

The realization that the apocalypse was real and that the day-to-day things that had made their lives more comfortable and safer were now gone was finally settling into the girl's minds. They couldn't take for granted modern medicines and the availability of doctors. People could actually die from a small scratch or an infected tooth.

Cole replied, "I guess we all have to come to grips with the fact that this is a different world and we're living back in the 1850s. We've all grown accustomed to being able to run to a doctor or an urgent care center for all our boo-boos and issues. All of those modern antibiotics and vaccines that tamed the viruses and germs are no longer available. All you have to do is look in Carole's medical bag, and you will see that she only has a few bottles of aspirin, several tubes of antibiotic salve, and bandages. We have to avoid getting injured."

Molly pulled the three of them together and hugged them for a minute before tears flowed from her eyes. "This is almost too much to take in. How can we survive and how can we avoid injuries?"

Cole squeezed his wife Gemma and kissed Molly on the forehead. "Molly, most people survived the 1850s, and we can survive also. I guess that we're going to have two months down time here in Dutchtown, and we need to make use of that time. We need to dig out all of Carole's books on medicine, herbal remedies, and old-time healing to help us prepare for our future. We also can't go charging into ambushes nor pick fights with strangers."

Gemma wiped the tears from her eyes and looked into Cole's eyes. "Honey this scares the hell out of me. What the hell do we do if one of the ladies gets pregnant?"

"Babe, I guess we'll just have to do it the old-fashioned way. Women have been having babies for millions of years without fancy medical facilities or wonder drugs."

Gemma gently punched Cole in the stomach. "And a lot of babies and mamas died back then."

Molly stuttered and then tapped Cole on the shoulder. "Cole we've been dancing around the elephant in the room, and we've got to do something about it now. This is the second time in a few days that Jack has almost gotten several people killed. We need to help him get well and let him and Carole do what they want to, but I for one do not want Jack with our group. He's going to get one or all of us killed."

"Molly I just had that conversation with Deacon, and we both agree with you that something has to be done. I plan to have a blunt talk with Jack as soon as he's able to hold a coherent conversation. He can either straighten his sorry ass up or get the hell out of our group. My patience is gone, and it's time to kick ass and take names. Oh Gemma, please talk with Jenny and make sure she's on the same page that we're on."

Cole caught Carole off to the side away from Jack and tried to talk sense to her. "Carole you know that Jack almost got several of us killed again by charging into that ambush. He agreed many times to stop anytime he saw something strange or different on the road and to let me assess the situation. We should've backed up and sent scouts in to see what was happening before being sucked into an ambush."

"But there were babies in the middle of the street," Carole cried out.

"Yes there were, and they were being used as bait to draw us into a damned ambush. We can't let our hearts overrule our heads, or we will all certainly die. Carole, the rest of the group has decided that if Jack ever does anything like this again, we will leave him behind. You would be free to come along with us, but I guess you will stay with your husband if he can't pull his head out of his ass. I'm sorry for talking so bluntly, but Jack is responsible for the deaths of Sarah and Pete and almost got the rest of us killed today."

Tears were flowing from Carole's eyes as she tried to compose herself. "Jack is a wonderful man, but it's killing him that he's not in charge and honestly doesn't know what to do in most of these situations. He can't come to grips with reporting to an 18-year-old boy."

Cole patted Carole on the back. "Jack and I had a serious talk after the last follow-up, and he agreed to follow my lead. Jack is a good man, but he doesn't have the experience that I've gained fighting the thugs and criminals up in Oregon since the lights went out. Deacon and I are going to sit down with Jack in a few minutes and lay down the law. We will tell him that if he can't fall in line, we will ask him to leave the group. I'm sorry Carole, but that's the way it has to be to keep the rest of us safe from his mistakes."

Carole cried as she replied, "I don't like it, but I understand. I will stay with Jack regardless of what happens."

Cole gathered the rest of his group as Carole went to tend to Jack and Madison. "Gang, I just explained the situation to Carole, and while she doesn't like it, she understands the situation. She will stay with Jack regardless of the outcome. Let's give her a few minutes to check on Jack and Madison, and then we will go over and talk to Jack. I'll do the talking; I just need your support if he gets pissed."

Cole led the crew over to the place under the trees where Jack and Madison lay on blankets on the ground. As they approached, Carole stood up with a frown on her face. "Cole, Madison has been unconscious for several hours, and Jack just passed out a few minutes ago. They both have high fevers, and there's not much I can do but give them aspirin and make them comfortable. I'll check my medical books to see if I should cool them off or keep them warm, but I'm out of any medicine that would help them. We have to make it a high priority to find antibiotics and other medicines."

Cole looked at the team as he shook his head. "Carole, obviously we need to stay here until their fevers break. Team, we need to scout for a place to stay short-term until they get well enough to travel. Gemma, you and Molly, will go with me, and we will scout the area for abandoned houses or cabins. Jenny, stay and guard our wounded and vehicles. Deacon, please look around the immediate area for any food or dangers as we scout the larger area. We all need to look for the antibiotics that Carole needs."

Cole led the women around the fringes of the town looking for abandoned homes and cabins. Many had been burned to the ground, and the others looted, and only a few would be suitable for their use. Several times Cole had to caution the ladies to lie down in the grass as people passed. Several of the groups looked like hard cases and were filthy. One group openly talked about making methamphetamine and trading it to other drug addicts in the area for sex, food, and weapons.

They traveled through the woods staying off the highways until they were on the north side of Dutchtown. The north end of Dutchtown appeared to be free of some of the scum they'd seen during their travels around the town. They lay on top of a grassy hill watching several homes in a valley when Molly got Cole's attention.

"Cole, look a family is coming towards us. They have clean clothes and children traveling with them. Let's stop them and try to gain information about the area."

Cole moved his binoculars to spy on the approaching family. They were about 500 yards away and appeared to have a mother, father, and three children in their group. The adults and the oldest boy carried rifles, and a younger boy had a shotgun. All of them had backpacks, and the father and oldest son carried large duffel bags.

"Girls, how can we get these people to stop and talk with us without scaring the hell out of them or getting our asses shot?"

Gemma pulled a white handkerchief from her pocket, found a stick long enough to make a flagpole, and tied the handkerchief to the rod. "Cole, don't say anything but one of us women need to approach them with the flag of truce and ask them to talk with us."

Cole turned to his wife. "Gemma, I don't like it, but I think you're right. They don't look like the kind of people who would shoot a woman. They do look like the kind of people who are running scared and would shoot a man that approached them with a rifle. Be careful."

Gemma rose up from the grass with the flag held high and began walking towards the strangers. It only took a few seconds for one of the kids to notice Gemma and point her out to their dad. The entire family dropped to the ground with guns pointed at the stranger. Gemma held the flag with both hands, stopped, and slowly turned around so they could see she wasn't armed. "Can I come closer and talk with you."

"Stop there. Don't come any closer. What do you want?"

Gemma now rethought her idea of approaching the strangers. She couldn't help but have a bit of fear in her heart as her hands trembled and her knees shook with the weapons pointed directly at her. She took a deep breath and said, "I come in peace and only have a few innocent questions for you. We mean you no harm and just need your help."

A man's voice came booming over the tall grass. "What do you mean we? I only see you. Is this an ambush?"

Cole was now afraid that his sweet Gemma might be in danger, so he stood up with hands raised high and spoke up. "I'm Cole Biggs, and I mean you no harm. Like you, we are only trying to survive and need some information about this area. Do you live around here or are you from here?"

The stranger was very cautious as he answered Cole. He stayed hidden behind a log and kept his family hidden from sight. "Man there are plenty of bad guys out here, and we don't know if you're one of them. We've been robbed, harassed, and nearly killed a dozen times over the last few months, so get the hell outta my face."

Cole now knew he wouldn't get any information from these people and they were probably just passing through as his group was. "Good luck and I pray that you get to your destination safely. We will back away and let you pass safely. We mean you no harm. Have a good day."

Gemma slowly backed up towards Cole's position with her hands still raised high. She backed into Cole who wrapped his arms around her making her feel safe again.

"Babe, I don't think we will ever do that again. Even the good folks are scared shitless and might shoot us just for asking a question. We were just talking about how to get better at this shit, and we've already screwed up. Any one of those kids could have an itchy trigger finger and blow the hell out of us. We sure as hell don't need more wounded people."

Molly came running to them and wrapped her arms around both. "I thought that crazy asshat was going to shoot you. How can we make people believe that were not trying to hurt them?"

"That my dear appears to be the biggest question of the day. I don't have a clue. I guess we just have to judge everyone else by what's happened to us. Almost everyone we run into has either tried to kill us, enslave us or rob us," said Cole.

After a short rest, Cole led the girls on around Dutchtown and found an old abandoned group of cabins circling a large lake. It appeared to be a rustic resort out in the woods of Missouri. Cole counted 35 cottages, an office, a large events building, and a rather large barn circling the lake. Most of the cabins had broken windows, and several had their doors bashed in. He and the girls cleared each cabin one by one just as Earl and Wes had taught him to do back in Oregon. He took no chances and decided not to divide his force even though it would've taken half as long to clear the area from all danger.

All of the buildings had been picked clean of anything usable over the last year since the shit hit the fan. Several of the cabins could be used for shelter if they were cleaned up. "Girls, come with me so we can scout the area around this resort for any dangers or supplies."

They thoroughly searched the area around the resort and found no dangers or food; however, they did find several farmhouses that had old gardens. All of the gardens had volunteer plants growing at random in the garden plots. They found numerous plants that had tomatoes, cucumbers, and potatoes growing wild. All of the farmhouses had fruit trees and blackberry bushes.

Molly looked at the plants, trees, and bushes. "Cole it will be several weeks before most of these plants bear anything edible. I hope like hell we're not here at harvest time because that would mean we're 2 to 3 more months behind schedule."

The humidity in southern Missouri was quite high and a light fog settled in as they walked at dusk. Gemma clamped her hand down on Cole's when a large owl hooted and suddenly flew past them. Both of the women screamed and ducked as the colossal bird flapped its wings above their heads.

"Damn, my mighty warriors are scared shitless by this bird. All of you have killed men and women in face-to-face combat but are frightened by a bird," Cole jested.

Molly jumped up and got in Cole's face. "You know that's not fair. Just the other day that spider web caught you across the brow and you looked like a ninja warrior jumping and dancing to knock the spider off your head. You were screaming like a child."

Cole continued laughing until his wound hurt. He finally composed himself. "Molly that's ancient history. I wish to hell that I'd had my camera phone recording you ladies jumping and dancing while trying to swat some monster out of your hair. Thank God, it wasn't anything serious because it was so damn funny. I'm sorry but..." Cole broke out laughing again. Gemma tackled Cole and brought him to his knees, and Molly piled on tickling him.

Gemma said, "We better stop, or he'll piss his pants."

Cole and his ragged team arrived back at the camp just as the sun went down. Cole and Deacon compared notes from their scouting trips and decided to move to the cabins early the next day.

☆

Chapter 2

Cole rolled over, and his arm didn't land on Gemma's side as he expected. He had only slept for about five hours when he woke up wide-eyed and rolled over to find Gemma gone. His mind was fuzzy, but he did remember that Gemma was on guard duty early that morning. Cole saw a soft glow to the east where the sun was thinking about rising for the day. While the air was clean and smelled pure, it was still sticky with humidity. The nighttime temperature only dropped to around 75°, which made sleeping barely tolerable. He pulled himself up and out of his hammock. He looked around the camp and saw Gemma patrolling around the SUVs.

A glint of light caught Cole's eye. He saw Carole using a small flashlight as she daubed Jack's forehead with a damp cloth. It had been a week since they'd set up camp at the old rustic resort. It was too hot to sleep in the cabins, so they slept outside in hammocks and pallets on the porches. This was only possible because Jenny had found several storage lockers with camping supplies, which included mosquito netting. The mosquitoes in southern Missouri attacked from dusk to dawn. They were also lucky because they found several cans of mosquito repellent and citronella buckets in several of the abandoned homes.

Cole slid his clothes on, tied his shoes, and then walked towards Gemma. She was wearing a tank top, shorts, and tennis shoes. Her hair was tied back in a ponytail, and it swung with every movement of her head. "Anything new or different tonight?"

Gemma looked up and saw Cole and a smile came over her face. "Nope, it was the same old same old all night long. Owls hooted, dogs barked, and a bunch of damn cats must've been having an orgy the way they were making noise. Come here and hold me if you can stand the smell."

Cole wrapped his arms around her and instantly felt her clammy tank top that was soaked with sweat and almost gagged at the aroma of Deep Woods Off coming from his lady. "Damn girl, you're almost as sweat-soaked as I am. I hope the skeeters didn't eat you alive last night. Judging from the pine scent of the mosquito repellent you fought a good battle."

Cole kissed Gemma and ran his fingers through her damp ponytail. "Babe, I guess we both stink and need a good bath. What do you think about us going to that creek about a mile north of here for a swim and a bath?"

"Yep, Hubble Creek or the lake would be great if we could go there alone," Gemma said.

"No chance of that today, sister," Jenny said as she walked up. "We don't have time for that fool around stuff today. Remember, Cole promised that we could send a team into Cape Girardeau to look for supplies. A nice swim and a bath after that would be fantastic!"

Cole frowned as he turned to Gemma. "Damn, little sister has us there. I have to hit the road to Cape Girardeau this morning. Ladies if it's okay with you, I'm going to take Deacon and Molly into town with me today. I think it's relatively safe here and you too can mind the store while I'm gone. Keep an eye out for trouble and stay sharp. I hope not, but I might need some firepower today."

Gemma and Jenny sulked a little bit and then Gemma grabbed Cole's arm. "Cole I know Deacon is bigger than I am, but I'm a better shot and twice as mean. I know you've noticed that he takes too long to decide when to pull the trigger. That could get my baby killed."

"Hey Babe, I totally agree with you. I plan to work with Deacon on this trip to improve his skills and his response time. You know I'd rather have you with me than anyone in the world."

"Are you sure you aren't doing this just to protect me from danger?"

Cole placed his hands on Gemma's shoulders. "Girl, I will always do my best to protect you, but this will possibly put you in more harm. We scouted this area several times over the last several weeks, but there are always people moving around and even possibly people hiding in the woods, so you really need to keep a sharp eye on the area. Deacon will never improve unless I work with him and help him improve his skills. This is what I need you to do to help me accomplish that task."

Gemma still didn't like it, but she understood Cole's thinking and wanted to support him as much as possible. "While you three are gone, Jenny and I will be stationed at opposite ends of the camp and stay on guard until you return. After breakfast, we will make arrangements so that we can stay in place until you get back. Cole, how long do you think you'll be gone?"

"Babe my wild ass guess is about 6 to 8 hours to search the city and find the supplies we need."

"Darling, please break the search of the city into three or four shorter trips. Please don't be gone more than 4 to 5 hours. I know you have faith in Jenny and me, but we would be scared shitless here alone by ourselves. You know darn well Carole is in no shape to help us if we're attacked."

Cole was impatient to scout the city but quickly realized she was right about the dangers of leaving them alone. "The more I think about it, I know you're right, and I'm so sorry for even thinking about leaving y'all alone that long. Now let's get some grub and get this party started."

After breakfast, Cole checked Molly and Deacon's weapons and equipment. Molly's gear was in good shape, her rifle and pistol were thoroughly clean, and she had the tools Cole had told both of them to bring along on the trip. Cole was disappointed as he inspected Deacon's weapons. They had not been recently cleaned or oiled. Small rust deposits had already started on the barrel of Deacon's rifle. Deacon didn't have several of the tools that Cole had asked him to bring along with them.

"Deacon your rifle is starting to rust, and your 9 mm is dirty. You didn't bring the pry bar or rope. Please, quickly go clean your weapons, and I'll fetch the pry bar and rope for you," Cole tersely said.

Deacon was mad at himself and said, "Cole, I promise to do better. Hell, I've been a football player all my life, and I never had to do anything this serious. Please help me, and I promise I'll do better."

"Deacon old buddy, I figured that out a while back, and we'll work on that. I need you to help me build my endurance and strength, and I'm going to help make a warrior out of you," Cole said as he laughed.

Deacon slapped Cole on the back. "We're going to make a damn good team my friend."

It only took Deacon a little over an hour to clean his weapons and be ready to travel to Cape Girardeau. The south end of the city was only about 3 to 4 miles from their camp. The lower end of Cape Girardeau consisted mainly of quarries, manufacturing, and petrochemical companies. Cole led his team along Highway 74 E until they saw the first large industrial complex. Even at 9 AM in the morning, the air was muggy and thick enough to cut with a knife. The sun was hot on their faces, which reminded Cole that they would need sunscreen.

Cole hoped that most people wouldn't think about scavenging industrial complexes for food or medical supplies. Earl had told him that all large industrial complexes had medical supplies and some even had nurses on duty. These places could be a gold mine of the medical supplies they desperately needed. Earl also told him that many were also large enough to have their own cafeterias and kitchens.

The buildings were scattered around a vast quarry. None of the group had a clue what this business did for a living other than making a massive hole in the ground. Molly pointed at the nicest looking building, and they walked along close to another building as they watched for intruders and other dangers. Cole was shocked when they found the front door was intact and locked. He didn't want to be the one to break their fancy door, so they went to the side of the building and broke a window to gain entrance. Cole cleared the window frame of glass and climbed through the window. He went through the office and opened the door for the others.

They began searching the office room by room and brought any treasures they found to the lobby. Initially, they only saw a few Band-Aids, bags of candy, and potato chips. They moved on to the back of the office where they found much nicer and larger offices. All of them had small refrigerators, and a few of them had cans of soda, whiskey, and a lot of spoiled food. They found a few backpacks with laptops and notebooks but nothing much else of interest.

Molly found the door at the back of the central office complex that led into a small cafeteria. There was a bank of vending machines at the end of the room. They still contained snacks, sandwiches, and canned food.

Molly was the first to see the full vending machines. "Holy shit we've hit the mother lode. I see canned chili, beef stew, chicken soup, and potato chips out the ass."

Deacon gave a hearty laugh. "Girl you got a potty mouth."

Molly took the butt of her 9 mm and broke the glass on the snack vending machine and threw a bag of corn chips to Deacon. "I know. I was raised better than that, but I ain't gonna stop cussing any time soon."

Cole looked at the cornucopia of snacks, canned goods, bottled water, and soft drinks and wondered how they were to get all of this back to their camp. "We should have driven one of the trucks over here. Let's look for some medical supplies and then come back tomorrow to pick most of this up. Molly, stop stuffing your face with chocolate and listen."

"Damn Cole, this Hershey bar is almost as good as sex."

Deacon laughed and patted Molly on the back. "Cole what will you do with us reprobates? This girl is about as common as they come."

Cole grinned as he shook his head. "Come on and stop screwing around and let's go find the medical supplies. A place this damned large at least has to have a first aid room."

Molly pointed at a notice on the wall. "I believe that evacuation plan has a little box on it that says FA. I'll bet my ass that FA means that's the first aid room. Follow me, boys."

Molly ripped the evacuation route plan off-the-wall and headed down the hallway. She went out the back door and crossed a small courtyard into another building. Just inside the doorway on the left was the first aid room. It wasn't only a small first-aid room with Band-Aids. It had a nurse's office and a stock room for medical supplies. The best part was that no one had ransacked the medical supplies before they got there. They loaded up two duffel bags with every antibiotic they could find then added items from the list Carole had given them.

Cole looked at the filled bags and stacks of supplies. "Ladies we need to head on back to the cabins. We have more than 20 men could pack. Let's get these oral antibiotics back to Carole so she can get them into our patients."

Molly hefted her backpack and one of the duffel bags. "Cole, what's the plan? It's still pretty early in the day. Are we coming back with the truck and trailer?"

Cole took the duffel bag from Molly. "Deacon and I'll carry the two duffel bags along with our backpacks. You carry your backpack and a couple of those small sacks. Let's think about it for a while before we come back here in the Bronco pulling the trailer. I'd like to go unnoticed as long as possible."

Molly dropped her bags and placed her hands on her hips. Molly frowned. "We can't just leave this stuff here, someone will steal it. Let's take the time to cart it over to the production floor and hide it under some of the machinery until we can come back and pick it up."

Cole replied, "Damn, you're right. We could be collecting the stuff for someone else to steal. We'll take back what we have to have each trip and hide the extra. Then we'll make one trip through with the Bronco and trailer and pick up all the rest that we need. That should keep this operation as low-key as possible."

They stayed off the streets on the way back to the cabins, which made walking much more difficult. The bushes and weeds along the roadside were thick and tangled. Molly had to stop often to rest even though Cole and Deacon carried three times the weight that she carried. Their last stop to rest was at the edge of a small clearing. They all sat on a fallen log. It was now midday, and the heat and humidity were stifling. Molly looked up at the sky and only saw a few passing clouds moving from west to east.

Molly said, "I'd kill for a chance to sleep in an air-conditioned room tonight."

Cole laid his arm across her wet sticky back and then took his handkerchief and wet it with water from a plastic bottle. He took the damp cloth and ran it across Molly's face, neck, and shoulders. "I hate this humidity, but I also know that we will be cussing the snow and cold this winter. Molly, I'm just thankful that I have my friends with me even if y'all stink and are all sweaty."

Molly nudged Cole. "Remember you promised that we could go swimming in the creek later today. I've been looking forward to that all day long."

Molly laughed and then grinned. "We can bring some soap and wash our clothes at the same time we swim. Cole, you and Deacon had better check that creek out and make sure there are no snakes or alligators."

Deacon jumped up and said, "Come on everybody get off your butt and let's get on back to camp. I got carried away and forgot we need to get these antibiotics back to Carole."

Deacon frowned the rest of the way back to the cabins because he knew he'd forgotten about Madison and Jack lying there with fevers. When the road to the cabins came into view, Deacon sprinted the last quarter-mile to hand the antibiotics to Carole.

Carole dumped the medical supplies out on the table and sorted through them. "Here's some Keflex and two bottles of Amoxicillin. Damn, we need something stronger than those two."

She kept sorting through the bottles and packages. "Thank God here's some penicillin."

Carole crushed the penicillin tablets and mixed them into a glass of water. Deacon helped her hold Madison's head up as they tried to get Madison to drink the medicine. It took some coaxing, but Deacon finally got her to drink all of the liquid. Deacon then helped Carole hold up Jack as she forced him to drink the vile tasting concoction.

Carole made both of them as comfortable as possible. "Thank you so much for finding these medicines. It will take a while to see how effective they are but this is the only chance these two have to survive."

Cole asked, "What was wrong with the Keflex and Amoxicillin?"

Carole responded, "Those are excellent drugs for ear infections and urinary tract infections but aren't much good for deep wounds. We definitely need drugs like them, but penicillin and several more modern antibiotics are what we really need."

Jenny had stayed out of the way, as Carole tended to her patients but flagged Cole down before they sat down for their noon meal. "Cole we have a situation. I only caught a fleeting glimpse, but someone is watching us from the woods to the north. I didn't want to leave my post, so I didn't investigate but watched for them out of the corner of my eye. I signaled for Gemma to watch for them, but she never saw them."

"Did you see how many there were and what type of weapons they had?"

Jenny was a bit frustrated. "No Cole. I told you I only caught a glimpse of them. Honestly, it was more like bushes being moved and shadows in the woods."

Cole apologized and started over. "I'm sorry for being abrupt, but this could be very bad for us. We'll discuss it over lunch with the rest of the team and determine how to deal with the situation. I have to remember that not everyone out there is trying to kill us."

Jenny laughed, "But Cole, most people have been trying to harm us. I for one am glad that you are very cautious."

Cole chewed and swallowed a small piece of cold rabbit. "Jenny has seen some suspicious activity at the north end of the camp. Gemma and I are going to leave the camp heading east as if we were going back into town. Once we're out of sight and feel safe to do so, we will circle around to the north to find out who's watching us. Deacon, I need you to stay at the camp with Molly and Jenny just in case they decide to enter our camp. I don't plan to contact these people or attack them unless they attack us first."

Cole and Gemma finished their lunch, gathered their gear, and walked out of the camp heading east. Cole encouraged Gemma to laugh and joke as they walked along the road. After about a half a mile Cole and Gemma made a sharp turn into the woods going north. They waited inside the bushes for 10 minutes to see if anyone had been following them. There was no one behind them. They slowly traveled north across farmland and forest until Cole thought they had gone a mile.

The woods were infested with biting flies and mosquitoes, which made the trip tenuous at best. The insect repellent kept the mosquitoes away; however, the flies drew blood with every bite. Seeing Gemma in such pain from the bites, Cole stopped at a small spring and gathered some mud in his hands. He rubbed the mud on Gemma's arms, legs, and face before applying it generously to himself.

They stood there looking at each other and broke out in smiles. Cole said, "You look so cute with that mud on you."

"I look like crap, and I know it. You are an angel for trying to make me feel good about being covered in mud. You are my sweetheart. Of course, you look like something the dog drug in."

Cole grinned and then laughed. "At least I don't smell like dog poop."

"No baby, you don't. But you do stink."

They carefully walked on through the bushes and weeds until Cole directed them to head west. They stopped every few minutes to make sure no one was following them while watching for ambushes ahead.

The flies still swarmed around them but couldn't bite through the thick mud. Cole had to stop several times to reapply mud as they traveled along a tiny creek because the mud fell off in cakes as it dried, exposing their skin. They continued to follow the stream as it wound its way to the west. The further they went the more prominent and broader the stream became. Gemma looked down into the bright and clean water and longed to bathe the mud off her body. Gemma was gazing at the pool when Cole tapped her on the shoulder and pulled her down behind a bush. He pointed across the clearing in front of them, and she saw several people who appeared to be robbing another group of people.

"Gemma I can't tell which of the two groups we are looking for. Who are the good guys and the bad guys?"

Gemma watched carefully and noticed several events that made it clear to her who the bad guys were. She pointed several times so Cole would see the same thing she saw. One of the men slapped a young boy and then knocked a lady to the ground. Cole shook his head in agreement and then motioned for Gemma to follow him as he moved closer to the people. Cole saw an old pickup truck looming in the woods ahead, and they hid behind it as they continued to watch the struggle.

Cole desperately wanted to stay out of the fight until he saw one of the men aim his rifle at a young girl. "I'll shoot the two on the left. You kill the bastard on the right."

Cole's AR-15 barked twice followed closely by Gemma's rifle shots. All three of the asshats fell to the ground wounded or dead. Cole ran ahead of Gemma to make sure they had killed the thugs. One of the other men jumped to his feet and tried to pick up a rifle. Cole yelled, "Drop that rifle, or I'll kill you dead."

The man dropped the gun and raised his hands to the sky. Cole and Gemma walked in with their rifles aimed at the group. "Keep your hands where I can see them. We don't know you, and we don't trust you. Why were these men attacking you?"

One of the men answered, "The bastards wanted our food and what few guns we have. We are good people and don't want no trouble."

Cole looked the group over, noticed that they were all clean, and appeared to be well fed. He knew he had to get better at this, but he still couldn't tell if these are good people or bad people. He took a chance. "If you are good people why were you watching us from the woods? Don't lie to me."

The man looked startled and was about to speak when one of the women spoke up. "Sir we have been camping on this creek for several weeks trying to make sure that we didn't draw anybody's attention. There are several groups of thugs operating in this area, and we thought you might be one of them. We planned to move into some of those cabins, and you beat us to it. We need to get our kids under a roof and try to make a proper home for them."

Knowing these little kids were sleeping on the cold ground tugged at Cole's heartstrings; however, he knew he couldn't let these people move in next door to them. Before he gave the strangers the bad news, he explained to Gemma that their group would have to be on constant guard against a potential attack from these people. He then told Gemma that he would have to order them to move on out of the area or face the consequences.

Cole called the strangers to attention. "I'm sorry that you find yourself in such circumstances, but you can't move into our camp. We don't know each other, and we don't trust each other. You would be looking over your shoulders afraid that we would attack you and we would be doing the same. We would eventually kill each other. The bottom line my friends is y'all need to move on and find you a place far from here to live. If we see you poking around our area again, we will shoot you without warning. Do you have any questions?"

The woman glared at Cole. "That's not fair we found the cabins first. We need them for our kids."

Cole replied, "Lady didn't you just hear what I said? You don't get a damn vote in this. You're gonna pick up your crap and get your asses outta here. I was trying to be nice, and apparently, that's not gonna work. Leave those men's guns and go to your camp and leave. If I see you tomorrow, we will unleash hell on you. You have three old revolvers, a .22 rifle, and two old hunting rifles. We have AR-15s and 9 mm pistols. You are outmanned and outgunned. Now go in peace and don't come back."

Cole and Gemma watched them from a safe distance as the group picked up their possessions and walked further west. They followed the group until the strangers stopped at a clearing that had several tents and three more families. Cole wasn't close enough to hear what was said but it was apparent the entire group was outraged. Cole didn't see any attempt by the group to pick up their things and break camp.

"Babe this is going to get ugly. These people don't plan on leaving, and I could be wrong, but I think they're going to attack us soon."

Gemma watched the people through her binoculars and then shook her head. "I agree. These people aren't attempting to leave the area. Let's attack them now and wipe them out before they can attack us."

Cole placed his hands on Gemma's muddy shoulders and looked into her eyes. "Babe, there are at least 12 adults and a half dozen kids in that group. I'll have no problem killing all of the adults if they need killing. Now, what do we do with the kids if all the adults are dead?"

"Oh shit! I hadn't thought of that. I just wanted the danger gone. What the heck are we going to do?"

Cole thought for a few minutes and then said, "We can't chance shooting around the kids. I think we should ambush them when they try to attack us. That would allow us to kill the worst of their bunch and leave the caretakers alive. Do you have a better idea?"

Cole and Gemma watched the strangers for another hour until they were satisfied the group was not going to leave that day. They headed back to camp stopping only to bathe in the creek. They checked to make sure no one was watching and then stripped their clothes off. They both washed their clothes the best they could in the water and hung them to dry on top of the bushes. Then both of them dove into the water and washed each other to remove the caked on mud. Cole never let his rifle out of sight, and both kept an eye on their surroundings as they played in the water.

Gemma swam up to Cole and wrapped her arms and legs around him. She kissed him and held him tight. "Cole this is the first time in several days that we've been clean enough to hold each other. I stink so bad I don't want to hold myself."

Cole smothered his wife with kisses. "You smell awful nice now."

They locked in an embrace and then made love in the water.

As much as Cole wanted to stay in the water with his beautiful wife, he knew they had to get back to the cabins just in case the strangers decided to attack that night.

☆

Chapter 3

Cole walked south through the bushes and small saplings trying to clear a path for Gemma who walked closely behind him. They both had numerous scratches and welts from the small limbs and branches hitting them as they journeyed through the backwoods of Missouri. Now that they had washed all the mud off, the flies and mosquitoes swarmed around them.

"Cole, please stop and spray me with some mosquito repellent. Those damn mosquitoes are eating my ass up."

Cole laughed. "Same here. Spray me when I get done with you."

Cole sprayed her until the can was empty. Gemma saw the can's sputter as the last few drops sprayed out on her legs. "Baby you sprayed all the mosquito spray on me. There's none left for you."

Cole looked into her eyes and lifted her chin. "Honey, I'd die for you so what's a few mosquito bites. Let's get moving."

They walked around the lake and came to the cabins from the North. Deacon immediately challenged them. "Hey what was all the shooting about? Are you okay?"

Cole wiped his brow and swatted a mosquito. "We found two groups of people and the best I can say is that neither one of the groups was our kind of people. We killed the worst ones that were attacking the other group and thought we had done a good deed. Then we found out that the group we saved wanted to run us out of the cabins and take this area over. We highly encourage them to move on or die."

Deacon shook his head and didn't know what to say. They walked in silence for a minute, and then Deacon said, "Are there any decent people left in this world?"

Gemma stopped and put her hands on her hips. "Yes, there are some good people left in this world. We are one of the best examples of those good people. I'm beginning to believe that all of the good people are hiding until things sort themselves out and the bad guys kill each other off."

Deacon quickly replied. "God I hope you're right. Madison and I found your group, and we all found Jack and Carole. We are all good people. Yeah I know, Jack can be a pain in the ass, but he is basically a good person. We just need to knock some sense into him and get him to obey orders, and he will do just fine. Surely we can find other people like ourselves as we march on to Oregon."

Carole and Jenny listened intently as Cole and Gemma told them about their encounters with the two groups of people. They were astounded that even after having their lives saved by Cole's group that they wanted to throw them out of the cabins and take them for themselves. Cole warned everybody to stay alert for the next several days to make sure that the group had moved on. They doubled the guards for several days and never saw those people again. Apparently, Cole scared the shit out of them, and they valued their lives more than those cabins.

For the next week, life at the cabins settled into a mind-numbing schedule of guard duty, eat, sleep, and swat mosquitoes. Cole didn't want to leave the cabins undefended, so no one strayed far. During that time, Madison and Jack began to wake up and show signs of improved health. They were still both very sick but improving. Carole and Deacon were thrilled with the change in their loved ones.

On the seventh day with no sign of the other group, Cole took Molly on a scouting trip around the area. The stranger's camp was abandoned, so Cole and Molly followed their trail several miles until they were satisfied the group had left the area. Cole took this opportunity to scout the north end of Cape Girardeau, which was vastly different than the southern half of the city. The city had gone through a business boom in the early 30s with several large manufacturing and chemical companies moving into the south side. They constructed vast operations, which resulted in the city doubling in size by 2035. The northern and western suburbs exploded as the city annexed the new neighborhoods. The city leaders saw the boom coming and annexed farmland and forests in a corridor about five miles wide around the Northwestern edge of the town. The bad news was that numerous trailer parks also opened on the fringes of the city. This made for cheap housing, but this area was very prone to destruction from tornadoes.

"Damn Cole, these houses go on forever. Do you think we will find anything in them? Many are burned, and most are gutted, and all have been scrounged through."

Cole stopped at the corner of the house and hid behind a bush. "Molly you're probably right, but we need to look through them. I'd hate to miss a large quantity of food or weapons. Come on girl, just suck it up, and keep looking. We will head back to the cabins around 2 o'clock and be home by 3 o'clock. Can you deal with that?"

Molly was deep in thought about losing Cole to her cousin when she heard Cole speak. "Hey girl where is your mind off to today? I just asked if you could deal with my plan."

Molly lied. "I thought I said yes. I guess I didn't say it loud enough, Cole. Yes, that sounds like a plan."

They continued walking across the top edge of the city until they crossed Highway 177 and walked through a thick stand of trees. They came into a clearing and saw what looked to them to be a subdivision made up of mansions. All of the houses were on 1 to 5-acre plots and were huge. Cole immediately wondered if any of these homes had secret rooms like the one they had encountered at the golf course in Ledbetter.

Molly tapped Cole on the back. "Cole, do you think any of these homes have safe rooms or doomsday bunkers?"

Cole replied, "Girl, I was just thinking the same thing myself. Let's quickly check several of them out for supplies while looking for hidden rooms. I wouldn't mind finding a vehicle to load up and take us back home. I don't know why but I'm a bit tired today."

"We've all been under a lot of stress for the last several years. Cole, you have saved all of our lives and carried us when we were too weak to travel. I think you just need some rest and relaxation. When we get back home let's all take a break for a day and just rest up."

They skipped the first several houses. Cole saw one that was larger than the rest and had a five car detached garage. Cole led Molly to the garage first and entered through an open man door. The door had been beaten with a sledgehammer until it was caved in. It was very dark in the garage, so Cole and Molly opened two of the overhead doors. The building had been looted, and items were strewn all over the floor. They were pleasantly surprised that there were still seven cars and trucks still in the building. The interior was decorated as though it was an old garage from the 1930s. There were several of the old visible gas pumps standing in front of a façade of a garage from the 1930s.

Cole ignored the cars and trucks to scout the offices and look for hidden rooms to no avail. There was a million dollars' worth of antiques and cars but no weapons or food. Just as Cole finished searching the rooms, Molly called for Cole to join her at the other end of the garage. There he found Molly standing beside a 1957 Chevy pickup truck that had an antique travel trailer hitched to it.

Molly opened the door to the trailer and invited Cole into the camper. "Cole, would it be possible for us to tow one of these trailers with us? It would be nice to sleep in this instead of on the ground when we travel."

Cole looked around the trailer and knew Molly wouldn't want to hear that towing the trailer would eat up a lot of gas. It probably weighed five times what their little cargo trailers weighed. Cole stepped out of the trailer and thought he saw something under it. He got down on his hands and knees and crawled under the trailer. "Hey, Molly I found something here. Crawl under with me."

Molly crawled under the trailer and saw what Cole had seen. "What is it a doorway or a trapdoor?"

"I think that's exactly what it is. The trailer is parked here over the door to hide it from prying eyes. I've heard of these holes in garage floors being installed as tornado shelters and bomb shelters. Let's move the truck and trailer and see what's under here."

Cole got in the truck, released the emergency brake, and placed the transmission in neutral. Molly opened the garage door in front of the truck and pushed some debris out of the driveway. Both of them strained against the back of the truck until it began to move. Unfortunately, the driveway sloped downward toward the house from the garage, so the truck and trailer picked up speed until they crashed into the swimming pool. Cole stood there with his mouth open in shock. "Holy shit! I never dreamed the bitch would get away from us like that. Oh well, the owner is probably dead or working his ass off in a FEMA camp."

They went back into the garage and tried to lift the door using the two D rings on one end of the door. The door wouldn't budge so Cole more closely examined the door. He couldn't find the keyhole or a hidden switch anywhere close to the door.

Molly looked around the garage for a strong magnet that might be used to flip a switch under the door. "Cole, look for a big magnet. Hey, also look for hidden switches."

They look for 30 minutes without success when Molly suddenly had an idea. "Cole, follow me back to the house. I have an idea."

Molly calmly walked towards the back door of the house on the other side of the swimming pool. The door was swinging open, and it obviously had been beaten with the same sledgehammer as the garage door. Molly backed up and looked out the door as though she was about to walk out to the garage. She reached above the door found a switch and pushed it.

"Cole I'll bet dollars to donuts that the switch I just pushed unlatched the door to the hidden room. I just hope there was still a power source to make the door open," Molly said.

Cole followed Molly back to the garage, and they tried to open the door again. They lifted the D rings, but the door still wouldn't open. Molly said, "Turn the D rings while pulling on them."

The door was stuck and hard to open, but it did open. Cole pulled his small flashlight from his pants pocket and shined it down the dark hole. There was a stairway with a handrail leading to the floor below. Cole went first with his pistol in one hand and his flashlight in the other. The room was enormous and was like a small house below ground. They walked around exploring each room and found three bedrooms, a large kitchen, and two bathrooms. They also found a large room at the back that contained substantial stainless steel tanks and several rows of racking. Each of the stainless steel tanks had their contents stenciled on their side. Water, diesel, and gasoline were marked on the three containers.

The racks held everything from canned goods, bags of rice and flour, and boxes of dry food. Cole was very disappointed that they didn't find any weapons or ammunition; however, they did find an empty gun rack.

There were gaping empty spots in the gun racks, which indicated the owners had taken all of the weapons and ammo. They also took an abundant supply of food with them when they fled. He was surprised they took the time to stage the trailer and pick up over top of the door. This meant that they had the time to plan and execute their escape without being noticed. Cole wondered what could have driven them from this luxurious home and stockpile of food. He didn't think long about it because their loss was his team's gain.

Cole and Molly checked out the vehicles and quickly noticed that all of their distributors had been removed making them useless. Cole promptly went back down into the hidden room and went through several unmarked boxes until he found the distributors. Cole tried three of the distributors in an old Ford pickup truck until he found the right one. He didn't know much about car mechanics but kept moving the distributor until the timing was close enough to fire the cylinders when the truck was pushed. Cole and Molly moved the truck to the open garage door, and Cole got behind the steering wheel. Molly pushed the truck out the door, and it picked up speed.

Cole turned the ignition on and popped the clutch with the truck in first gear. It sputtered, ran, died, and finally fired up and ran. Cole barely avoided crashing into the swimming pool and drove the truck back into the garage. "Well, that worked better than I expected. I thought for a minute that I was going to be at the bottom of the swimming pool with the trailer. Let's grab some of the food and supplies and get on back home. Hey, what are you laughing about?"

Molly was laughing so hard she couldn't catch her breath. "Cole that was so funny. You were screaming all the way down the hill towards the pool. You only stopped screaming when you crashed through the fence did a sharp U-turn and headed back up the hill to the garage. I don't know what you owe me but you owe me, or I'm going to tell the others about you screaming like a little girl being teased with a spider."

They loaded the back end of the truck with cans of gasoline, food, and medical supplies before leaving. They drove northwest almost to Jackson before heading south taking several back roads to avoid the populated areas. They never saw anyone during their trip back to the cabins, but several others saw them. They didn't notice the Humvee parked under the overpass where they crossed Highway 55. The FEMA agents were taking a break in the shade when they heard the pickup roar overhead. They jumped in their vehicle but had to drive a quarter-mile the wrong way to get up on Highway 55. By that time, the pickup was long out of sight and was on a back road heading south. The Humvee cruised up and down Highway 34 but never found the pickup.

Cole parked the pickup about 500 yards from the cabins to make sure none of his friends took potshots at them. Cole walked into the camp and told his friends that Molly would soon drive a pickup loaded with surprises into the camp. He looked back up the road and waved at Molly to join them. Molly came roaring up the road in the pickup with the exhaust bellowing. Cole quickly admonished her for making so much noise and possibly drawing attention to them.

Gemma ran up to Cole and gave him a big hug and Molly her middle finger. Molly got out of the pickup truck and returned the bird to her cousin. "You're just jealous that you weren't with Cole when we found all this food and supplies."

"Molly you know I was just busting your balls. I could never be jealous of you, and any time you spent with my wonderful husband. Besides, remember he doesn't even like you," Gemma laughed.

Molly only laughed and bit her lip. She remembered that Cole had been very interested in her when they were sleeping together in the same bed at the FEMA slave camp. Molly didn't pursue the relationship only because she was focused on getting her two younger cousins out of the FEMA camp and to safety. She just realized later that she had made a big mistake because this brash young man had won her heart before she even knew it.

Molly and Cole unloaded the truck and handed the supplies to the others to store in the cabin Cole and Gemma occupied. It had an extra bedroom that was perfect for storing the supplies. They held back several boxes of macaroni and cheese along with six cans of jalapeno Spam.

Jenny cried out, "I love mac & cheese, but I could do without the Spam. What other delicacies do you have in these boxes? I see Cheerios, rice, beans, and oh my God, there are several cans of coffee. I think I've died and gone to heaven."

Molly swatted her cousin on the butt. "You'll eat the Spam and like it young girl. A little girl like you needs her protein and jalapenos to grow up big and strong. No kidding everyone, we found the mother lode of prepper supplies. Now we have to figure out how much we need to draw off the supplies and how much we will need to take along with us when we get back on our trip to Oregon. If anyone saw us returning from our scavenging trip, they might try to take our stuff."

They had just placed the last box of food in the cabin when Carole yelled for them to come to her. She pointed at the woods to the north. Gemma raised her binoculars and said, "Oh my God, it's a bunch of little kids coming this way. Cole, they look like the kids from the group we ran off. Let's see there's one two three... crap... There are five of them. What are we going to do with them?"

Molly quickly replied. "They're not our problem. We can't be responsible for every kid in this screwed up world. We can barely feed ourselves, what are we going to do with a pack of kids?"

Cole interrupted the conversation. "Whoa, ladies. Now Molly, what would you want someone to do if that were little Gemma and Jenny wandering through the woods afraid and alone?"

Molly rolled her eyes and placed her hands on her hips as she glared at Cole. "That's not fighting fair. They're not Gemma and Jenny nor are they our concern. If we start picking up every kid and lost soul we run into, we will get ourselves killed or starve at best case."

Cole was now looking at the kids through Gemma's binoculars and said, "The oldest is a boy about 12, and a little girl is carrying a baby almost as big as she is. Wild dogs or coyotes will be dining on these kids by the end of the week if we don't do something."

Madison had been listening to the conversation from her lawn chair on the front porch of her cabin. "Deacon, we can't let these kids starve nor have wild animals eat them. I vote that we take them in and care for them and feed them until we decide what to do with them."

Deacon scratched his head as he walked over to Madison and took her hand. "I've always wanted a couple of kids. Madison and I will be responsible for two of them." Carole spoke up, "Jack and I will take the little girl and the baby."

Cole watched as the kids continued marching towards them. "Now wait just a minute. We have to look at this from all angles. This could be just another trap, and their parents could be looking at us from the woods. Let's not decide these kids fate until we know what the hell is going on. Molly, you and Deacon slowly leave the group and come back around behind the children on the right side. Gemma and I will wait a few minutes and then circle around to their left side. The rest of you watch for an imminent attack."

They searched all around the children and didn't find any adults planning to attack Cole's group. Cole and Gemma greeted the children and asked them where they were going. The oldest boy answered, "Sir, I was hoping that you would help us get to my Uncle Charlie's place. Those people killed my parents and took all our stuff. My sister and I hope that Uncle Charlie will also take the others in."

Gemma reached out for the baby. "Can I hold the baby? She looks hungry."

The little girl said, "We haven't eaten in three days. Do you have any food?"

"Yes we have some food, and while you eat, we'd like to hear your story. Come on let's go down to our camp."

Gemma carried the baby while Deacon carried the little girl back to the cabins. They introduce themselves while Jenny and Carole warmed some rabbit and soup for the kids. The baby was 18 months old and able to eat solid food. Gemma changed the baby's diaper and brought her back to eat with the others.

The oldest boy's name was Bobby, and he spoke for the group. "That's my sister Anna, and those mean people killed our parents and took us over a month ago. About three weeks ago Darrell, Betty, and the baby Millie joined us. We were told that the mean people found them wandering in the woods. Darrell told me that they were attacked while sleeping and his mom and dad were captured. The next day two black trucks showed up and took their mom and dad away."

The black truck comment peaked Cole's interest. "Did the trucks have any markings or signs on them?"

Bobby looked up from his meal. "Yes. Both trucks had F E M A on the doors and hood. The men were dressed in black and had the same word on their chests. They all had rifles like the one you have."

"Son of a bitch, FEMA is operating in this area. Your parents are probably alive and safe at one of their camps," Cole said.

Gemma thought for a minute and said, "Cape Girardeau still has quite a few people in the area. I'll bet FEMA is harvesting those people to work in their camps. We need to move on quickly."

Carole shook her head vigorously. "We can't move on because Jack and Madison are only about half recovered and leaving now might kill them."

Cole waved at everyone to stop talking. He turned to Bobby. "Bobby where does your uncle Charlie live?"

"He lives in Millersville. I think that's north of here. Maybe on the other side of Jackson," Bobby replied.

Cole announced to the group. "I don't like it, but Carole's right. We need to lay low here and camouflage the entrance to the cabins. We also need to hide the trucks and erase any evidence we been here that could be seen from a helicopter. Two of us will take the kids to Millersville and hope we can find their uncle. We will take our new pickup truck and take a load of supplies for that family. I hope that induces them to take all of the kids."

Jack cleared his throat and waved at the others. "Cole, perhaps the rest of you should leave Carole and me here and go on your journey to Oregon. We were not entirely sold on going to Oregon until those FEMA assholes burned our cabin and took our food. It only makes sense for you to go on. Now don't interrupt, I've screwed up twice and can never make up for the loss I've caused. The group shouldn't suffer because I got shot doing something stupid."

Cole walked over and sat down beside Jack. "Jack everything you say is true. The group shouldn't suffer because you did something stupid and it's my job to make sure this never happens again. We will not leave you and Carole, and you are free to go to Oregon with us; however, you can't keep making dumb mistakes, or we will leave you. If the group agrees, I say the past is history, and we need to move on. We will stand here and fight if necessary, but we're not leaving you."

The others all agreed and gave Jack a pat on the back and Carole a hug.

Cole continued going over his plans. "Tomorrow Molly and I will make a trip in the pickup back to the prepper stash and pick up some food for the kids and their new family. Then the next day, Gemma and I will head north with the kids. I plan to leave early tomorrow morning and hopefully return that night but be prepared that we could be away for a couple of days. I want to avoid all of the cities and travel slower than normal to be on guard for roadblocks."

Jack felt much better that night sitting around the campfire as he forced himself to read another of his mom's letters.

Dear Jack:

I hope all is well with you and your family. I talked with Joe this morning, and he promised to start preparing for the apocalypse. I'm sending him and you several cases of the Wise-72 hour meals. This will help jumpstart your survival prepping.

Joe is my favorite grandkid, and he really cares for me. Talking with you and Joe is very important to me. Alfred is a faithful companion and takes care of my day-to-day needs, but you two are blood kin, and our conversations mean so much to me. I hope you and Joe talk to each other several times a week. I know that talking to me may not be high on your list, but it does make my day when you call. I wish you had moved your family out here to Oregon and went to work for the family company, but alas, that didn't happen.

Your sister's husband is a worthless piece of shit and almost ruined Building # 3 before my chief of operations fired his sorry ass. Now she's bugging the crap out of me to give him another chance at another job. The asshole is a slug and couldn't pour piss out of a boot with instructions on the heel.

Between you and me, this makes me feel better about yanking their chains on the nonexistent treasure and not leaving them squat in my will.

Speaking of my will, I know you and Joe don't care for Harp Enterprises, so I'm leaving the company to all of the workers. Of course, I'll leave you and Joe some money and other property, but your damn sister won't get much.

I hope...

Jack read the part about not inheriting the company and became livid. He tore the letter up without finishing it and tossed the box of letters in the fire. Even though he had known for over a year that his mom didn't leave him part of the company it still pissed him off. The letters caught fire and blazed.

Cole was shocked to see Agnes Harp's letters to her son burning in the fire. He remembered Joe's letters from his Grandma Harp, and how much Joe revered the letters. Without thinking, Cole reached into the fire to save the letters. He was only able to save one-half burned letter. Cole held the letter and looked at Jack with disgust. "Jack, how could you burn your mom's letters? Your son Joe loved Grandma Harp and cherished her letters to him. Joe found great wisdom and comfort in her letters."

Jack took several seconds to compose himself before speaking. "Cole, I'm happy that you look up to my son Joe and found my mom's letters to be so valuable. While I love my mom, we didn't have the same relationship that my son had with her. The letters don't mean that much to me. Frankly, some of them upset me, and I don't need the hassle. That's why I burned them."

Everyone around the campfire was surprised to see tears in Cole's eyes as he clung to the letter. Gemma made him hold his hand out so she could check his burns. Luckily, for Cole, he only received a couple of slight burns and just received First Aid.

Cole went to bed early that night, clutching the burned letter from Joe's grandma. The letters from Joe's grandma had meant so much to everyone in their group. Joe shared most of them with his team, and Agnes Harp kept them in stitches and shared her wisdom on survival preparation. The entire crew benefited from the bunker that she had left Joe. It was their safe refuge when times were tough.

Gemma came to bed about an hour later and saw Cole tossing and turning in his sleep. She couldn't imagine what he was thinking and going through. Then she saw he had the letter clutched in his hand.

Cole fell asleep very quickly and immediately had a dream about Joe and his Grandma. In the dream, Joe told him that he should carefully listen to his grandma's advice and wisdom. Then Agnes Harp walked up to Cole in his dream. She said:

Dear Cole:

Cole, Joe tells me that you have become very close to him. He also told me that for a young lad you have become a fierce warrior and a strong leader. My son Jack is neither, so I need you to watch out for him. Oh, I know that he can be an ass sometimes, but please keep watch over him as you do the rest of your people. Now let's get down to business.

I know it may seem strange to be taking direction from an old dead woman, but I'm not through stirring up shit in your world. You have several problems that you must overcome. The trip to Oregon might kill all of you. You won't make it there this year so by early fall, you need to find a hole and crawl into it until springtime.

I know this may be a bit personal but don't let any of the women get knocked up. Don't blush. We both know what causes babies. A baby or several babies on this trip could cause a year's delay or more. Well, I've had my say for the day so you can go on to sleep now.

Love Grandma

Cole suddenly sat up in bed as Gemma watched. "Cole, what's wrong?"

"Please don't think I'm crazy, but I just had a conversation with Joe's grandma. I think she gave up trying to talk to Jack through the letters. She wants to share her wisdom with me. Damn, I think I am crazy."

Gemma had to think about this one for a minute. "Honey, I don't think you're crazy. I think it's your subconscious finding a way to deal with the issues and problems bouncing around under that thick skull. Now if I find you talking to yourself, I'll get worried. Just don't put too much emphasis on a dream. Lay back down, and I'll take your mind off that dream."

Cole remembered something he just heard in his dream. "We must be careful, we don't need any kids until we get to Oregon."

☆

Chapter 4

Cole and Molly quickly left on their drive to the north end of Cape Girardeau. They took a different route, which swung further north of the city and stuck to back roads. They found a place where they could cross Highway 5 by cutting two fences and then driving through a pasture and onto a dirt road. They crossed all of the major roads using this technique to avoid roadblocks and other people.

Cole drove to the north side of the subdivision and parked on the other side of a copse of trees to hide the truck. They walked carefully into the neighborhood and only saw a small pack of dogs on their way to the house. They quickly entered the garage and moved the vehicle from over the hidden door. They opened the door and entered the room below. Cole and Molly chose the canned goods and dry goods that they wanted to take with them. Molly added two first-aid kits, and they hauled all of the supplies up the steps. Cole was about to open the garage door when Molly tapped him on the back and stopped him. "Cole, did you hear that noise? I think I heard a vehicle out there."

Cole slipped out the man door and walked around the side of the house. Sure enough, there was a black vehicle sitting in the middle of the street. Cole didn't see any of the occupants. He looked around and didn't see anyone, so he rejoined Molly in the garage.

"Molly there's a damn FEMA Humvee parked in the road. I didn't see any of the troops, but you know they're snooping around. We need to lay low and avoid them if possible."

Molly was pissed at the situation they found themselves in that afternoon. "I thought we were done with those FEMA jerks. I guess they're going to make our lives miserable forever. Let's just go find them and kill them and get it over with."

Cole chuckled. "Molly, what do you think will happen when these guys don't show up at the end of their tour of duty?"

"I know their boss will send someone to look for them."

Cole replied, "Damn Skippy he will. Those FEMA sum bitches will be all up in our asses, and we won't be safe here."

"Yeah, I know. I guess we need to get some crackers and peanut butter and pig out until they leave."

Cole shook his head as he grinned at Molly. "Molly as much as you eat I'm surprised your ass isn't as big as a barn."

Molly suddenly had a mean looking smirk on her face. "It's not like there's much else to do around here. Hey, you used to like my ass when you were snuggling up against it back at the FEMA camp."

Cole about choked on his peanut butter and crackers. "Molly, please don't ever talk about back then. If Gemma heard you, it would break her heart, and she would probably kill both of us."

Molly stared at Cole and said, "Cole it's not like Gemma and Jenny didn't know what we were doing back in that bedroom. Hell, Jenny even got after me several times for not having sex with you."

Cole looked down as he played with his fingers. "Molly, I'll admit that I wanted you and would've done about anything to sleep with you at that time. I'm glad I didn't because I really wanted Gemma from the first time I met her and she felt the same way. I think things happened for the best, and I love Gemma more than anything. I'll always care for you, but I love Gemma. Now let's find something else to talk about."

Molly smiled at Cole. "I know you're right about this, but both Jenny and I are jealous of you and Gemma. Jenny's Pete was killed, and you were the only man in my life for the last year. It's not like we're going to meet Prince Charming in the Missouri woods."

Their conversation ended when they heard boots scuffling at the entrance to the garage. Cole drew his knife, scurried to the backside of the door, and waited on the man to enter. Molly hid behind the old Chevy and trained her pistol on the doorway. Suddenly a beam of light pierced the darkness and a FEMA trooper cautiously entered the garage. He flashed the light around the room and had a pistol in his other hand. Cole slid in behind him and yanked the soldier's head back as he drew his knife across the trooper's neck in one motion. The pistol and flashlight fell from the trooper's hands as he stood there gurgling blood and bloodied foam from his wound. Then the man collapsed to the garage floor. He was dead.

Cole looked outside of the garage and didn't see anyone, but he knew there was at least one more FEMA trooper nosing around. "Molly we have to find and kill the rest of them, or we are in deep shit."

Molly replied, "They have to be close by this house. Let's go hunting."

Cole and Molly left the garage and entered the house without making a sound. Before they moved a few feet into the house, they heard a noise upstairs. They could hear two men talking. They heard, "Look, Ralph, I don't give a crap what you think. We need to find a couple of good-looking women and ditch FEMA. We have a truck full of food, water, and our weapons and ammo. We could take over a small town and live like kings. If we stay with FEMA, we will eventually get killed by some redneck with a shotgun."

"Rod, it's not that I don't agree with you, but those FEMA assholes won't stop until they find us. That fucking FEMA leader won't stop looking for us until we're hanging from a tall tree. He is still obsessed about that group that disappeared from the convoy. The only way I'll go along with you is if we take off now and drive 500 miles west or south to make sure we are far away from that bastard."

Molly poked Cole on the shoulder and whispered in his ear. "Cole let's kill them and then I have a plan."

"What's the plan?"

Molly told Cole to hide around the corner and then suddenly she spoke up in her most sexy voice. "Hey, is anybody here."

They heard the two men running in the upstairs hallway toward the stairs. The men abruptly stopped, and one peered around the corner. He saw Molly and asked, "Hey baby what are you doing?"

While she waited on the men to respond Molly had let her hair down and took her T-shirt off. She stood there wearing only her shorts and a black sports bra with her long red hair flowing over her shoulders. The men saw her and tripped over themselves trying to get down the stairs. They made the mistake of not checking their surroundings as they ran down the steps to ravage the young lady. Cole took aim at the first man, took a deep breath, and squeezed the trigger. Before the man knew he was shot, Cole had moved his aim and killed the next man with two well-aimed shots.

Molly saw the first man lying at her feet with a hand raised towards her as if to ask, why. Molly kicked the man in the side. "You two men have learned a valuable lesson. Don't fall head over heels over a piece of ass. Die bastard."

Molly drew her pistol and fired in one motion sending the man to hell. Cole looked at her. "Molly you wasted that bullet. Did that make you feel better?"

"Cole if you'd seen the look on their faces, you would've also shot them. Where are all the decent men in the world?"

"Most of them are trying to survive with their girlfriends or wives. The others are looking for a good woman."

"Are you saying I'm not a good woman?"

Cole looked exasperated. "Molly, you are a good woman and any man would be glad to have you. You're only 20 years old, and most of the men in the world died last year. You're going to have to look a little harder and not be so damn self-absorbed. You could've had me, but you chose to focus totally on your family and getting back to Oregon. To find and keep a good young man you will have to balance him in with your other priorities. Hell, I'm only 18, and I don't have all the answers, but that's what I think."

Molly leaned over and kissed Cole on the forehead. "Cole, I was stupid and let you slip through my fingers. Don't worry I would never say anything in front of Gemma and have moved on. I do appreciate your advice and will take it to heart. Let's roll."

Cole picked up one of the AR-15s and said, "Molly this is going to be loud, but you need to learn to shoot this before we leave this house."

Cole trained Molly on the weapon and then drew a target on the wall at the end of the hallway. She took aim and placed all three shots into the six-inch circle. Cole then drew a smaller circle about 2 inches across and had Molly take three more shots after giving her more instruction. Two of the three bullets struck the center of the circle with the third on the circle.

Molly jumped with joy and thanked Cole for the instruction. Cole then showed her how to load the magazines. They stripped the clothes from two of the FEMA agents and dressed in their uniforms.

Cole helped Molly put on the tactical vest and then showed her how to store the magazines for her new AR and her 9 mm pistol.

They wrapped all three bodies in several layers of plastic and placed them in empty 55-gallon drums in the shelter below the garage. Next, they loaded the pickup truck with the supplies and the FEMA trooper's weapons and ammunition. Then Cole found a tow bar and hitched the old truck to the back of the Humvee.

"Molly do you really think this is going to work? Stuff all of that red hair up in that helmet or they'll know you're a girl."

Molly waved a whiskey bottle at Cole and then stuffed her hair into the helmet. Molly then acted as though she was drinking from the whiskey bottle. "I really do believe we can pull this off and misdirect FEMA. Fire that Humvee up and let's have some fun."

Cole got behind the wheel and pulled away from the curb heading south. They passed a group of people, and Cole slowed down and asked if the women wanted to join them. He waved a whiskey bottle at the men and asked if they would trade one of the women for whiskey. The men were afraid of the FEMA troopers, so they kept their mouth shut. Cole threw a half-empty whiskey bottle at them and drove off. He turned on Highway 61 and ran down the full length of the city weaving from side to side playing his part of the drunken FEMA trooper. They each threw several half-empty whiskey bottles at people they passed. Cole hoped the people would tell the story to the FEMA Troops that came searching for the missing men.

Cole stopped in some woods just before the highway 55 Junction and unhitched the pickup from the Humvee. He then hid the Humvee deep in the woods. They waited to make sure no one was watching and drove off southwest on a side road. It took a while as they doubled back on dirt roads to make sure no one followed them but they finally made it to the road to the cabins. They removed the makeshift camouflage that hid the road and Molly drove the pickup down to the cabins while Cole replaced the camouflage.

Deacon and Gemma had their rifles aimed at Molly as she got out of the truck with her hands up and then removed her helmet. "Damn boys, don't get trigger-happy it's just me Molly. I'll explain the FEMA duds when Cole gets here. We had a few problems."

Carole and Jenny had prepared a tasty supper of canned ham, spaghetti, and canned green beans. They ate while Cole and Molly filled them in on their day's events. Everyone was speechless at first and then laughed at how Molly had lured the men to their demise. Madison sat at the picnic table for the first time since she had been wounded. She asked, "Do you think your ruse fooled them? Is there any way they can trace you back to our location?"

Cole fielded the question. "There is no way that anyone could answer that question and be sure they give you the correct answer. We did everything in our power to avoid killing them, and then we covered our tracks, as well as anyone could have under the circumstances. We'll have to stay on guard just like we always do and unfortunately, we just have to wait and see."

Gemma hugged Molly then Cole and stood up. "They both are my heroes, and I appreciate what they did today."

Bobby spoke up. "I wish we had had brave people like Molly and Cole to stop the bad guys from killing our parents."

Cole patted Bobby on the back and said, "Thanks son that means a lot to me."

Cole gave Gemma and Jenny one of the troopers AR-15s and gave Carole and Madison 9mm pistols. Thanks to FEMA, their arsenal grew that day. Cole trained all four how to use the weapons and conducted target practice later that day.

The time flew quickly that evening as Gemma and Cole prepared to take the kids to Bobby's Uncle Charlie. Jenny and

Carole got the kids into bed early because they knew it could be a rough trip in the morning.

All of the adults were awake before the sun rose and Carole quickly had a pot of coffee brewing. Carole warmed some stew while Gemma added some Beanee Weenees and canned Spam for their lunch. Jenny woke the kids up and got them ready for the day, and then Carole fed them breakfast.

Cole placed a tarp over top of the cargo so prying eyes wouldn't see the boxes of food. They loaded the kids in the cab with them and drove off with Gemma holding the baby. A few years ago, this would only be a half-hour drive, but now it could be a two-day drive if they got there at all. Cole and Gemma both had two 9 mm pistols since there was no room for their rifles in the cab of the truck. Cole had placed their rifles and two shotguns in the bed against the cab under the tarp just in case they needed them.

As usual, they took the back roads on either side of Highway 25 as they headed north to avoid being seen by any FEMA agents. It was a little cooler that morning as they drove before the sun was fully up. The air was much cleaner now than it was before the shit hit the fan thanks to the reduction in pollution and farming. Gemma also noticed she only heard the tires on the pavement and the birds singing as they drove along. Billions of people had to die to yield clean-air and eliminate noise pollution. Gemma would trade all of that to change things back the way they used to be. It might be quieter, and the air cleaner, but death lurked around every corner. If it wasn't someone trying to shoot you, a rusty nail could infect and kill you.

The drive was uneventful until they were west of Jackson and encountered a roadblock made up of old cars. Cole quickly pulled off the road into a stand of trees and hoped they hadn't been seen. "Gemma, please stay here with the kids and protect them while I scout out the roadblock."

Cole was only gone for about 15 minutes when he came back to Gemma. "Babe, they're just too damn many of them for us to try to fight our way through. We're going to backtrack and go around the SOB's."

They backed up and drove about half a mile before swinging due west until they got to highway 335 and turned north. Cole immediately took a side road heading northwest to stay off the main road. Two hours later, they found themselves at the Highway 72 and Highway 8 junction.

Cole looked at Bobby and said, "Tell me what you said last night about where you think your Uncle Charlie lives."

"All I know is that his place is just out of town on the west end. When you leave town, Dad always made the first turn to the right after a big creek. Then the farm was straight down the road on the left just past a big black barn."

Cole bypassed most of the southern part of Millersville but had to get back onto Highway 72 W to make sure he didn't miss the turn after the creek. Cole stopped just short of the turn on to 72 and scouted the area in both directions before proceeding. Cole didn't see anything dangerous, so he returned to the truck and made a left turn onto Highway 72. They only traveled half a mile before they crossed the creek and saw the road on the right side. Cole turned the truck down the dirt road and started looking for the black barn. In a few minutes, he saw a pile of rubble on the left side of the road. "Bobby I think that was the black barn. Someone burned it to the ground. Look up ahead on the left, and there's a farmhouse about 500 yards off the road."

Bobby pointed and got excited. "That's my uncle's place. I can see his windmill and his old red farm truck."

Cole didn't like what he saw because there was no concealment or cover between them and the farmhouse. Crops had been planted all around the back of the farm but nothing between the farmhouse and the road. "Gemma I need a white flag. Do you have a piece of cloth that I could use as a flag?"

Gemma reached into her back pocket of her shorts and pulled out a white handkerchief. She kissed it for luck and handed it to her husband. Cole cut a limb from a bush and tied the cloth to the end. He left his rifle with Gemma and walked down the road to the farmhouse waving the white flag with only his 9 mm pistol on his hip. Before too long, Cole saw movement in one of the windows and at the front of the shed to the right of the house.

Two men came out of the shed armed with shotguns. They walked towards Cole and stopped about 50 feet from him. One of the men said, "Who are you and what you want. Stay where you are."

Cole kept the flag in the air with one hand and raised the other empty hand to make sure the two men stayed calm. "Hello I'm Cole, and I'm here to see Charlie."

"What business do you have with Charlie?"

"We have his niece and nephew. We rescued them from a group of thugs."

One of the men stepped forward. "What about my brother Raymond and his wife?"

Cole hated telling the man that his brother and sister-in-law were dead. "I only have bad news for you on them. The thugs captured them, and the kids think they're dead. I believe the thugs sold them to FEMA to become slaves."

The big man had tears in his eyes. "What makes you think that my brother was sold into slavery? I know FEMA has done some bad things around here, but what makes you think they are taking slaves?"

"Because several of us have just escaped from a FEMA slave camp over in Kentucky. FEMA has dozens of these camps all across the eastern part of the United States. I worked in a coal mine while my wife and her sisters worked on a farm. We were held inside a fenced in compound with guards all around. They made us work from morning to night and anyone who didn't work disappeared. I call that slavery."

The big man said, "I'm Charlie, and I'd like to see the kids. You can put your hands down but keep them away from that pistol."

The man walked up to Cole and asked where the kids were located. Cole looked back over his shoulder and pointed to the pickup truck. "The kids are up there in the pickup with my wife. I'll signal my wife and get her to bring the kids down here. I need to tell you that there were some other kids rescued with yours. There were three more kids with them, and they all need homes."

"I'll gladly take my brother's kids, but my wife and I already have three kids and can't take anymore. I'll bring this up with my friends."

Cole waved at Gemma and beckoned her to drive the truck down to the farmhouse. The truck sped down the road and lurched to a stop. The kids piled out of the vehicle and began running towards Cole and Charlie. Bobby and his sister ran to their Uncle Charlie and almost knocked him down hugging him. A woman and three kids flew out of the farmhouse toward them. Bobby looked up and said, "Aunt Janie, please let us stay with you. Our mommy and daddy are dead."

Gemma got out of the truck holding the baby's hand as she walked towards the others. The little flaxen-headed pixie smiled and laughed as she joined the group. Two other women and their husbands walked into the crowd, and one of the women picked up the little girl. "Oh my, this little girl is an angel. Are you her mother?" She asked Gemma.

Gemma saw the woman had fallen in love with the little pixie. "Oh no, I don't have any kids. Cole and I just got married last month. We rescued these children from a nasty group that had killed or enslaved their parents. We are looking for families to take the kids. We are traveling back home to the West Coast, or we would love to have them all."

The woman held the baby close and looked at her husband. "Darling we lost our little Jesse six months ago, and this baby needs a home."

The man took the baby from his wife's arms and cuddled it for a few minutes. "She sure is cute; does she have any brothers or sisters?"

Little Bobby spoke up. "This is her brother and older sister they need a home also. Jake, please keep them."

This went much better than Cole had hoped for, and soon it was apparent that all of the kids had found a new home. It was now lunchtime, and Charlie's wife invited them to stay for lunch. They walked to the back of the house and found three large picnic tables with umbrellas. Cole and Gemma were treated like family and helped set the table and then dish out the food.

Cole looked back over his shoulder and saw acres of corn, beans, and potatoes. Much closer to the house was a vast garden growing everything from tomatoes to watermelon. Cole was astounded that FEMA hadn't found them yet. "Have any of the FEMA troops showed up at the farm yet?"

A frown came over Charlie's face as he turned toward Cole. "We've had a couple of run-ins with them, but they haven't found our farm yet."

Cole thought this was strange. "Have you seen any helicopters buzzing around?"

"No, we've only seen a few of the Humvees. And we hid from them because several of the people passing through told us not to trust them."

Cole laughed. "Not only don't trust them but avoid them if you can. They are capturing people and turning them into slaves to work in their farms, factories, and mines. We've heard several of the corrupt FEMA leaders are trying to start a new country on the East Coast. They have made themselves the dictators of this new country.

They are also tearing down homes and factories to help build their country. They will probably take over this area sometime before winter sets in. Don't be here when they come."

Charlie and several of the men laughed at Cole. One of the men said, "That'll be the day. Look around you man. We have food, water, and shelter. Five families are living on this farm that know how to use a gun, and we can defend ourselves."

Cole knew when to cut his losses and not to argue further. "You and your families will be in our thoughts and prayers, and we wish you the best. Thank you for making good homes for the children and inviting us to share your meal. We need to get back home now before dark."

Cole and Gemma didn't talk much the first half hour after they left the farm. Cole was anxious that the FEMA assholes would overrun the farm, capture the adults, and make them slaves. "Babe, we warned them about FEMA, but they wouldn't listen. Is there anything I could have said differently to change their minds?"

Gemma quickly replied, "No Honey, you did the best you could. They are like many other people and can't believe their own government could be a danger to them. I just hope for the sake of the kids that FEMA never finds them."

Cole squeezed his wife's leg. "We better pray that FEMA never finds us. Babe, I'm afraid we're going to be stuck here for a while. I think Madison and Jack will need another three to four weeks to heal properly before we can hit the road again. I'm worried that FEMA could appear any day now. We need to gather more supplies quickly and hide until those two can travel."

☆

Chapter 5

    Cole looked across the floor of the dirty cabin and thought about the time wasted in these cabins waiting on Jack and Madison to heal. He also thought back to when Jack made several poor decisions, which resulted in Pete and Sarah being killed. Against Cole's advice, Jack led Cole's team into an ambush. Cole and the girls had warned Jack not to go blindly into the city. Jack ignored their opinions and headed into the town like a bull in a china shop. The result was that the group of innocent people thought they were being attacked and shot at Jack and his team who then returned fire. Cole's team was performing overwatch and had to respond with fire to protect their fellow teammates. They killed several on the opposing side. Thanks to Jack's impatience and lack of planning, Jack and Madison were also wounded.

    Both Jack and Madison's wounds were infected, and this threatened their lives. While the wounds were severe, they weren't that bad if they had had the proper antibiotics and medical supplies. With modern antibiotics and adequate care, Jack and Madison would've been healed by now. Instead, they barely survived the last two months.

Cole lay in bed holding Gemma in his arms as he tried to sleep. Sleep wouldn't come to him that night because he was all keyed up about leaving the cabins and heading out in the morning for Oregon. Jack and Madison finally healed and were fit to travel. This came none too soon because they had seen and heard FEMA helicopters in the distance two weeks ago.

Cole finally fell asleep and very quickly, grandma revisited him in his dreams.

Dear Cole:

Cole it's going to be morning very soon, and you're going to have to jump out of bed and lead this crew west. I need you to wake up in a good mood and cheerfully lead the others. Crack a few jokes and lighten the mood because this will make them feel safe. If you go around like a grumpy Gus, they will be afraid.

I know this trip has you worried. Deep back in your mind, you wonder if FEMA has attacked Charlie's ranch. You will never be certain if the location is safe or dangerous until you've scouted it out and know FEMA's exact location.

I want you to know that I'm very proud of how you and Molly handled the situation in the garage and house that day you were getting supplies. You both dealt with FEMA and took out those soldiers without being harmed yourselves. You also handled Molly very well. You know she still loves you.

I know Joe shared some of my letters to him over the last few months. I doubt if he shared the ones where I was telling him to forget his cheating girlfriend and find a new woman. You have Gemma and don't need Molly clinging to you. Now I'm not telling you to piss her off or run her off, but you need to distance yourself a bit from her unless you want Gemma to cut your balls off. Don't give Molly any hope to cling to.

Cole, I'm very proud of you. You continue to do a great job leading this group and aren't afraid to listen to their suggestions. Be careful out there tomorrow. Danger is lurking around every corner.

Love Grandma

Cole looked at the old wind up alarm clock and saw it was 2 AM in the morning. They were all supposed to be awake at 2 o'clock and on the road by three that morning. Cole wanted to make sure they were many miles west of the camp before the sun came up. They would travel without their lights on since there was a full moon. The fact that FEMA was scouting the area scared Cole more than he would admit to anyone.

Cole turned the alarm off so it wouldn't startle Gemma and gently rubbed her back to wake her up. "Hey Babe, it's time to get up."

Her eyes opened as he kissed her on the neck. "Cole it can't be time to get up; I'm so sleepy. Let me sleep another four hours please."

"Sorry Honey, but it's time to get up and on the road. I also need to tell you about my conversation with Cole's Grandma."

Cole slapped her on the butt and jumped out of bed to beat her to the bathroom. She walked into the room as he was relieving himself and said, "Darn you, Cole, you could have peed outside and let me have the toilet. That was just mean."

"Hey Babe I tried waking you up, and you wanted to sleep longer. Next time you'll get up."

She laughed. "Or I could just make your life miserable. If you don't put that toilet seat down, I will make your life miserable."

Cole quickly dressed and ate some crackers and cheese before gathering his gear. He carried several boxes to the Bronco and dropped his gear behind the back seat. He then returned to the house and helped Gemma move her equipment to the truck. Molly and Jenny had decided to drive the old pickup truck so they could haul more of the supplies. This left Cole and Gemma riding in the Bronco by themselves. Deacon, Madison, Jack, and Carole would be in the other Bronco. Cole saw that all of them were busy adding their personal items and gear to their vehicles.

A few minutes later, Cole rounded everybody up and gave them the final directions before heading out. "As we discussed yesterday, I'll lead the column and Molly and Jenny will guard the rear of the column. If anyone sees anything suspicious or dangerous, honk your horn twice, and we will pull off the road to regroup. If you think we need to haul ass to get away from danger honk your horn five times. Are there any questions?" There weren't any questions, so they climbed into their vehicles and left their home for the last two and a half months.

They were barely a mile down the road when Gemma asked, "Well, what did Grandma have to say this morning?"

"Well, Grandma or perhaps me... Crap! Anyway, one of us is apparently worried about the trip and Charlie's farm. She assured me that we've done the best we can and that I'm a good leader. She also told me that Molly and I did really well handling FEMA on that supply run."

Cole didn't share Grandma's comments about his relationship with Molly and the warning to distance himself from her. Gemma patted Cole on the thigh. "Now wait a minute. You sound like this is a conversation between you two. I didn't hear you talking in your sleep."

Cole thought for a second. "Babe, it's not like that. I'm not speaking words that come from my mouth. It's more like she reads my mind."

Gemma laughed and giggled for a minute. "Because she is you and lives in your mind. I swear Cole this is just your subconscious dealing with issues that are troublesome to you. Please don't even think that you're communicating with the dead."

"Gemma I know I'm not talking to a ghost or a dead person. Sometimes I feel like it's talking to a person sitting across from me just like we're talking. Mainly, she's giving me advice on how to survive but sometimes gives me personal advice."

That one went over Gemma's head for a minute, and then she reacted. "Just what kind of personal advice is Grandma giving you?"

Cole had never lied to Gemma before and didn't plan to start now. "I guess I shouldn't have said personal. What I meant to say was advice on dealing with people like her son and others in our group."

"And what advice is she giving you concerning me?"

Cole took Gemma's hand. "That one's easy. She told me to love you and keep you safe from all enemies. Oh, and not to have any babies until we get to Oregon."

Their route would take them on Highway 72 past Charlie's farm, and they had agreed to stop for a few minutes to check on Bobby and the kids. The going was slow, but two hours later, they arrived at the turn to Charlie's farm. They were shocked to see that several of the houses and barns on Highway 72 had burned to the ground. They also saw several pickups with bullet holes and one that had been blown up. They turned down the road to the farm and saw a burned out Humvee.

Cole drove down the driveway toward the farmhouse, but nothing but rubble remained. He stopped in front of the burned-out home and looked around to find several grave markers. He took his flashlight and shined it on the crosses. Tears came to his eyes, and he fell to his knees when he saw Bobby's name on one of the grave markers. Gemma and the others joined Cole at the grave and cried along with him.

Cole searched around the house and outbuildings to see if anyone survived and found tire tracks from Humvees and hundreds of spent machinegun brass. Cole alerted the others. "We need to get the hell out of here. FEMA attacked and killed these people. Come on people move it. Let's hit the road."

They traveled Northwest on back roads for the next two days in their attempt to avoid major cities and highways. They only saw a few people during the daytime but did see a few campfires and lights in windows while driving at night. Cole only wanted to drive at night in his original plan, but the attack on Charlie's farm made him anxious to get as far west as possible. He wasn't happy that several of the roads heading northwest had been blocked by fallen trees and landslides. This forced them to go further north toward Jefferson City than he felt was safe. They wouldn't have to go into the city but would have to take the bypass around Jefferson City or side roads just inside the city limits to get back on their planned route to Highway 70.

They arrived on the outskirts of Jefferson City early on the third morning just after midnight. Cole told Gemma that he would take Molly with him to find the best route around the city before the group made the trip the next night. "Babe, I want you to make sure that everyone gets rested up while Molly and I scout the city."

Gemma tried not to show her jealousy as she placed her hands on her hips and turned to face Cole. "Darling, why can't I go with you to do the scouting? You have trained me well, and I can handle myself pretty darn good."

This took him by surprise. "Babe, yes you are learning quickly; however, Molly can... I guess the best way to put this is that she can kill bad guys without hesitating. Honey, you may never become good at killing in hand-to-hand situations."

Gemma thought for a few seconds, and a grin came over her face. "It's a darn shame when you're jealous of your best friend and husband when all he really wants is a better killer by his side and not sex."

Cole was surprised that Gemma was jealous of Molly and him. "Are you really jealous of Molly?"

"Honey I try not to be but let's face it. Molly doesn't have a boyfriend, and she likes you a lot. I'll never get out of my mind that you two shared that bedroom for over a month. I'm sorry, but I can't help being jealous. I understand why you want to take her instead of me, but it still hurts a bit. I guess I just have to practice stabbing and shooting to get to go with you in the future."

Cole started to bite his lip and not ask; however, curiosity got the better of him. "Are you jealous of Jenny and me?"

"Oh no, I could never be jealous of Jenny and you. Jenny and I are almost like the same person. Wait a minute, don't get any ideas there big boy. Maybe I should be jealous, but I'm not."

Cole had a million thoughts rambling around in his mind but decided to keep his mouth shut. Gemma stopped Cole when he started to leave and said, "Cole I need a few minutes of your time. There's never a good time or place to cover this topic so I'll just dive right in. You are my hero and have saved Molly, Jenny, and my lives numerous times. We couldn't survive without you. Now the hard part, if anything happens to me, I want you to keep taking care of them. I hope we find them good husbands in the near future, but it's not likely to happen on a trip of this sort. Please make sure they get to Oregon and take care of them. This would mean a lot to me, so please don't give me an off-the-cuff answer. Think it through and only commit if you can look me in the eye and promise you'll do it."

Cole's first reaction was to say what the hell is this about? He thought for a minute before answering her. "Babe, first thing is that nothing is going to happen to you, but if it does, you know I will take care of the girls. You don't have to worry about that."

Gemma gave Cole a quick kiss and sent him off into the darkness. She watched him help Molly with her gear and then watched them leave in the old pickup truck heading towards Jefferson City. Gemma tried not to think about it; however, she knew that every time Cole went on a mission that he might not come back. She also wondered if the trip to Oregon was worth the pain and heartache. Every time they were attacked or had to kill to survive, Gemma wanted more and more to just find a place and settle down. She thought their lives were much more important than where they lived.

Cole drove down the dusty old dirt road until they had to stop because a tree had fallen across the highway. Cole got out of the truck and walked to the other side of the blockage. He saw several trees were blocking the road. He was very disturbed when he saw the tracks the bulldozer had left when it knocked the trees down.

Cole signaled Molly to join him. "Molly, I thought there were too many damn roads blocked and began wondering what could cause this. Look at these tracks on the ground. That's the kind of tracks a bulldozer leaves. See the scrapes on the trunk of that big tree where someone knocked it over and pushed it across the road with a bulldozer. Molly, I think FEMA is either blocking the way west or funneling people into Jefferson City."

"Why would they block the way west?"

Cole pondered the question for a few seconds. "Molly it's all about increasing the number of people in their slave camps. By blocking the roads, they're funneling travelers into ambushes where they can be captured or killed. The bastards are also collecting the vehicles for their own use."

Molly replied, "Well that stinks. So what do we do? Go much further south and around the blockades or fight our way through."

"Molly we can't fight them because they have us outgunned and outnumbered. We're going to have to find a way around the blockades."

Something caught Molly's attention, and she turned her head to listen back in the direction they had come from. Cole, there is a vehicle approaching."

Cole knew there was no time to move the truck to safety, so he called Molly. "Follow me, Molly; we have to head into the woods."

Cole quickly ran to the other side of the massive tree that was blocking the road. He then led Molly into the woods and hid behind a logjam about 100 feet from the blockade. They only waited a few seconds before an old beat up pickup truck led a Humvee through the roadblock. Two men got out of the old pickup truck and pointed at Cole's truck. One man said, "See, I told you so. There was a man and a woman in the truck when it went by me a few miles back. Now give me the reward."

The FEMA Sergeant laughed. "You know that's bullshit. There is no reward unless we get the people. Do you see any people? Now get your sorry asses out in the woods and find those people. Bring them to us, and you'll get your reward."

The two men walked into the woods heading in Cole and Molly's direction. One man had a shotgun, and the other had a .38 revolver strapped to his hip. Cole drew his knife, pointed at the two men, and made a slashing sign across his throat. Molly drew her knife and gave Cole a thumbs up. Cole had Molly stand behind a tree while he circled back behind the men. As soon as the first man passed Molly, Cole slipped up behind the second man and grabbed his head. In one motion, Cole cupped his hand over the man's mouth and slit his throat.

Molly grabbed her man by the throat as she kicked him in the back of the knee and thrust her knife into his kidney. She stabbed him five times quickly as he dropped to the ground. She kicked his shotgun away from him and looked back at Cole. They had silently dispatched the two men.

Cole placed his face close to Molly's ear. "Good job girl. The men never got a word out. Now let's go back and kill two FEMA troopers. We will shoot them and get the hell outta here. Check the men for any ammunition, and we will take their guns with us."

Cole led Molly through the woods so they could come back from behind the Humvee and attack the men. It took several minutes, but Cole and Molly were hiding behind the Humvee. The men were sitting on one of the fallen trees discussing their mission. "I have to give the boss a lot of credit for this roadblock idea. I would've never guessed how many people are traveling west. Joe, we have rounded up 87 people this week alone. We also have gained six trucks and three cars."

The men laughed and then chatted about how comfortable their lives were back at the FEMA camp. Cole was ready to shoot them when one said. "The boss had better get more guards at the new camp in Westphalia, or we will lose all of those new slaves. I'm wondering if we're short on people. Most of the guards for the Westphalia operation were stripped from the FEMA camps over in Western Kentucky. Rumor has it none of them were replaced. Our leaders need to stop this Western expansion until we can get more recruits."

Cole signaled to Molly to take the man on the right, and he would take the other one. He pointed to his head to indicate to Molly to take a headshot on her target. They both aimed and fired at the same time, but then Cole fired again. Molly's round blew the back of the man's head off. Bone and blood exploded into a fine red mist as the man fell dead to the ground. Molly turned to see Cole's man writhing on the ground with a shot to the shoulder and leg.

Cole kicked the man's weapon away and yelled, "Tell me what I want to know, or I'm going to blow your damned head off."

The man begged for his life. "I'll tell you anything you want to know just, please don't kill me."

Cole poked the man's wounded shoulder with his rifle. "How many prisoners and guards are at the camp in Westphalia?"

"As of yesterday, there were 298 prisoners and 13 guards."

Cole asked, "How many women and children?"

The man's face turned ashen. "There are no children below 13 years old. There are about 190 women, and the rest are men."

The answer shook Cole. "What are y'all doing with the children?"

Cole could see the fear in the man's eyes. The man answered, "FEMA doesn't pay for anyone younger than 13 years old."

Cole was filled with rage. "So y'all just leave the kids with the slavers and buy the adults? What do the slavers do with the kids?"

"I'm telling you the truth, I don't know. Honestly, I didn't want to know."

Cole drew his knife and in one motion stabbed the man in the throat severing his jugular vein. Blood sprayed from the wound and covered Cole's face. With each beat of the man's heart, more blood sprayed out. Finally, there was no more blood. Molly ripped off a piece of the other man's shirt and used it to mop the blood from Cole's face. She poured water from her bottle onto another piece of rag and finish cleaning his face.

Molly scolded Cole. "Honey, that man could have had AIDS or some other infectious disease. You need to be more careful when you kill people. Infected blood could kill you as quickly as a bullet. Gemma would be devastated."

Cole's head hung low as he thought about the fate of those children. Some would be adopted, but he was afraid that many were in the hands of perverts and pedophiles. He looked up at Molly. "Molly when I thought about those children, I flew into a rage. I wish I could've killed him over and over just to watch him die several times."

Cole leaned against the Humvee as he tried to regain his composure. He tried not thinking about the children without success. Molly sat down beside him and laid her head on his shoulder. "We need to quickly move on before someone finds us here with all these dead people. What's your plan?"

"I plan to kill as many FEMA assholes as possible."

Molly massaged Cole's neck. "Cole that plan sounds more like a vendetta than a plan. You are our leader, and we can't have you going off the rails on some kind of crusade. So big boy, pull your head out of that dark, smelly region and let's get our asses in gear and get out of here. We can discuss killing FEMA men later."

Cole and Molly stripped the men of their weapons and ammo before Cole disabled the Humvee. Cole also took the men's tactical vests and two sets of body armor before leaving. They headed south on backcountry roads in their attempt to avoid other people and FEMA. Molly was talking a mile a minute in her effort to keep Cole from thinking about the abuse of children. Unfortunately, she also kept them distracted from watching the road ahead.

Cole had glanced in Molly's direction as he laughed at what she'd said. He looked up to see a sharp turn ahead when suddenly a black Humvee sped around the curve on two wheels. Cole quickly darted off the road into the woods before being noticed. The Humvee was followed by a bus full of people that were also going too fast for the curve. The Humvee spun out and wrecked against a tree throwing one of the occupants onto the road. The bus tipped over on two wheels and ran over the man lying in the street before rolling over on its side. The bus then slid on its side crashing through the brush and small trees on the side of the road.

Cole quickly parked the truck and urged Molly to follow him. "We need to kill all of the guards before they know what hit them. You take the Humvee, and I'll take the bus. Hey, wait! Put on the body armor and tactical vest so we can pass for FEMA assholes. This should confuse them enough that they will be slow targeting us. Let's go hunting."

Molly ran through the woods on the opposite side of the road until she was directly across from the overturned Humvee. She ran across the road and stripped the half-alive FEMA trooper of his weapons, and then she ran to the back of the Humvee. She saw two men in the Humvee. The one in the back was bleeding from a gash on his head, and the one in the front had a broken forearm. Neither was able to fight. Molly looked back at the bus and saw Cole aiming his rifle at one of the guards. She waited until Cole fired his weapon at the guard. She heard the blast from Cole's gun and shot both of the men in the head.

Cole ran across the road using the bottom of the bus for concealment from the guards who had spilled out of the bus onto the ground. Cole heard several of the guards moaning and groaning as they lay on the ground nursing their injuries. Cole looked in the window of the rear door and saw that all of the guards were out of the bus, and many of the prisoners had injuries. Cole peered around the corner of the bus and counted five guards and a driver. One of them decided to go check on the men in the Humvee. Cole ran back around the bus until he was even with the front window and shot the man dropping him to the ground.

Cole then used the front of the bus as cover to engage the rest of the guards. He couldn't see Molly approaching from behind as he picked off the guards one by one. Just as he killed the last guard, there was a blast a few feet behind him. He heard a noise above him and saw a man fall off the side of the bus to the ground with his AR-15. Molly had killed the man before he could kill Cole.

Molly ran up and kicked the man to make sure he was dead and then looked at Cole. "Well, I hope that pays off some of the debt I owe you. You normally save my life when there's a fight."

Cole and Molly walked around the front of the bus and saw a man trying to get out. Cole yelled, "Hey, go back inside until we're ready to get you out. I'm going to open the back doors so y'all can walk out without climbing. I'll shoot anyone who pokes their head out of the windows."

Cole went to the back of the bus and pried the doors open while Molly held her AR pointed at the people on the bus.

Cole said, "I'm sorry, but we don't know if any more FEMA agents are hiding in your group. If there were, it would behoove you to point them out now. Does your group have a leader?"

A large heavy built man stepped forward on the other side of the doorway. "I'm the leader of this group. Thank you for freeing us from FEMA. Did you turn the bus over?"

Cole watch the man as he talked and noticed the man was wearing a clean freshly ironed shirt and pants. "Sir, how long have you been a prisoner with FEMA?"

"I was captured several months back over in Kentucky along with most of the people in the bus. If you let us go, we plan to head back home."

Suddenly the man lunged at Cole with a bayonet. The man quickly overpowered Cole and tried to drive the knife into Cole's chest. Cole had one hand on the man's hand keeping the blade from stabbing him and his other hand on the man's throat. It was clear that Cole was losing the battle when a shot rang out. Cole looked up and saw Molly's gun still smoking. Before Cole could get out from under the man, two more men rushed Molly knocking her to the ground. One of them grabbed her AR-15, and the other raised the knife to stab her. Cole drew his 9 mm from his side and shot the man trying to stab Molly. The other man turned and aimed the AR-15 at Cole. Cole whipped his leg around and kicked the man behind the knee dropping him to the ground. Cole then shot the man at point-blank range in the forehead.

Cole jumped to his feet and pointed the gun at the remaining people on the bus. "I'm going to start shooting every one of you unless someone points out the rest of those damned FEMA agents. A woman waved at Cole and pointed at the man beside her. "There's the last of the son of a bitches."

The man tried to run to the front of the bus, but Cole shot him in the back. The man dropped to the floor, and the rest of the people cheered. Cole told everyone on the bus to sit down until he could check on Molly. Molly was unconscious but breathing. Cole shook her until she woke up. Molly's eyes opened but not as fast as her mouth. "What the fuck happened?"

"Molly you saved my life again, but then several men ran out and tried to attack us. I shot the one trying to stab you and knocked the other one down until I could shoot him. All of the FEMA agents are dead now. Are you okay?"

Molly was a bit unsteady as she stood up and leaned on Cole until she regained her balance. She hugged Cole and kissed him on the cheek. "Cole you are my hero. I don't know what I'd do without you."

"Molly, we make a great team, but we need to get better at this crap, or we're both going to die. Let's go check on the people on the bus."

Cole asked the people to come out of the bus in a single file with their hands up so he could check them for weapons. There were

8 men and 11 women in the group. All were battered and bruised, but only two had broken bones. One lady had a broken finger and another a broken forearm. They found several first-aid kits and did the best they could to set the broken bones.

Cole asked again if they had a leader. This time one of the ladies spoke up and said, "I guess I'm their leader. I'm Staff Sgt. Janet Jared and the only one of the group with any previous leadership experience. I was an MP in the Army."

Cole looked at the lady. "Janet, where were y'all heading when the bus wrecked?"

"They were taking us to work on a farm for the day. I think it was about another five to 10 miles up the road. They will be looking for us shortly. We need to get the hell out of here."

Cole asked, "Where will y'all be going?"

Janet replied, "If you let us have most of the guard's guns, we are heading back to Westphalia to take over that camp and free the prisoners. Most of us have friends and relatives back at the camp. We won't leave them there without a fight."

Cole looked back at Molly and then back to Janet. "Of course you can have the guns, except for one AR-15. Let me talk with my friend here, and perhaps we can help you."

Cole took Molly to the other side of the bus. "Molly ever since I heard about the camp at Westphalia I wanted to attack it and set the people free. There are only 13 guards. What do you think about us providing transportation for this group over to Westphalia? We could use all three of our vehicles and the two trailers to haul them over there. I would only take volunteers from our group and let these guys do most of the heavy lifting in the battle."

Molly grinned and patted Cole on the back. "Cole I was thinking the same thing. I wish someone had helped us escape over in Kentucky. All we really need is three drivers, and you and I are two of them. I know Gemma or Jenny will volunteer. Let's get this show on the road."

Cole's face brightened up as he spoke. "Thanks, Molly I knew I could count on you. We need to get these people as far away from here as possible and hide them until we can take them to meet the others. Let's go check that Humvee to see if it's drivable."

Cole and Molly walked back over to the bus and saw their new friends had stripped the FEMA agents of all their gear and weapons. Cole stepped up to the leader. "Janet, please have someone check the Humvee to see if it's drivable. We need to get your people as far from here as possible, and then I have a plan to take you over to Westphalia."

Janet waved at the group and said, "Leroy, take Jim over to the Humvee and see if you can get it running."

Cole knew it would be tight, but he was sure the Humvee and pickup could haul all of the people back to the camp. He heard a rumble and then saw the Humvee turnaround in the road and head towards him. It had the one side bashed in and had lost a window but appeared to be running without any issues.

"Janet, load up your people. We're taking you home with us," said Cole.

☆

Chapter 6

Cole and Molly watched as the former prisoners loaded up into the Humvee and back of Cole's pick up. "Cole, you know that Jack will shit a brick when he hears our plan to raid the FEMA camp."

"Yes, I can't wait to see the look on his face. Molly, only 13 guards are watching over the camp. We have to free them or no one will."

As usual, they took back roads on the way to the stand of trees where the others camped and waited. They saw no signs of FEMA soldiers along the way. Cole asked Janet to park the Humvee a short distance from the camp so they wouldn't scare the crap out of his friends. Cole drove the pickup into the camp and waved at his wife, Gemma. "Hey, darling I missed you. Please round up the others, we've met some friends and brought them home with us."

The others came running and were surprised to see the bed of the pickup full of people. Deacon was curious. "Cole who are these people and where did you find them?"

Cole shook his friend's hand. "Deacon, the short story is that we freed them from FEMA, and there is another truckload of them waiting on my signal to join us. Hey everybody, there will be a Humvee coming down the road full of freed escapees from a FEMA prison bus. Please don't shoot at them."

Cole reached in the pickup's window and honked the horn twice. A few minutes later, the Humvee rounded the turn and drove into their camp. This started Jack and several others into a heated discussion. Jack said, "We can't feed all of these people. We can't take in every lost person and stray that we find."

Cole walked over to Jack with clenched fists. "Jack please shut up until you know what you're talking about. Everyone on our team, please listen to our plan. First, these people won't be staying with us. We will feed them today while we regroup and work on our plan. Second, I just found out there is a FEMA camp in Westphalia with around 300 people. These people left that camp in a work bus that crashed. Molly and I killed the guards and freed these men and women. Third, the camp is very lightly guarded with only 13 guards. They plan to attack and kill the guards to free those people. Fourth, Molly and I are volunteering to help with the attack. I would like several of you to volunteer to help us. This is not an order, and you don't have to help."

Jack immediately started grousing and complaining. "Cole you don't know what you've got us into. If we help free those people, FEMA will chase us down and kill us all."

Gemma walked over to Jack. "Jack, you and Carole have never been prisoners in a FEMA camp. The rest of us have, and we prayed every day that someone would help free us. If you and Carole don't want to help and feel your safety is threatened, you can take some supplies and leave us now. Jenny and I volunteer to help these people."

Deacon stood up and stretched out his 6-foot 5-inch frame above Jack. "Jack I'm sorry, but you're wrong. I won't speak for Madison, but I'm in with Cole and the girls. We have to help free these people from those filthy bastards. I couldn't go on down the road and live with myself if I didn't try to help."

Before Jack could say anything, Carole walked up to him and whispered. "Jack, stop being an ass. Those people need our help, and I'm gonna do my best to help free them. I hope you join me and have my back."

Jack was at a loss for words. He stood there shifting his weight from foot to foot and then said, "I don't like it, but I'll support the team. Just let me know what I need to do."

Cole slapped Jack on the back and replied, "Thanks old buddy; you're doing the right thing. Now, let's rustle up some grub for these people. I'm hungry."

Molly laughed at Jack as she saw him watching the people eat. She whispered to Gemma. "Jack is counting every mouthful of food that he thinks these people are taking away from us."

Cole stood up and banged a spoon on a glass to get their attention. "Janet, I need you to choose the leaders of your group so we can have a meeting and build a plan of attack. We will need several people to become snipers, an infiltration team, and foot soldiers for our attack on the camp. Let's quickly finish eating, and we will meet at the back of my pickup."

Cole had a brief meeting with his team. "Madison, Jack, and Carole, I want you three to become our lookouts and to shoot any guards trying to escape from the camp. I'll tell you where to take up your position after we scout the camp. Gemma, you and Jenny will be our snipers, and your mission will be to kill every guard you can as fast as you can when we give the signal. Molly and I will help infiltrate the camp and take out their communications. That's when I'll give the signal for the snipers to do their dirty work. Does anyone have any questions?"

No one noticed, but Gemma pinched Cole when she heard Cole was paired up with Molly again. Gemma asked, "Cole I think we need to take the two 30.06 hunting rifles along with our ARs. Is that okay?"

"Of course that's okay. The hunting rifles will be much more accurate at long-range than the .223 bullets."

There were no other questions, so Cole took the crew to the back of his pickup and waited on Janet's team. They arrived a few minutes later. Janet shook everyone's hand on Cole's team and introduced her team. "This is George, and he's an expert hunter and will lead our snipers. Carl used to work for the Bowling Green police force and will lead our foot soldiers. As I mentioned before I was an MP in the Army and will lead our part of the infiltration team. Oh, I have a rough map of the camp that we put together."

This pleased Cole, and he thanked Janet. Cole then went over his thoughts on a plan of attack. The main points were listed. First, they would attack just after the sun came up. Second, they would sneak in and disable the camp's communications, while killing as many guards as possible. The infiltration team would also hand out pistols to some of the prisoners to help fight the guards. Third, the snipers would pick off any guards that showed themselves. Fourth, the lookouts would kill any guards trying to escape.

Cole asked, "Is there any way to get a message into the camp? It would be nice if you had some trusted people in the camp that were ready and prepared to help us overcome the guards."

Carl spoke up, "Yes there is. I have a man on my team who has snuck in and out of the camp several times without being caught. I can have him sneak a message into several people we trust. He could also take in several pistols and knives."

The thought that they could arm the people inside the camp before the attack was a big relief to Cole's team. Cole thanked Carl for his input. "Carl, that's fantastic. You guys might have them all killed before we even attack. Would they know where any of the long-range radios or other communication devices are located? I'm not worried about the short-range walkie-talkies."

Carl replied, "Yes because we've been planning to escape before we met you. Oh, I forgot to mention that we have several men and women with military experience among the prisoners."

Cole was astounded and had a shocked look on his face. "That's a game changer. We need to modify our plans to include your military people destroying the communications and killing as many guards as possible. How many do you think you have that you can trust?"

Janet and Carl had a short sidebar, and then Janet apologized. "I'm sorry I failed to mention our people with military experience inside the camp. There are 23 known people with military experience. About 15 of them were actual combat soldiers in Iran and Turkey during the last war. If we can get guns and knives to them, they should be able to kill most of the guards by themselves."

Cole thought for a minute and then gave some orders. "I need both our teams to give me a list of all weapons in our possession. We need to know how many guns and knives we can sneak into the camp. Okay, everybody, break out your guns and lay all extra weapons on a blanket behind my truck."

Twenty minutes later, they had counted all weapons and found that there were no extra weapons if every one of them was given a weapon. Cole and Janet had a brief discussion and came back to the group. Cole said, "It's more important to get weapons into the camp then to arm every one of us. About half of you have no experience fighting or have ever killed a person. We will take those guns and knives and sneak them into the camp."

Several of the men and women in Janet's group bitched about losing their weapons. Janet gave them a pep talk. "Look, people, you know darn well we will be more successful with those guns in the hands of our experienced military people that are already in the camp. I promise when this is done we will give them back to you. You do realize that without weapons you will be held in reserve in a safe location. Now quit griping and get with the program."

They planned to attack in two days, which would give them time to work out kinks in their plan and to smuggle their weapons into the camp.

After they broke up for the day, Cole took Gemma and Jenny away from the camp for some hand-to-hand combat training. They arrived at an open spot in the woods not far from the camp. Gemma said, "Cole now that you have us out here, why are we here?"

"Because I promised to teach you how to fight so you could better protect yourself and go on missions with me."

Jenny laughed. "And why am I included in this training?"

Cole returned the laughter and lightly punched Jenny on the shoulder. "Because your sister once told me that y'all are almost like the same person. I think it would be dangerous on my part not to train you equally in the skills of warfare and survival. Once I get you two up to speed, I'll include Molly on advanced training. Let's face it, ladies; we have another 2000 miles of dangerous territory and people to fight our way through. We four are going to be together for a long time and need to watch each other's back and be prepared to kill to protect each other."

Both Gemma and Jenny hugged Cole and then knocked him to the ground. They bounced up off the ground ready to fight. Cole promptly threw both of them to the ground. "As I just said you both need a lot of training. An attack like that might seem funny to you two knuckleheads, but it would get you killed. Now Jenny, sit on the ground and watch while I abuse your sister."

They spent the next two hours with Cole demonstrating how to break holds and how to use the enemy's weaknesses against them. Toward the end of the training, the girls were exhausted but tried not to show it. They could now throw Cole to the ground and block most of his punches. Cole spent half the time teaching them that they needed to forget about fighting like a man. They were so much lighter and not as strong as most men, so they needed to surprise their enemy with a vicious attack and disable them quickly. He showed them how to break noses, bust kneecaps, and smash genitals to even the playing field.

Gemma came up from behind and smashed Cole to the ground. She then sat down on top of him. Cole was winded but soon got his breath back. "Girls that's all for today, y'all are just getting too damn tough for me. One thing I can't stress enough is that you should never kick your coach with a real kick to the nose, kneecap, shin, or balls. Hell for that matter, never kick me at all. I'll make a practice dummy for you lady warriors."

Jenny piled on top of Cole along with Gemma. "Boy that was fun today, what are you gonna teach us tomorrow?"

Cole flipped her over and trapped her head between his knees. "I might teach you how to wrestle tomorrow. I'm not hurting you, am I?"

He loosened his leg grip on her and allowed her to sit up. She hit his leg with her small fist. "That wasn't fair I didn't know we were still fighting."

Cole replied, "Always be prepared to defend yourself when we are training, you're going about your normal day, or taking a dump in the woods. Always be prepared to defend yourself. Tomorrow, we will work on knife fighting and more hand-to-hand combat."

The time passed quickly as Cole spent his time meeting with the leaders of the various teams and training the girls in hand-to-hand combat. He also gave all of the snipers a refresher course to help sharpen their skills. Cole knew that he was not an expert in hand-to-hand combat or knife fighting, but he did pass on everything he knew to the girls and several of Janet's people who joined them to increase their survival skills.

Cole had Molly join them and used her to train some of the new people from Janet's team. By the end of the second day, Gemma and Jenny were as proficient as Molly in the art of stabbing, choking, and slitting throats. Everyone that took the training felt good about their new skills; however, they were now bruised and battered. Cole felt much better because he knew his wife and the other two were much better able to defend themselves now.

Gemma and Cole lay on a blanket looking up at the stars while swatting mosquitoes. Gemma told Cole how much the girls and she appreciated the training. "Cole, please teach us everything you know. I hope I never have to kill anyone again, but I do want to be prepared to protect my family and pass the training down to our kids."

Cole rolled over and kissed Gemma. "You said, kids. You know something I don't know?"

Gemma squeezed Cole's hand and said, "Would having a kid be so bad."

"Gemma, you know I'd love to have babies with you but now is not the time. If it does happen, we will love our baby and raise it the best we can with all the shit going down."

Gemma held Cole close to her. "No, I'm not pregnant, but I do want to have a baby as soon as possible. I don't think there will ever be a good time to raise kids for the next hundred years. When we do have kids, I want to be able to protect them and train them to protect themselves."

Cole held his wife as he pondered their future. "Gemma we haven't talked much about our future. Molly and I have always been dead set on getting to Oregon. I really do miss my family and friends, but now you and the others are my new family and friends. We're not going to make it to Oregon this year before the snow flies. I would like to make it to Denver and find a place to hold up over the winter. Then we can tackle crossing the Rockies in the late spring and summer. If one of you ladies gets pregnant, we have to cancel the trip until the baby is old enough to withstand the rigors of the trip."

Gemma frowned at her husband. "Is that your way of reinforcing the point that we don't need any kids, yet?"

"Babe, I'll be honest with you. I really do want to have children with you, but until we are settled in one place, it could be hazardous for the kids. Take tomorrow for example. Both of us could be killed tomorrow and then who will take care of our kids if we were both dead?"

Except for Janet's infiltration team, they all turned in early that night. Cole didn't get much sleep thinking about the attack on the FEMA camp and starting a new family. Both were equally scary to Cole, but he knew he had to come to grips with both situations. Gemma wasn't even 20 yet, so they had plenty of time for kids. He just couldn't imagine raising children while on the road fighting for their lives every day.

Cole fell asleep thinking about his mom and brother, Charlie. He wondered how Joe, Cobie, and Cloe were doing out in Oregon.

He thought that surely things were getting better for them since they had killed off most of the bad guys in the area.

He dozed off and suddenly saw Joe's Grandma in his mind.

Dear Cole:

Cole, I'm sure that Joe told you that one of the reasons I wrote the letters is that I'm dying of cancer and taking these damn chemo treatments. I wanted to write as many letters as possible to Joe and his dad before I died so I can share my wisdom with them. I wrote each of them over 130 letters in the last six months of my life. Since you are now speaking to a spook who can live forever, I'm not in any damned hurry. Son, you're stuck with me.

You only have a few more minutes to sleep, so I'll make this brief. Don't believe anything you hear and only half of what you see today. Go in guns blazing and let God sort them out. You and your people are more important than any of these others and certainly more important than those FEMA assholes. I didn't like FEMA when they were well-run by our trusted officials so you know darn well I don't like them now when they're run by thugs and crooks.

May God be with you, son.

Love Grandma

The guard woke everyone up by 1 AM so they could have breakfast and then drive the 20 some odd miles over to Westphalia. Cole could tell Gemma was still a bit icy towards him as they ate their breakfast. He tried several times to start a conversation with her without success. She would only give yes and no answers. They had loaded the vehicles the night before and were ready to go as soon as everyone was finished with breakfast.

Cole led the way with Gemma and Jenny in the front of the old pickup truck. The two Broncos and Humvee followed closely behind loaded with people. Cole noted that Gemma and Jenny talked about the attack and several personal issues, but Gemma didn't direct any conversation at Cole.

An hour later, they were south of Westphalia and heading northwest on a dirt road so they would come up to the camp from the East. They stopped and hid in the woods about half a mile from the camp. The infiltration team had placed a wooden cross with a red ribbon on the side of the road. This was Cole's sign to pull off the road and wait on word from the infiltration team. They didn't have to wait long because one of the infiltration team members came out of the woods as soon as the trucks were parked. The woman reported to Cole. "Boss, it went better than we hoped. They were ready for the weapons and eager to join us. They will begin their skullduggery at 4 AM sharp. Our team is also in place and ready to slit throats and free prisoners."

Cole thanked the woman and sent her to rejoin her team.

The FEMA camp had been quickly constructed beside the local high school so FEMA could make use of the school for offices and sleeping quarters. There was only one row of 8-foot tall fence around the complex. The razor ribbon and guard towers had not been installed yet.

Cole positioned his lookouts in several places around the complex and gave them their final instructions. Shoot first and ask questions later was Cole's motto of the day. He still remembered Grandma's words. Cole then sent the snipers to their vantage points overlooking the school and huge courtyard. None of the houses or buildings around the school had been burned or severely damaged, so it was easy for Cole to place snipers on top of the four tallest buildings.

Cole finished giving the snipers their directions and asked Gemma to stay behind for a second. "Darling I know you're mad at me, but this is a perilous situation today, and I don't want the last time I see you for you to be mad at me. I love you so much and would do anything for you."

Gemma took Cole in her arms and kissed him. "Babe, I love you very much and will get over it quickly. I'm not mad at you, but I am very mad at this screwed up situation we find ourselves in today. Why did the world have to end for me to meet the man of my dreams?"

Cole kissed her. "Thanks, I needed that. I love you Gemma, and you'd better get moving to your position. Happy hunting."

Cole walked over to the men and women, which he called his foot soldiers, and gave them a short pep talk as they waited to go into action. He wasn't good at public speaking, but he did crack a few jokes and tell them what Wes and Earl had told him before going into battle several times. They were soon laughing, and the tension was broken. Cole then reminded them of the job at hand. "I know some of you have never fired a shot in anger or killed anyone. That will change today. Your friend's lives in the prison and our lives depend on you pulling the trigger when faced with the enemy. Remember those are the bastards that imprisoned you and made you into slaves; kill the sons of bitches."

Cole looked down at the watch that his mentor, Earl, had given him months ago when they were out on a mission. It was 3:59 AM and his stomach was tied in knots. When the hand ticked 4 AM, Cole led his men to the gate to the FEMA camp. As they ran to the gate, they heard several shots ring out, and the two guards dropped. Cole took the bolt cutters and cut the lock on the gate letting his motley crew run through and join the attack.

Half an hour before the rest of Cole's team attacked, the infiltration team began working their magic. Janet had four of her team and a dozen of the prisoners killing guards and disabling the communication gear. The men and women who had been prisoners at the camp for several months knew where the guards would be and where they slept. The hatred they had for these guards was immense, and their anger was satisfied that night. The guard in charge of communications was quickly dispatched with a knife, and the captain over the camp died shortly afterward. There was no better way to describe the fury of killing other than it was pure bloodlust. The infiltration team members who had been abused by the guards for months now killed and tortured each one of the son of a bitches.

Cole led his team through the gate and sent Molly's team to the left as his team sprinted to the right end of the high school. All of his team members were ready for action and looking for a fight. They saw no one. Not one guard came out to confront them. The snipers had no targets. The lookouts didn't see any guards trying to escape. Janet's infiltration team had killed every guard. The battle was over before it started.

Cole saw Janet walk out of the administration building. "Janet, what happened to all the guards?"

"Sorry Cole, but we killed all the bastards before you got here."

Cole was shocked and then relieved. "I love it when a good plan comes together."

Janet then said, "All we have to do now is to free the prisoners. I know that sounds easy; however, not all of the prisoners are model citizens. We have to be careful and not trade one slave master for another."

Cole replied, "I guess my guy's job is done, so we will get back home and get ready to head on west."

Janet asked Cole to wait. "Hold on for a minute. We found their armory and their fuel dump. Your team needs to take some of the weapons and as much fuel as you can carry. There are dozens of 5-gallon Jerry cans full of diesel and gasoline. Carl will give you six AR-15's and two M4s with plenty of ammunition."

Cole thought a minute. "That sounds more than fair, but could you spare any food from their cafeteria. Dry goods, canned goods, or even MREs would be appreciated."

Janet quickly replied, "I know we're short of fresh foods, but I think we have a ton of military MREs that we can spare. I hope that helps you."

Cole's face beamed with delight. "That would be excellent. As I mentioned, we have a long trip ahead of us, and the MREs are perfect for us. Thank you and good luck to your team. I highly recommend that you get away from here as fast as possible. The FEMA commander for this area still has people looking for us, and he will crap his pants when he hears that a whole FEMA camp escaped on his watch."

Janet tapped Cole on the shoulder. "We will be gone tomorrow. Cole, we have a small group of people who are from Seattle. They would like to travel with you as you head west. I can personally vouch for them."

The request surprised Cole. "I'm sorry, but I'll have to know a lot more about them before we can add them to our group. Can they handle a gun and protect themselves? Do they have any survival skills?"

"Paul fought in Iran and was a doomsday prepper for several years before the lights went out. He has trained his wife and daughter to shoot and survive in the woods. Brad has recently learned how to handle weapons but is new to survival skills. He is still learning."

Cole stroked his beard as he thought about this new dilemma. "Janet, if you don't mind, I'd like my group to meet them to determine if they're a good fit for us."

This disturbed Janet. "Cole that bothers me that you won't take my recommendation for these people."

Cole was expecting her reaction and replied, "Janet, I trust your judgment even though I haven't known you for very long; however, the people in my group may have to live with these people for many months on our trek to the West Coast. They must have a say in who joins our group. Are you okay with this?"

"I guess when you put it that way, I have to agree. I'll get them brought up here immediately."

A thought came to Cole's mind. "Janet before I forget, do you feel that you have any spies in your group? There were a few in the FEMA camp that we escaped from."

Janet pondered the question for a minute. "I don't know of any, but FEMA did seem to know more than they should have known about what was going on in my close-knit group."

Cole brought his team together at a picnic table by the basketball court. He explained to them Janet's request for these people to join them. As he expected, Jack put up a fuss. "I don't like this one bit. We don't know them, and it gives us more mouths to feed. I'm against it."

Deacon raised his hand to speak. "Cole this does take us by surprise, and I guess Janet took you by surprise. I agree with you that we should interview these people before making a decision. While there normally is safety in numbers, a large group would be easier for FEMA to find. I'll try to keep an open mind."

The rest of the team had their doubts about any strangers joining them but were open to interviewing them before deciding. They quickly put together a list of questions to ask the new people. They ranged from, have you ever had to kill in self-defense to what did you do to try to escape the FEMA camp.

Carole cleared her throat and nodded her head in the direction of the admin building. "Here comes the new crew."

The group stood up and welcomed the newcomers to the table, and everyone introduced themselves. Cole saw a big smile on Molly's face when she saw Brad, who was very handsome and had an athletic build. Cole thought that this could be a problem between Jenny and Molly.

Cole banged his knuckles on the table and brought the meeting to order. "I hope Janet told you that this meeting is to decide if y'all are a good fit for our team. She has already vouched for you, but we are a tightknit band of people with a long way to go and don't need any disruptions. We also can't babysit any people who can't carry their own weight. I know my words may piss you off, but that's life. We are going to try to get to know you very quickly and ask a lot of questions. I suggest you do the same with us because after you get to know us, you might not want to go with us. Any questions so far?"

A man named Paul spoke for the group. "Our group has the same concerns, and we take no offense from your caution. I suggest that your group start the discussion with three questions, and then we will ask your group three questions. I also suggest that if we don't like the answers, we keep it to ourselves until all the questions are asked. There is no way any group of people would be a perfect match for another group, so I recommend moving through the questions and then deciding if there are enough positive matches for our groups to join."

Cole replied, "That sounds like a good plan. Before we get started, I want to cover the group's rules that you would have to live by."

Paul was visibly disturbed by Cole's comments. "Wouldn't we have a say in how the group was managed?"

Cole knew this was coming and quickly responded. "Yes, everyone is free to give input, but I make the final decision. Let me cover the rules quickly. I am the leader of the group. I make all the final decisions. I listen and take advice but still make the final decision. You as an individual must be prepared to fight and kill to protect the group. You must pull your own weight and contribute to the group's success. Everyone fights and everyone pulls guard duty. You are free to leave the group anytime you want to."

Paul's face had now turned red, and his fists were clenched. "How is it that a young boy is the leader of the group and has such power?"

Deacon quickly spoke up. "Because he has proven himself time and again by killing our enemies, saving many of our lives, and giving us excellent leadership. Cole may be young in age, but he is very wise and experienced in survival."

Before anyone else could say anything, Jack stood up. "I too questioned a young lad becoming our leader. I was wrong, as you are wrong. One of you may be a strong leader and can take your group to the West Coast. This group will follow Cole into hell and back. He saved my life twice and kept me in this group even though I made some poor decisions that caused harm to the group. Your group is free to head west on its own, or you can join us if you accept the rules Cole covered."

All of Cole's team applauded Jack's endorsement of Cole. This surprised Paul and his small group. Brad spoke up for the first time. "I personally don't care who our leader is, as long as they are competent, fair, and get us to the West Coast safely. I guess we need to back away and decide if we can accept those rules."

Paul took his team across the courtyard and discussed what they heard. Cole's crew could tell they were having a lively discussion by just watching the body language. A few minutes later Paul brought the crew back to the table. Paul tried not to have a scowl on his face as he sat down at the table. "We can live with those rules, but I have reservations about the leadership."

Cole stood up and said, "I expect my orders to go unquestioned, and you lead me to believe that you will be second-guessing all of my orders. May God go with you during your journey, but you won't be going with us. Team, we'll head back to camp and prepare to move out."

All of Cole's people stood up, wished the other group well, and walked away. Paul shouted out to Cole. "You'll regret not taking us with you because you need a strong leader."

Gemma replied, "We have an excellent leader and wish you well. See you on the West Coast, if you make it there."

Cole told Janet the results of the meeting and said goodbye. She replied, "Cole, I think you're making a big mistake. Paul would've been an excellent leader for your group."

Cole responded, "What exactly did Paul do during the war?"

Janet's face turned red. "He was a supply sergeant at the depot in Kuwait. Cole that doesn't mean he doesn't have the leadership qualities that your team needs."

"Janet, has he been in hand-to-hand combat? Has he snapped a man's neck and broken his spinal column? Has he killed dozens of thugs from 200 to 1000 yards? Has he led men on patrols and raiding missions? Janet, in the last year and a half I have done all of this including leading men and women to their deaths in battle. I've had excellent mentors and learned quickly as we fought for our existence when we were always outgunned and outnumbered. Paul is a desk jockey, and I hope they do well, but he is not the one to lead our group. May God go with you and your group? Our thoughts and prayers will be with you."

Paul's group drove away from the FEMA camp that afternoon. They took one Humvee and an SUV pulling a trailer on their trip to Seattle. Janet watched them leave and wished Cole's group had gone with them. She was very much afraid that Cole's group wouldn't survive the journey due to their poor decision.

☆

Chapter 7

As Cole and his crew loaded their new supplies and weapons, Carl drove up in a Humvee. "We have a few extra of these Humvees and thought you might want one."

Cole and Deacon laughed at the same time. Deacon thanked the man, as he shook his head no. "Sorry, but those things are FEMA magnets. They stand out like a sore thumb, and all of the FEMA spies will track our every move. Your group needs to ditch them as soon as possible. Thanks but no thanks."

Carl laughed and said, "I told the bosses the same thing and was told that I was a worrywart. I do have a few surprises for you in the back of the Humvee. There are several walkie-talkies, boxes of antibiotics, and several bags of hygiene products. I'm breaking away from the group and heading down to Mobile, Alabama with a few other rednecks. I'm getting away from the rest of these people as fast as possible. Be safe my friends. Bye."

Cole asked. "Carl, were you surprised that we turned down Paul and his group?"

"Yes, frankly I was surprised. Paul has had his nose so far up Janet's ass and became one of her top supporters. I was afraid her

99

recommendation would be enough for you to take them. The jury is out on Brad. I don't know why, but I just don't like him. I think you're better off without them and they sure as hell aren't going to Alabama with us."

Cole shook the man's hand. "Thanks and we really appreciate the supplies."

They arrived back at their temporary camp a couple of hours later. They were all exhausted even though the FEMA troops hadn't put up a fight. Cole thanked everyone for the great job and the vote of confidence during the meeting. He then divided the team so that most of them could get some sleep while the others pulled guard duty. They even spent the next day resting instead of packing up and leaving.

Cole did make use of some of the time training his friends on their new weapons and walkie-talkies. Deacon and Cole kept the M4 fully automatic rifles and passed out the ARs to the ones who didn't have one. All of the others now had AR-15s and by the end of the day were proficient in taking them apart and reassembling them. Cole had them practice by dry firing since he didn't want to draw attention to their group.

They loaded everything up that night and prepared to leave early the next morning. Cole and Gemma were sound asleep when Madison woke them up and reported that FEMA helicopters had just flown through the area. Cole woke everyone up and told them to prepare to bug out. They had a cold breakfast and were on the road by 3:30 AM.

Cole now knew that they had made a mistake by taking time to rest. They traveled without their headlights on and drove due west as fast as they could. A few minutes after they left the camp Gemma pointed east, and Cole saw a searchlight from a helicopter scanning the ground a few miles from where they just left. Gemma laid her head on Cole's shoulder. "Baby, we were damned lucky to get away from there. We shouldn't have stayed the extra day to rest."

"I know. I think I was trying to be nice to the group because they all supported me against Paul. I have to get back to making the tough decisions even though it hurts people's feelings. That's what a good leader does."

Gemma laughed. "You saw right through me, didn't you?"

They drove on until the sun came up, and then pulled into the woods for a rest. Gemma and Jenny offered MREs and coffee for breakfast. Cole and Jack scouted the area to make sure it was safe. They heard Carole yell something, so they went to join her. She was standing in the middle of a small apple orchard behind a farmhouse eating a juicy red apple. Carole saw them come running. "Boys come on over here. These apples are delicious. We need to take several bags of them with us."

Cole went back to the trucks, found two empty bags, and took them back to Carole. Jack and Carole filled the bags with apples while Cole walked up to the back of the farmhouse. He was worried that someone might think they were stealing apples, but there was no one there. They filled the bags and headed back to their vehicles when suddenly they heard gunfire on up the road.

"Gemma, come with me," Cole said.

They walked through the woods alongside the road about half a mile until they saw two Humvees sitting in the middle of the road with several bodies lying behind them. Gemma whispered in Cole's ear. "Cole, that's Paul and his wife lying dead."

Cole grimaced and then felt sorry for the dead. "I knew those Humvees would attract too much attention, but Paul would never listen to me."

Gemma quickly replied, "Cole, we both saw that coming. It's just a shame. It could've been avoided if Paul hadn't been so pigheaded. I wonder if any of them are still alive. I see four bodies there."

"Babe, how many of the FEMA men do you see?" Cole asked.

She answered, "I only see three men and one vehicle parked in the woods. Let's be careful if you plan to attack them."

Cole replied, "No, it's their lucky day. I don't want to bring any more attention to this area than we have to. Let's go back to our vehicles and hope these assholes move on."

They started to sneak back in the woods when Cole saw movement on their left side. Cole signaled for Gemma to stop and wait on him. He quietly moved deeper into the woods and came back around to his left where he saw two people huddled under a bush. It was Paul's daughter, Joan, and Brad hiding from the FEMA troops. Cole moved closer and whispered to get their attention. They saw him, and he waved for them to follow him. He led them back to Gemma, and they high tailed it back to Cole's group.

As soon as they stopped, Cole questioned them. "What happened back there? Why did they ambush and kill your parents?"

Between sobs, Joan tried to tell them what happened. "The men in black stood in the middle of the road and challenged us to stop. Dad gunned the motor and tried to run them over. They opened fire on us, and we never got a shot off."

Cole could tell that Brad was very angry and upset. Brad interrupted Joan, "If Paul had just stopped, he and your mom would still be alive. I told Paul a dozen times that FEMA wants us alive not dead. If we don't stand a chance to kill all of them, we should never shoot."

"Brad, that's not fair. Dad just couldn't handle us all being captured and made slaves again."

Brad dropped his head and wrung his hands. "I guess he likes being dead better than being a live slave."

Cole waved his hands and interrupted the argument. "What's done is done and throwing blame around won't solve anything. Stay with us until you to figure out what you're going to do. Gemma, please get them something to eat and drink."

While Brad and Joan ate, Cole held a short meeting. "We're going to be stuck here until these FEMA creeps pull out. Get some rest and make the best of it. We could easily overpower and kill the three FEMA troopers; however, I don't want to draw any more attention to this area. So let's cool our heels here, Jenny, and I will keep an eye on the FEMA guys. I'd also like to bury Joan's parents. If possible."

Cole and Jenny walked back to the ambush site on the opposite side of the road but a bit deeper into the woods to help make sure they had missed any hidden enemy. Much of the brush and undergrowth had been burned away by a recent fire. Numerous rains and the winter snow had washed away most of the smell, but their clothes were covered in the charcoal residue. Cole noticed the forest was still alive in spite of the fire. There were many new plants, and vegetation sprouting up all over. Cole thought that this was evidence that the Earth would go on regardless of man's futile attempt to wipe his own race from the earth.

Jenny was disgusted to see that the bodies and shot up Humvee had been shoved off the road. The FEMA thugs were gone, but the shell casings and blood on the road were evidence of their handiwork. Jenny asked, "Cole, what has happened to our government? If these FEMA thugs are organized enough to take over everything east of the Mississippi to Charlotte, they are a threat to the entire country. Why can't the US government help us? They should've shut down this rogue FEMA operation."

Jenny saw Cole's head move from side to side as he struggled for an answer. "Girl, I have no idea. It's as if the federal government and state governments disappeared. I once heard Joe and Earl discussing this topic. They concluded that our officials and law enforcement people just went home to take care of their loved ones. The want-to-be dictators and thugs saw this as an opportunity to start their own kingdoms. We may never know what really happened, but that's my best guess."

Cole walked out of the woods and onto the road as he searched for any signs that there might still be FEMA thugs in the area. Satisfied no one remained he walked over to the bodies to check them out. Paul and his wife had been executed with a bullet to their brains. Cole didn't recognize two other men whose bodies were stacked beside Paul and his wife. Cole felt terrible as he checked the bodies for weapons and ammunition. He found two pistols and four magazines for the pistols.

Cole went back into the woods on the opposite side of the road to search the area where the FEMA thugs had parked their vehicle. "Jenny look for anything that we could use that they might've dropped."

They found the tire tracks and several wrappers and containers from discarded MREs but nothing else. They loitered around the area for another hour before deciding to go back to join their friends. Cole enjoyed the walk with Jenny and found it very difficult to avoid confusing her with Gemma. He knew they were identical twins, but even their mannerisms, voice, and thought process were the same.

"Jenny, what do you think about Brad? He seems to be an okay guy, but I can't get a good read on him."

Jenny turned and smiled at Cole. "I hadn't given it much thought. He seems like a nice guy."

"Don't bullshit me, girl, I saw you checking him out. You know I can read you as well as I read Gemma. You two are more than identical twins. You could be the same person. If I hadn't seen you both together, I would think that was only one of you posing as two people," Cole said as he laughed.

Jenny stopped and placed her hand on Cole's chest. "What makes you think I'm Jenny?"

That night Cole quickly fell asleep and had another Grandma dream.

Dear Cole:

Joe was right about you. Ya' done good today. Aren't you glad you trusted your gut reaction on Paul and his wife? That SOB was a hardheaded know it all who would've been dangerous to the group. You sensed that and led your group in the right direction.

Cole, you must have more faith in your judgment. Yes, I know you're only 18 going on 19, but Joe, Wes, and Earl did a great job mentoring you. They only had you for a short time but look how far you've come. Don't just say you're the leader, leaders lead. They have to be decisive while supporting their team. Yeah, you'll make some errors and bad decisions; however, as long as you learn from your mistakes, you can keep this group safe and together.

Now, for some of my wisdom. That Brad guy is not what he seems, and he has his eyes on Molly and Jenny. Watch him closely. The girl, Joan, is a whiny ass bitch. She will drag your group down if you let her. Keep an eye on those two and if you can get rid of them peacefully, do it. Mark my words, those two are trouble. They will get someone killed in your group if you don't deal with them.

Now for a bit of advice on the twins. They are a bit frisky and mischievous. So check for those freckles on Gemma's neck before you get into trouble. LOL

I hope our conversations don't seem too weird to you because I enjoy them greatly. I watched from above as Joe read my letters with pride knowing that I was helping him just a little bit. His dad, on the other hand never was much to take advice from his father or me. I have to guess that when you wake up and remember this conversation that you really think you're going crazy talking to this old broad or started believing in ghosts. Think whatever you want to as long as I can help you and yours survive.

Love Grandma

The band of survivors continued northwest for the next two days and finally arrived at highway 70 just north of the city of Sweet Springs, Missouri. They stopped there for the night and camped beside a small lake southeast of town. They took turns bathing and swimming in the lake before supper. Cole and Gemma checked out a small abandoned cabin and found an aluminum Jon boat and several spin casting rods. Cole told Carole that they were going to have fish for supper.

Carole laughed at Cole and said, "I'll be ready to make some soup, just in case you come up empty."

Gemma looked at the rods. "Cole, I don't know how to use these. Dad always had those Zebco rods and reels. I can fish pretty good with those pushbutton reels."

"Don't worry, darling, I'll show you how to use it, and you'll be a master at it in a few minutes."

Cole checked the rods out and tied an artificial lure on the end of each line. He cast the first one and got a bite but didn't catch the fish. He reeled the line in and showed the rod to Gemma. "Look, Babe, hold the handle in your left hand. Now stick your left index finger above the bail and flip it with your other hand. When you go to cast you just release the line from your finger at the top of the cast. Now give it a try."

Gemma's first cast hit the water in front of her, and she made an ugly face at Cole. She tried again, and the lure went straight up in the air. She smiled at Cole and made another cast this time the lure sailed out into the lake and made a ripple as it landed. Gemma began reeling the lure when suddenly the tip of the rod yanked downward. She fought the large bass into the shore and Cole took it off the hook for her. Gemma had a big grin on her face and said, "I learn quickly don't I? See if you can beat that big boy."

Cole laughed and grabbed his rod. "I'll quickly catch a largemouth bass much larger than that dinky minnow and then we need to switch to Crappie lures. Bass are fun to catch but don't taste all that good. Crappie tastes great and has a nice white flaky texture."

Cole fished for half an hour for bass and only caught four small fish. Gemma caught one more big bass and a couple of small ones. Then they switched to smaller jigs and caught two dozen nice size Crappie for supper.

They walked back to camp hand in hand when suddenly Gemma dropped to her knees and pointed into the woods. Cole saw a man hiding behind a tree watching something on the other side of a bush. Then Cole saw that Molly and Jenny were bathing in a spring that fed the lake.

Cole asked, "Gemma is that man peaking at Molly and Jenny? I can't tell from this angle."

"Honey I can't tell either, but you are getting an eye full of my naked sister and Molly. Let's move just a little closer. Hey is that Brad?"

Cole didn't have his binoculars with him, and all he saw was the backside of the man. Gemma stepped on a dry limb, and it made a cracking sound. The man's head popped up, and he ran off in another direction. Molly and Jenny heard the man crashing through the woods and covered themselves with their shirts. The man was gone so quickly that Cole decided not to chase him down.

Molly saw Cole and Gemma approaching. "Hey, we're taking a bath over here. How about a little privacy?"

Gemma yelled back. "A man was peeking at your naked butts. I stepped on a limb and scared him off before we could figure out who it was. I almost think it was Brad. Oh, and you both gave a great show for my hubby."

Cole added, "And Jenny you are identical to Gemma even down to the mole on your right butt cheek."

Jenny's face turned red as she ducked behind the bush to put her clothes on. "Damn his sorry ass. He started to follow us out of the camp, and I told him to go back because we were going to take a bath. The pervert must've followed us."

Gemma shook her head and said, "We can't be sure it's Brad, but we will need to keep a close eye on him."

When the four arrived in camp, Brad was sitting next to Deacon and Madison. Brad's clothes didn't match the ones the peeping Tom was wearing. Cole and Deacon went looking for the man without success.

Cole tried to teach Gemma how to clean the fish, but she disappeared quickly. Cole finished cleaning the fish and took them up to Carole to cook. Carole had found some cornmeal in her supplies and made hushpuppies to go along with the fish.

Everyone enjoyed the meal and ate until they were full. Cole finished eating and took first turn on guard duty. He walked past the red Bronco and noticed it was leaning. He examined the passenger-side tires and found both of them flat. There was just enough daylight left to see that both tires didn't have nails in them. He then observed his pickup and the other Bronco only to find that they were okay. Cole went to the group and filled them in on the situation.

Brad raised his hand to be recognized. "I would think we could find some Fix a Flat or Slime somewhere in town. Both work great on small punctures. I guess we also need to find a portable air compressor."

Jack replied, "That's what I was thinking. We need to send the team in early in the morning to search the gas stations and stores for those items."

Without drawing attention, Cole caught each of his team off to the side after supper and filled them in on his concerns about Brad. He told them about Janet mentioning there might have been a spy in her group and wondered if she had tried to pawn Paul and Brad off on them to protect her group.

Deacon listened quietly then spoke up "Cole I looked at the tires also and couldn't find any nails. I think someone let the air out of the tires through the valve stems. If that's true, we just need to inflate the tires. Cole, I have a small portable air compressor and four cans of Fix a Flat in our truck. I don't think we should inflate the tires until we know for certain if Brad is the spy and let the air out of the tires."

Cole replied, "Good catch Deacon. That makes me wonder if he was so eager to go into town just to lead us into a trap. He could be working for FEMA or be an actual FEMA agent. We need to get rid of him and the girl. Molly, Gemma, Brad, and I will go into town. Molly's only job will be to keep an eye on Brad and shoot the bastard if he tries anything. Deacon, keep an eye on Joan and don't let her out of your sight."

Everyone agreed with Cole and as quietly as possible, they put a plan together for the next day.

Cole slept through the night with no interruptions from Grandma. He woke up clear-eyed and on a mission to find out if Brad was a friend or foe. Cole had a secretive planning session with Deacon, Molly, and Gemma before breakfast. He told Deacon that he should try to air up the tires as soon as Brad was out of the camp in the morning.

They left before the sun was up that morning. Their camp on the lake was only a quarter mile from the eastern edge of town. They walked around the northern end of the lake and headed west. The trees were dense, and the brush was thick which made movement slow and tedious. Brad offered several times to take the last position in their column, but Cole told him that he was used to Molly guarding their backs and didn't want to change at that time. Molly watched for every suspicious move or attempt to signal others from Brad but didn't see anything suspicious.

The first buildings they saw were a bar and a large shop behind a farmhouse. A sign on the shop said "Red's Welding and Fabrication." The place had been abandoned for quite some time, but Cole did search the shop for what they needed. The place had been rummaged through several times, and they found nothing usable, so they went on into town. They snuck along house to house while keeping a low profile and only saw a couple of people outside.

It didn't take long for Molly to notice that Brad now appeared jittery and kept looking back to see if she was behind him. On several occasions, Brad offered to drop back and take Molly's place.

They finally stumbled upon a home that had somehow been overlooked. The upstairs and ground floor had been thoroughly searched and trashed; however, the basement was a different matter. Cole entered the hallway and saw it was full of trash and human excrement.

Gemma held her nose. "It smells like poop in there."

The smell was horrendous, and he started to leave, but then he noticed a mattress leaning against the wall. He shoved the mattress out of the way and saw a hidden doorway. He drew his pistol and slowly turned the knob to expose the basement steps.

Cole couldn't see anything through the darkness, so he shined his small flashlight into the void. "Holy shit! The basement still has some good shit down here. Come on down and let's see what we have here."

Cole began searching the shelves and boxes as Gemma and Molly joined him. There were four sets of large shelves, and three were filled to the ceiling with canned goods, boxes of dried food, and cases of water. They also found boxes with everything from Life Straws to magnesium fire starters. This was a preppers dream.

They were so excited that no one noticed that Brad had slipped away in the excitement. Molly was stuffing canned hams, canned chicken breasts, and other delicacies into her duffel bag when suddenly she looked up. "Gemma where did Brad go?"

"Oh crap, I don't remember seeing him since we came down into the basement."

Cole looked disgusted because he knew they'd all gotten excited and forgot about Brad. "Girls let's finish filling our duffel bags and then perform a quick search for Brad. If we don't find him, we will go back to the camp, drop these bags off, and come back for more. These supplies are more important than finding Brad. When we do find him, he better have a damn good answer for disappearing."

They carried their duffel bags upstairs and then searched the house and up and down the street for signs of Brad without success. Now, they were confident that Brad was up to no good. Gemma was the only one who gave him any benefit of the doubt. "You know we should remember that he could have been kidnapped."

Molly and Cole both replied together, "Sounds like BS to me."

They arrived back at camp after the first trip and asked if anyone had seen Brad. No one had seen Brad, but Deacon had several concerns. "Cole, about an hour ago we heard a vehicle crash through the woods Northeast of here. Joan has also been acting strange, and I wonder if we can trust her."

Cole opened his duffel bag to show Deacon the contents. "Deacon I'm afraid that you're going to have to keep the group hidden in the woods nearby the Lake and take the risk. This food is too big of a prize to walk away from. Keep Joan on a short leash and sit on her if you have to restrain her. We're going to try to make several trips today. We'll keep an eye out for Brad, but I believe he is gone for good."

They made three more trips that day and never saw Brad. Now everyone in the camp was satisfied that Brad worked for FEMA. They were almost back to camp on their third and final trip when they heard gunshots.

☆

Chapter 8

Jenny tried to prepare a light lunch as she kept an eye on Joan. Jenny looked up from her work and noticed that Joan had disappeared. Jenny looked over by the vehicles and saw that Deacon was inflating the tires on the red Bronco. The small air compressor took a while but did a great job. She saw the movement out of the right corner of her eyes and thought she saw Joan holding something to her ear.

Jenny waited to get Deacon's attention and pointed at Joan hiding between two bushes. Joan turned her head and saw them watching her. That's when they both saw that she had a small walkie-talkie in her hand. Jenny and Deacon drew their pistols and ran towards Joan. Joan quickly pulled a handgun from her waistband and shot twice before they could react. One bullet struck Deacon in the shoulder, and the other missed Jenny by a few inches. Joan yelled into the walkie-talkie, "Come on in, they caught me."

Joan waved at Jenny to drop her gun, "Drop it, or I'll kill your sorry ass."

Jenny dropped her gun as Madison ran up with her guns ready. Joan yelled at them, "Drop your guns or I'll kill Jenny."

She saw Deacon lying on the ground and Jenny standing with her hands up in the air. She dropped her pistol. Madison asked, "Joan we saved your lives. Why are you doing this to us?"

Just as the girls thought that Joan was going to kill them, Brad came up from behind one of the vehicles with his gun pointed at Joan. "Drop your gun. Now we know for sure you're a FEMA spy."

Several shots rang out from behind Brad and Joan fired her pistol several times. At the same time, two FEMA Humvees rolled into the camp and slid to a stop. Gunfire erupted everywhere.

Cole, Gemma, and Molly were only a few hundred yards from the camp when Joan shot Deacon. They dropped their bags and readied their rifles as they ran towards the camp. Cole barked orders along the way. "Molly you take the right side. Gemma, take the left side. I'm going up the middle. Try to use whatever you can for cover. Good luck, girls."

Cole was three steps ahead of the girls as he broke free of the forest and saw Deacon lying on the ground between the two Broncos. From his angle, he saw Brad shooting towards Jenny and Madison. Cole dropped to his knee and aimed his AR-15. He squeezed the trigger, and the bullet struck Brad between the shoulder blades. Brad's rifle clanged against the truck as his body hit the ground. The truck had a large spot of blood and bits of flesh dripping from the door.

Molly sprinted around the end of the blue Bronco and immediately engaged three of the FEMA thugs. She fired on the run dropping two of them and then fell to the ground behind the front wheel of the Bronco. She kept firing until she hit the man in the leg as he shot at her and hit her on her hip and calf. Molly shot one more time and hit the man on the side of the head, which exploded in a red cloud and bits of bone exploding outward. The man stood there in disbelief that he had just died. Molly struggled to stay focused as she saw four more of the FEMA thugs shooting at

Gemma, Jenny, and Madison. Molly passed out as she dropped one of the four to the ground with a lucky shot.

Cole took a bullet to the side and one in his left shoulder before he realized the men had outflanked him. He killed one of the last three men before he passed out. Jack and Carole had been out picking berries and just arrived at the camp in time to surprise the enemy from behind. Jack shoved Carole to the ground behind a tree and lay prone behind a log as he fired his AR-15 at the last two men. He took them by surprise, killed one immediately, and wounded the other. Jack jumped up and charged the man firing wildly. The FEMA thug reached for a hand grenade on his vest, pulled the pin, and tried to throw it at Jack. It careened off the old pickup truck and hurled towards Jenny and Madison. Gemma saw it and tried to swat it away with her right hand. The hand grenade exploded under the blue Bronco and caused the gas tank to explode only a dozen feet from the three women.

Madison only received two small grenade fragments in her left hip since one of the twin's bodies had blocked the grenade explosion. She was dazed from the blast but quickly recovered and began barking orders. "Jack, Carole, come here quick. More FEMA troops will be here shortly. Carole let's stop the bleeding, load the living up in the red Bronco, and get the hell out of here before FEMA gets here. Let's go, chop chop."

Cole lay there with his mind searching through foggy memories trying to process what happened. Unrelated events from years ago kept trampling on recent events confusing him even more. The one thing that rang true in his mind was that he was pleased that he had shot that damned traitor Brad. That memory reminded him that he'd been shot during the fight. Then he heard Grandma speak.

Dear Cole:

I know you're in pain and your mind is having trouble coming to grips with what just happened. You have been shot and peppered with shrapnel, but you are one tough son of a bitch and will live through this horrible time. Your wife needs you. Your team needs you, and your loved ones need you. It's time to wake up.

Love Grandma

Cole tried to work up enough energy to interrupt Grandma and tell her how much he hurt and couldn't move. He struggled to open his eyes to confront her but fell back exhausted. Cole then said, "Grandma, I hurt and can't move. You're asking too much of me. I need to sleep."

Cole passed out and remained unconscious for a long time until Grandma nagged at him again to get his ass out of bed and lead the crew. Cole woke up to see his beautiful Gemma wiping his forehead with a damp cloth. "Gemma I love you. Are you okay?"

This was the first time the young woman had seen her new patient. It took her breath away when she saw him for the first time. She thought that she knew him at one time in the past. "I have some pain from my burns and shrapnel wounds, but I'm okay. Why do you call me Gemma? The others told me that they didn't know which of the twins I was, and I lost my memory. You were married to Gemma, weren't you?"

Cole's mind was clearing of the fog as he heard the beautiful lady's story. "Let me see your neck. I can tell from your freckles. You and Jenny can't fool me."

The lady's smile turned to a frown as she turned her neck towards Cole and pulled her collar down. "Cole it's not that simple because the hand grenade and explosion injured my shoulder and burned my neck. I was unconscious for several days and woke up without my memory. Everyone has been so nice to me as they tried to jog my memory but nothing helps. I know I love you, but then both of us loved you according to my cousin Molly."

She jumped up and ran away leaving Cole more confused than ever. Carole heard the commotion and rushed over to Cole's bed. "Cole, I'm glad to see you're awake. We almost lost you a couple of times over the last three weeks..."

Cole couldn't believe what he just heard. "I've been unconscious for three weeks. Where's Gemma?"

Carole placed a damp cloth on his forehead. "Cole, you were shot twice and peppered with shrapnel from the hand grenade. The grenade also blew up one of the Bronco's gas tank, which caused burns on several of our people. When you are better, we will fill you in on what happened."

"No please tell me now, I have to know. One of the twins was just with me, and she doesn't know if she is my wife or Jenny. That must mean one of them is dead, which one survived? Was anyone else wounded?"

"Brad and Joan were killed early in the fight. Joan killed Deacon, and I'm sorry to say the grenade killed one of the twins and injured several of our team. Until she can remember who she is, we can only guess which one died. Madison and Molly were both wounded, but they are recovering rapidly. Molly can't wait to show you her bullet wounds. Son, you're going to have to be patient as you recover. It will be many weeks before you're back to normal. I know how confusing this must be to wake up to something so tragic. I may seem calm now, but I have been dealing with this for almost three weeks."

Cole's mind couldn't process everything he just heard and almost went into shock. He looked up and smiled at Carole. "At least I killed that traitor, Brad."

Carole suddenly took a deep breath. "Cole, I'm sorry to say that Brad wasn't a traitor. He didn't work for FEMA, and the big surprise was that he worked for that group out West. The Mountain Men sent dozens of their people to the east to find out what FEMA was doing and to figure out how to stop them."

Cole's ears turned red, and he stuttered. "How do you know this? I saw him shooting at the girls."

"Brad didn't die right away. Molly saw him shoot and kill Joan, who was trying to kill Jenny and Madison. He saved their lives. He told us that his current mission had been to ferret out FEMA spies who were infiltrating survivors trying to escape the East. FEMA is gathering every person between 13 and 60 years old to work in factories and farms. They are also forcing people to fight for them."

"I shot an innocent man?"

Carole quickly answered. "No, you thought you saw the threat and tried to help Jenny and Madison. Don't dwell on it because it will eat you up. Now go back to sleep and get some rest."

Cole's mind was racing a mile a minute. "Where are we and how did we get here?"

"Cole, Jack, and I loaded everyone up in the undamaged Bronco and its trailer. We drove night and day to escape the reach of FEMA. We only stopped long enough for bathroom breaks and tending to the wounded. You were the most injured of the group, and we were very much afraid we would lose you during the trip. I'm sorry to say it Cole, but we had to take that chance to save the rest of us."

Cole interrupted. "Carole, don't worry. I would've done the same. We don't leave anybody behind, but we can't sacrifice the entire group for one person. I thank you for everything you've done for me and the others."

"Thanks, Cole that means a lot to me. Anyway, you're now lying on a bed in a ranch house in Colorado. The closest city is Burlington, and there are very few people around here. The only ones we've been in contact with tell us they've never seen FEMA in the area. We plan to stay here for several more weeks as you heal, and then go to Colorado Springs and see if Fort Carson or the Air Force Academy is still under the control of the US Military.

Cole, Brad also told us why we couldn't reach anyone on the long-range radios. FEMA is jamming all of the long-distance radio bands. He said he lost touch with the Mountain Men when his team came down this side of the Rockies."

Cole was very tired and couldn't keep his eyes open as he mumbled. "Well, at least that explains that mystery. Tell Jack to do what he has to do and that I trust him."

"That will mean a lot to him. Now get some rest. Hey, hold that order. Here comes a nice lady with some broth for you."

The young woman sat down next to Cole and said, "I have some delicious deer stew for you. I mashed up the potatoes, meat, and carrots so you'll get more than just flavored water. Here let me prop your head up, and I'll feed you."

The touch of her hands on Cole's head sent a tingle down his spine. He thought that this had to be Gemma but honestly couldn't tell. "My mind is having trouble getting wrapped around knowing you but not knowing who you are."

Tears ran down his face as Cole said, "Carole called you nice lady. What name do you want to be called? I'd love to call you Gemma, but that wouldn't be fair if you actually turned out to be Jenny. I know this has to be confusing to you but until you regain your memory, how do we address you?"

The nice lady laughed. "Molly told me that when we were growing up, she couldn't tell us apart, so she called us Brat 1 and Brat 2. Molly is calling me Brat, and you can call me Brat too. Now let's get some nourishment into you."

Cole chuckled and reached for her hand. "Brat, I feel funny calling you that, but a person should be able to choose their own

119

name at a time like this. I want you to know that I made a promise to Gemma a few days before she died... err... Anyway, what I mean is that I promised her that I would take care of her twin sister if anything happened to her. So you might be Gemma or Jenny, but I'm still going to take care of you as long as you let me."

Cole's eyes teared up at the prospect that his dear wife could be dead. He was still in shock and quite confused. He was also in denial and had a hard time processing the news.

A few minutes after Brat left, Molly came to Cole's bedside. She bent down and kissed him on the cheek. Cole looked up and saw her eyes were wet and she looked exhausted. Molly took Cole's hand. "I'm so glad to see that you're awake now. We were all so worried about you."

"Carole told me that you and several others were also wounded in the fight. How are you doing?"

Molly proudly showed Cole her wounds and added that he couldn't see the one on her butt. Molly laughed and then choked up knowing that they were dancing around the main issue. "My wounds weren't very severe and other than a limp and some pain, I'm doing very well. Cole, I know Carole and Brat have filled you in on the battle and our losses. I haven't cried yet today, but if I make it to the end of the day, that will be one in a row. Losing one of the twins who had been like a sister to me was bad enough but not knowing which one is dead is like torture. It may be even worse for you. Seeing Brat but not knowing if she is your wife or not is cruel at best. I just don't know how to deal with it going forward, and I'd hate to be in your shoes."

Molly's head dropped to her hands as the tears flowed freely and she sobbed. Cole took her hand and tried to console her as he openly cried. "I know that what I'm about to say may not sit well with everyone, but we're not out of danger yet. We have to suck it up and move on with our lives. Several days before the fight with the FEMA thugs, Gemma made me promise that if anything happened to her that I would take care of Jenny and you. I will do my best to fulfill that promise. Molly, I need your help in dealing with how to handle Brat's memory loss and what I need to do about her."

Cole tried to present a strong front but broke down and cried along with Molly for several minutes. Molly finally stopped crying. "Cole, I've had three weeks to think about this, and I believe there's only one way to go forward. Get some rest, and we'll talk tomorrow about my plan."

Cole became a bit stronger every day as days turned into weeks as Brat fed him and changed the bandages on his wounds. He healed quickly thanks to the excellent care and Penicillin. She tended to his needs and spent a lot of the day with him when she wasn't on guard duty or performing her chores. Soon they were flirting with each other and forming a strong bond. Cole was still confused about what to do but implemented Molly's plan, and it was working.

Molly also visited him twice a day to fill him in on everything going on around the camp. She gave Jack good reviews on how he handled everything after the battle and going forward. She filled Cole in on the hard work they were all doing to survive. Jack and Brat hunted every day while Madison and Carole tended to the rabbit traps. Molly was still recovering from her wounds but would soon be out hunting with the others. Madison didn't talk much as she continued grieving for Deacon. She cried uncontrollably at times and stayed to herself most of the day.

Jack and the others visited Cole several times per week to see how he was doing but kept most of the day to day issues from him. After another month, Cole was walking around the house and occasionally outside for short walks. He was much stronger, so he asked Jack to call a meeting to set short-term and long-term plans. Cole also asked Jack to continue to lead the group until Cole was back to full strength.

Jack was very humble in Cole's presence. "Cole it pleases me to no end that you have faith in me to lead our group. I have learned a lot from you and will do my best not to make any stupid mistakes. I certainly won't go rushing into a situation anymore without a proper evaluation of it first."

Cole shook his friend's hand and patted him on the back. "Jack you always have been a strong leader but didn't have the survival and military training for our situation. You have learned quickly and will do well in the future. Never forget to rely on the others and me for advice. Now, what are your thoughts on what to do until spring when we can cross the mountains?"

Jack replied, "We have 5 to 6 months before we will be past the potential for spring snowstorms. Molly, Brat, and I have been out scouting this past week for a better location to live this winter. I think that next week you should be strong enough to travel to several of these locations and help us pick the best one."

Cole replied, "Please narrow your selection down to the best two, and we will go look at them the day after tomorrow. I have to get my ass away from this bed and walk a lot more. I don't need my cane to steady myself anymore, and unless we're climbing mountains, I'll be good to go. How safe are we in this house? I know you told me there are no FEMA troops around but are there other dangers?"

*

Chapter 9

Cole had walked around the house many times the last week regaining his strength. The home was an older ranch house that had been built over a century ago. The same family had lived there for six generations. It had been modernized but still had two huge fireplaces and a water pump at the kitchen sink. The pump had been left for decorative purposes but still worked. The house had been perfect for them as their wounded friends mended.

Cole walked around the outside of the house as he waited for lunch to be served. The area around Burlington was very flat, and the ground was covered in those huge circles where farmers had irrigated their crops. Cole felt he could see forever as he looked west towards Colorado Springs. He walked away from the house toward the two barns south of the house. He went in the open door of the largest barn and saw the red Bronco and two other vehicles. He suddenly heard a noise behind him and turned to confront Brat as she walked in the door carrying a bag of tools. She smiled at him as he took the heavy bag from her. Brat pointed at the back of the F250 4 x 4 truck with the camper shell on the back. "Please place the bag in the camper. We probably need to bring your bags down here sometime this week. Jack thinks you will agree with his plan to head up to Colorado Springs, so we're loading up all of the extra stuff now to be ready to leave at a moment's notice. You're going to ride with me so I can keep taking care of you. You need to be careful lifting and don't overexert yourself."

Cole noticed that the bandages were gone from her neck and hoped he could tell which twin had survived. He moved closer and stared at her neck. Brat pulled her collar down to give him a better view of her neck. "I hope this ugly scar doesn't scare people. It covers where Gemma's freckles would have been. Sorry, but you're stuck with me, the Brat."

Cole cautiously took Brat in his arms and hugged her. "Don't worry about the scar and just be yourself. You are a beautiful person, and a little scar won't make a difference. Don't think about what Gemma or Jenny would've done. You have to find yourself, and I believe you will become the best of both of them."

"Cole that was very sweet. I see why Gemma fell in love with you. We have a two-wheeled dolly over in the corner, and we will use it to haul the heavy stuff back to the truck."

They finished loading the truck and then went back into the house to the kitchen. They washed their hands at the sink and then sat down together at the table. Jack said grace before they ate and then said, "Madison, this is the best rabbit stew I've ever eaten. Cole, Brat trapped the rabbits, and Madison prepared the stew."

"Deacon loved rabbit stew," Madison said before beginning to cry. She left the table for a few minutes to compose herself.

Jack began the discussion about relocating. "Now moving along, I talked with Cole about finding a place to hole up for the winter. I told him about Colorado Springs, and he thinks it's worth pursuing. I told Cole that all of us agree on the move. Cole, please tell them your thoughts about us moving to Colorado Springs and if so, how do we proceed?"

"Jack, I've been out of the loop and have to rely on your judgment. What does each of you think?"

Molly was the first to speak. "I like the idea, but we need to proceed cautiously. Our neighbors think the area is safe, but their information is two to three months old. Let's do what we've always done and send a small scout team in to check the area out before exposing the rest of the team. I'm in."

Carole was the next to speak her mind. "I really like this area, and this house we're living in now. We can grow gardens in the spring, and there's plenty of game. The downside is that Burlington has been picked clean and I think we'll run out of food before winters over. Our decision has to be made with the thought of where can we find enough food to survive the winter."

Cole held back and waited until the last one had given their opinion. "I think that there's been a powerful point made about the lack of food in this area. I don't know if the six of us can survive on jackrabbit meat alone. I know that it's been a long time since the shit hit the fan and that Colorado Springs and Denver may also be picked clean of food. We know we can't stay here and the other options except for Colorado Springs are no better than staying here. My opinion is that we should all leave the area and travel to a safe location close to Colorado Springs. Perhaps we stop 5 to 10 miles out and send a scouting team into the city. We should look for those friendly veterans who took over the area. We should observe them, and if we like what we see, then we can ask them if we are welcome. Anyway, that's my opinion."

Jack quickly agreed, and they continued getting ready to leave at the end of the week. Included in their plans was to send teams into some of the cities they passed on the way to hunt for supplies, weapons, and ammunition. They planned to travel at night with their lights off to avoid attracting attention. They would scout a few of the towns during the early daylight hours to help prevent conflicts with the locals. They would have to stop to search for supplies during the night at the others. The drive was only 130 some odd miles, and they didn't want to speed past a potential treasure of supplies. Highway 70 only had eight small towns and villages between them and their potential new home.

Madison asked Cole a question. "When do you plan to take over leadership?"

"Madison that's a great question, and I wish I had a good answer for you. While I'm feeling better every day, I have to say I'm still weak and need too much of your help to take back over. Besides, Jack is doing a great job and has my full support. Let him get us settled in our new home and then we'll have this discussion again."

The time flew by as they loaded up their vehicles for the trip. The red Bronco broke down and was now dead. They had to rely on Brat's F250 and a Dodge 2500 4 x 4 to get them to their new home. Both had horse trailers hitched to them to haul their supplies and extra diesel fuel.

Jack wisely had the team search the abandoned farms for food and other supplies. He also had them search the fields for vegetables and any edible grain that had sprung up from the last planting. During the four weeks scrounging the fields, they found half a trailer full of everything from potatoes to turnips. There were dozens of orchards in the area, and many of the trees still had apples, pears, and peaches on their branches.

Molly and Brat had converted an old refrigerator into a smoker. They used a steel garbage can for the firebox and ran a pipe from the top of the garbage can into the bottom of the refrigerator. They had smoked rabbit, deer, and even some quail meat so that it would be preserved. Carole even showed the crew how to make pemmican, which would even last longer without refrigeration than the smoked meat.

Cole helped Brat load the packages of preserved meat into the trailer hitched to the back of her F250. A thought came to him. "I don't remember hearing any gunfire. How did you kill the deer, rabbits, and such?"

Brat began to answer as she pulled a strange looking rifle from the back seat of the truck. "We probably shot the deer while you were asleep, but we mostly trapped or shot the small game with this pellet rifle. This one shoots a .22 caliber pellet at over 1000 feet per second. We've also been experimenting with some bows and arrows, but none of us is very good at it. You once told us that you were an excellent shot with a bow. Do you think you could teach me when we get settled in Colorado Springs?"

"I'd be pleased to, and I'll also pick up where we left off on your survival and combat training."

Brat smiled and continued loading the trailer.

Cole remembered what Brat had said and asked, "You said that I told you I was an excellent shot with a bow. You said to us, so that means you heard me say that. Who was standing next to you?"

"Damn, I don't remember. Crap, if it were one of us, then I'd be the other one. Good try, but I don't remember. Cole, I've given up on finding out who I am and am focusing on moving forward."

The end of the week came quickly, and except for Madison who was pulling guard duty, they all slept in that morning. They needed all the rest they could get since they were going to drive all night. They had a late breakfast around noon and began checking to make sure they had everything loaded. Then Cole insisted that they clean and inspect all of their weapons. Jack and Brat performed a final inspection of the vehicles and checked all the liquids and spare tires.

They took turns napping that afternoon even though sleep eluded most of them. They were too keyed up about their new adventure, and while none would admit to it, they were worried about dangers along the way. They ate supper at twilight and had a final meeting before driving away.

Early on, Brat had let Cole know that the truck was hers and that she would drive it most of the time. She proudly showed Cole the mounts for her shotgun and AR-15. The mounts on the passenger side contained his favorite pump 12 gauge and his M4. Then she showed him another mount on each door that held a 1911 .45 and two extra magazines. "We don't have a lot of ammunition for the .45s, so I mounted them on the doors for emergencies."

Cole pulled his M4 from the mount, jacked a shell into the chamber, and did the same with the .45 and the shotgun. "You've done a great job with the truck and armament. Where are the hand grenades?"

"Thanks for the compliment, and I did know that you are kidding about the hand grenades. Well, it's just about dark, climb in, and strap yourself down. This should be a smooth ride tonight, but let's be prepared for anything."

They all looked back at the ranch house as they drove away that crisp, clear fall night. They wondered if they would ever find a place they could call home. Cole didn't feel anything as they drove away from the house. The only thing he missed was Gemma's warm embrace and companionship. He was growing closer to Brat but tried to force himself to think of her as Jenny to help him get over losing Gemma. He felt deep down inside that Gemma was gone for good and he must move on.

Brat looked over at Cole and tried to remember everything she could about him. She had been trying this exercise with the others. It didn't work because she only knew what she had seen since she woke up after being unconscious and what they had told her. Every now and then, she had a flash of a memory that was someone's face or something she'd seen. The problem was that she couldn't remember seeing it and even if she did, the same memory could be either Gemma or Jenny's memory.

Carole and the others hadn't told her much about Cole before the day she met him. When she saw his face, she felt a powerful emotional attachment and feelings for him that surprised her. She tried to hide it, but she was a nervous wreck because nothing gave her clear signs that indicated if she were Gemma or Jenny.

Cole sat there trying not to stare at Brat without success. He quickly decided to focus on going forward and not the past. "Brat, tell me about yourself."

She turned to face him. "You know more about me than I do."

"No, just start talking and tell me your likes and dislikes. I think that you were born last month and are a new person. You might never regain your memory so why not become the person you like the best."

Brat chuckled as she dodged a limb on the road. "My favorite color is green. I like puppies and kittens. I love old pickup trucks and butter pecan ice cream. I like you and my other friends. I don't like spiders and snakes. I don't like mean people. I love babies and want three of my own. Were you and Gemma planning to have children?"

"Yes, we planned to have them after we got home to Oregon. I have to say that Gemma would have started a kid long before we arrived back home. Her mothering instinct was very strong for such a young lady."

"I know that both of us twins were a lot alike and shared the same views. I'm afraid I agree with Gemma or me, oh you know what I mean. I would want to start a family now. Has there ever been a good time in history to start a family where everyone was safe from harm?"

Cole told Brat about his history before the SHTF and the past year. Then he told her a detailed story about his history with the twins and Molly. He left off the parts about getting too close to Molly in an attempt to reduce any jealousy in the future. Cole was deep in thought about Gemma, Jenny, Brat, or whomever this lady was sitting next to him when he saw the sign for the city of Bethune up ahead. "Look that's the first city that Jack wanted to explore. Get ready to pull off the road."

They had taped over the taillights so the brake lights would not be seen and draw attention to them. They did leave two small holes in the tape so the following vehicle wouldn't run into the back of the lead vehicle. Brat saw the little red lights and slowed the vehicle down. She followed Jack into a copse of trees about a quarter mile from the tiny village.

They knew the houses would have been searched many times for food, so they planned to concentrate on food manufacturing facilities and warehouses when possible. It was soon quite evident that there were no large facilities or warehouses in the small town. They found a farm implement store and checked it out. The front door had been bashed in, and the office had been torn apart. They searched the building but only found a few hand tools that Jack wanted to keep. Every machine in the break room had been turned over and looted. They did find two winter coats hanging in the employee locker room that would come in handy. They never saw any lights in the city or any evidence that there were any residents.

Highway 70 was mostly open for traffic; however, several wrecked cars blocking the highway slowed their progress. The night sky was cloudy, and it was very dark, which made travel difficult at best. They stopped for a bathroom break after midnight and Cole took over the wheel when they got back on the road so Brat could rest. They arrived at Limon at 3:30 AM after traveling slowly through the night.

Cole followed Jack's truck into a small railroad yard that was crammed with overseas containers and semis with trailers. They parked their vehicles between some containers and got out to stretch their legs. Cole walked up to Jack with a big grin on his face. "Jack this could be a gold mine. Most of these containers haven't even been opened."

Jack replied, "We can only pray there's something usable in them and not a bunch of machinery or building supplies. Brat, you and Madison stand guard while the rest of us open trailers and containers. I only have one bolt cutter, so I'm going to cut the locks on the closest 10 trailers, and we will see what's in them."

Jack proceeded to use the large bolt cutters to cut six of the locks, but the others just had a thin metal strip through the lock hole. Cole and Molly held their breath as Cole opened the trailer door. They were floored by the rancid odor from rotting meat. Cole then noticed that they had selected a refrigerated trailer. Jack had the same issue with his first trailer. They skipped all of the refrigerated trailers going forward. The next trailer Jack opened was stacked high with sewing machines in their cartons. Cole's next trailer contained 26 pallets of baking soda. Cole checked several more trailers without success. They were now finished with the trailers and moved on to the overseas shipping containers.

Their luck with the containers wasn't much better, but at least they did find one container that was full of canned goods, and another had clothing. They opened another seven overseas containers and found everything from disassembled ATVs to Grandfather clocks. This was disappointing, to say the least.

It was now 9 AM and time for them to hide and get some sleep. Jack walked over to Cole with a disgusted look on his face. "That was almost a big waste of time wasn't it? The canned goods will come in handy, but they're mostly vegetables. Some canned hams, spam, or roast beef would've been nice. Our clothes are somewhat ragged, but it looks like a container full of women's sportswear. The ladies will tear into that container."

Cole agreed with Jack and pointed to the main building, which contained a cross-dock operation. "Let's park the trucks behind the building and get some sleep. I'll take first watch for four hours, and then I'll get some sleep."

They parked their trucks behind the building and then searched the building to make sure it was safe. They were lucky that the vending machines still contained potato chips and candy. A small thing like that was perfect for their morale. Cole munched on several candy bars and a bag of potato chips as he watched for any danger.

☆

Chapter 10

Just before noon, Cole heard a sound at the front of the building and went to check it out. He had his M4 ready to shoot thugs and FEMA troops when he saw a teenage boy and girl on bicycles. He watched them and heard the boy say, "I'll check the trailers while you check inside the building. These trailers have to have something in them to eat, or we're going to starve."

The boy noticed that the trailer doors had been unlocked, but he was so hungry he began opening door after door in a desperate attempt to find some food. He cursed aloud every time he saw the machinery or rotten food. Jack had placed a lock on the trailer with the canned goods. The boy saw the lock and went back to his bicycle to fetch a hammer. The boy beat on the heavy lock without success and looked like a whipped dog. Cole felt sorry for him.

Cole snuck up behind the boy and poked his rifle in the boy's ribs. "Son, I mean you no harm, and you look like you're starving. That trailer contains our food, but we will share it with you. Call your friend over here, and I'll let you fill your saddlebags and baskets with canned food."

The boy's eyes were huge as he stared at the rifle. "You can shoot me now, but I won't call my girlfriend over here to die with me."

Just as the boy finished speaking, Brat and the girl walked toward Cole and the boy. "Cole, look what I found sneaking through the building. It looks like you found her boyfriend. What should we do with these two hungry kids?"

The boy spoke up. "We're not kids, I'm 17, and Mary is 16. We are getting married soon. Do you have any food to spare?"

Cole laughed at the kids because they were only two years younger than Brat and he. "I'm sorry, but I'm not laughing at you. It's just that you're not much younger than we are and we've been married for several months."

Cole caught his mistake but didn't say anything to Brat. "Before we decide to share our food with you tell us about yourselves and who else is with you. I'm not giving food to a bunch of criminals and thugs."

The girl was upset at being called a thug. "Bill and I are not bad people, and we are here by ourselves. The group we were traveling with was attacked by those FEMA assholes. We only escaped because we were... err...away picking blackberries about half a mile from our camp. The men in black took all of the adults and gave the kids to some mean looking people."

Cole looked over at Brat and shrugged his shoulders. "Why should I believe you?"

The boy had tears in his eyes. "Mister you don't have to believe us but could you let us go? We don't mean you any harm we're just out looking for food. Look, there are our bags, and you'll see we don't have any weapons. The FEMA thugs took all of our parent's weapons, and I never had a gun."

Cole reached into his shirt pocket and handed each one a candy bar. "Here, you two munch on these while I open the trailer doors and get you some food. You'll have to stay here with us until we leave tonight just in case you are lying to me. We have already loaded down our vehicles and can't carry anymore, so you can have everything left in this truck. Finish your candy bar, and we will fix a meal for you."

Brat went back to her truck and retrieved a package of the smoked meat for the boy and girl. Brat said, "This meat will tide you over until you can catch your own rabbits and perhaps a deer or two. I'm sorry to say, but the trailer is mainly full of vegetables."

The two kids ate like they've never seen food before. Cole had to slow them down so they wouldn't get sick from overeating. Cole looked at the young pair of lovebirds. "Where was your group heading when the FEMA thugs attacked? What was your plan to survive?"

The boy swallowed his mouth full of cold green beans. "My uncle planned to get as far west as possible to get away from FEMA's slave camps. We were barely getting by day-to-day by eating berries, wild plants, and rabbits we trapped. I guess Mary and I will continue on west and try to find a place to live. We really thank you for the food, but we need to move on now."

Cole quickly replied, "Wait here just a minute while my friend and I discussed this situation."

"Brat, what do you think about the kids joining us? I have a good feeling about them and worry that they will soon be dead if they don't join another group or us."

She replied, "Cole, this is one of the reasons that you are such a good man. Even when the world is trying to kill us and we're barely surviving you think about others safety. Do you really think I'm Gemma, and we are married or was that a slip of the tongue?"

Cole didn't know how to answer the part about being married. "Honey, I would just hate to be out there alone at 17 years old with a pregnant girlfriend and no one to help me. I just replied without thinking about us being married. Brat, you know that the two of you were identical in every way except those freckles. Every time I see you, I want to kiss and hug you, but then I just don't know what the hell to do. Let's talk about this when we get back on the road again. I don't know what to say, but it's been torture being with you but not being with you. If you get my drift?"

Brat hugged Cole and said, "I know exactly how you feel."

Brat and Cole went back to Bill and Mary to fill them in on their decision. Cole started the discussion. "Would you two like to come with us and join our team? We only have a few rules, but we also demand your 100% loyalty to our team. In return, we will be loyal to you and help you learn what you need to survive. Think it over for a few minutes and let us know your answer."

Bill and Mary looked at each other as their heads nodded. "Sir, we would like to join you and your team. We know we don't stand much of a chance of surviving ourselves. We both grew up in the city, and our parents didn't fish or hunt. We were both excellent high school students, but we don't know anything about the woods, hunting, or fishing."

Cole said, "I'll have to get the blessing of the rest of our group, but I'm certain they will be glad to have you with us. This won't be a walk in the park, and you will have to work hard and pull your share of the load. I don't have a lot of time for people that whine and complain, so get that out of your system before we leave tonight."

Brat walked over to Mary and hugged her. "Mary do you have any idea when the baby is due?"

Bill was shocked and took Mary's hands. "You're pregnant?"

"Yes I am, and I was afraid to tell you. I hope you're not mad at me."

Bill was in a state of shock as he answered. "Mary, I love you, and I'll love our baby. Why didn't you tell me?"

"I was afraid that you would be mad at me for failing to use protection and wouldn't want the baby or me."

Bill hugged his girlfriend closely. "I love you and would never leave you or our baby."

Brat moved over to Cole's side and held his hand as the two lovebirds discussed their baby. All Cole could think about was Grandma's advice about none of the women should get pregnant. He knew this could hinder their trip to the West Coast. Brat read the look on his face. She whispered, "Cole you know the baby will be born in about four to five months. It will be able to travel in the spring."

Without thinking Cole answered, "Babe, I guess you read my mind. I hope you're right about the timing on the delivery because I've already committed to them joining us. I don't want to upset the others."

"Honey you know that Molly will agree with us and I'm pretty sure it's a slam dunk with everyone except Jack. I can't read him sometimes on the issues like this. I guess we'll know in a few hours."

Cole thought for a few seconds. "Babe, I guess I'm just worried that I turned the reins over to Jack and then I'm making decisions that he should be making."

"Honey, why don't you take the others into the warehouse and get some sleep? I have the next guard duty and will wake you up when I wake Jack up."

"Babe that sounds like a plan and the sleep will do me good. Be careful and keep your eyes open. Don't let anyone sneak up on you," Cole said and then kissed her goodnight.

Cole very quietly slipped into the warehouse and looked for a place to sleep. He noticed the others had made pallets out of old cardboard sheets and did the same to make his bed. He was tired, but his mind kept going over what just happened. The funny thing was that he was more worried about him saying Babe and Brat saying Honey, than he was about his decision to let the kids join them. He fell asleep thinking about Brat and began wondering if he really cared whether she was Gemma or Jenny. He thought that perhaps it didn't matter in the end.

He felt a hand on his shoulder and moved his hand to his 9 mm pistol. He opened his eyes and saw Brat kneeling over him. She smiled and gently shook his shoulder again when he closed his eyes. "Wake up sleepy head. You have to talk to Jack before he meets our young couple."

Cole was half-asleep as he jumped up and gave Brat a long kiss on the lips and then ran barefooted over to Jack. He tapped Jack on the shoulder just as Jack saw the couple sleeping. Cole spoke up before Jack had a chance. "Jack there is something we need to talk about, and I think you're looking at it. I apologize, but I overstepped my bounds and led this young couple to believe they can join us."

Jack answered, "Slow down Cole. Did you promise them or only said it was possible."

"I did the right thing and told them that the rest of you would have to approve it, but they had a good chance of joining us. FEMA attacked their camp while these two were out picking berries and killed or captured the rest of their group. They were starving when they came up to search the trailers. Brat and I fed them and let them sleep. I meant well, but I should have talked to you first."

Jack had a frown on his face as he looked from Cole to the young couple and back. "Cole I'm not upset if that's what you're worried about. I do want to talk with the couple before we vote on them joining us but I do trust your judgment and expect everything will go okay. I can't speak for the others, but you know we all have a big heart. Shouldn't you be asleep?"

"Yes, and I'm still tired. It was quite out there during my shift, and I don't think Brat had any trouble either. We'll get some shuteye and discuss it further when everyone wakes up. If that's okay with you?"

Jack put his shoes on and grabbed his gear to take over guard duty from Brat. Cole went back to his mat and found Brat had made a mat next to his. He lay on his mat facing her when abruptly her eyes opened. She moved closer to him and placed her head on his arm. "Cole, I know it's weird for you not knowing if I'm Gemma or Jenny, but I know I love you. I want us to be together forever."

Cole pulled her closer and kissed her. "Babe, we are going to be together and forget about who you were. I love the person in front of me now."

Cole wrapped his arms around her, and she was soon fast asleep as Cole lay there with his eyes wide open.

Molly and Carole woke up around 7:00 PM and immediately saw Brat snuggled up to Cole. Carole pointed at them and waved at Molly. "I'm so happy that they appear to be getting along so well. I don't know which one of the twins she is, but does it really matter as long as they are happy together?"

Seeing the two together gave Molly mixed feelings. While she was happy for them, she couldn't help but be jealous. She never wanted anything to come between Gemma and Cole, but down deep inside she saw the current situation as an opening for her with Cole. The frown on her face told Carole all she needed to know, so she backed away from the topic. "Molly, help me fix some supper for the sleepy heads."

Everyone except the new couple, Brat, a
awake for an hour when Brat's eyes opened. Cole
her back, and he had his arm over her waist as he s.
lifted his arm and tried to get up and leave him as.
barely sat up on her cardboard bed when Cole stirred. ˎ
up for her, pulled her down to him, and kissed her. Bra
say something when Cole placed his finger on her
whispered, "Not now, Babe."

Cole took her hand and helped her stand up after the
their shoes on. Cole walked over to the new couple and nudgeᴑ
on the back with his shoe. "Wake up lovebirds. Let's get so.
breakfast and figure out what to do with you two."

Carole was on guard duty and had already eaten breakfast.
Jack asked the couple to tell everyone their story during breakfast.
The two took turns telling the story. The couple's group had a rough
time since the lights went out. Their group started out with over 20
people but lost eight due to sickness and attacks by criminals and
thugs. Bill and Mary had been high school sweethearts and stuck
together through all the trials and suffering. The FEMA attack ended
their hopes of keeping their families together.

Jack shook his head when they were finished with their
story. "It's amazing you survived at all without much in the way of
training or survival skills. What can you contribute to our small
group that would make us want to let you join us?"

Bill turned to face Jack. "You already know that we don't
have any skills that you need. We can make up for that in hard work
and willingness to learn. If you could just give us quick training to
make sure that we aren't a liability and can help keep the group safe,
we will quickly learn everything else you teach us. We will also be
happy to take all the crappy jobs and work our butts off to earn a
place in your group. If that's not good enough, we understand, and
we will part ways."

141

Carole said, "You had me at doing all the crappy jobs. I vote et them join us. Darling, I'm sorry, this is your show to run, but t's my vote."

Jack replied, "Everyone in favor of Bill and Mary joining us, aise your hand."

Every one of the group raised their hand and accepted Bill and Mary in their group. Carole then took Mary off to the side and immediately began giving her vitamins and advice on becoming a mother. Carole and Jack became very close to the young couple over the next few months.

Molly and Madison moved their gear into Brat's truck so the new couple could ride in Jack's truck. When Cole realized that they had company for the rest of the journey, he caught Brat and took her to the other side of the warehouse. Brat started to ask a question, but Cole kissed her for a long time. Cole again placed a finger on her lips. "Babe, I love you with all my heart, and I'd like to forget everything in the past and move on to a future with you."

Brat was very happy and excited that they were moving forward. "This makes me very happy but what happens if I turn out to be Jenny? Will you still love me?"

Cole answered without hesitation, "Yes, and all of you unconditionally. If your memory comes back, only you will know who you actually are. I could never tell the two of you apart, but I honestly thought that it would be easy to tell who you are once I spent some time alone with you. That certainly didn't turn out to be true. I'm sure you love me, and I love you so who cares who we are as long as we love each other. I think we should just forget Gemma and Jenny and move forward as Brat and Cole. What do you think?"

"Cole I still see you crying as you grieve for Gemma. I will always miss my other half and don't know when I'll stop grieving for her. I guess what I'm trying to say is that I think you're right that we do love each other and should make a great life with each other. Let's start new right now and just be ourselves going forward. Let's don't question who I am, the important thing is I belong to you, and you belong to me."

Brat grabbed Cole's hand in hers and pulled him out to meet with the others. She banged her hand on the door of her truck and said, "I have an announcement. Cole and I are married. We will be living together as man and wife. I hope this doesn't startle anyone or cause any concern, but that's the way we want it."

The group looked confused at first and then Carole started applauding. Everyone joined in clapping their hands and took turns hugging the new couple. Molly hugged her cousin and wished her well.

Jack asked, "I know this might confuse our new young couple, but Brat do we need to have a wedding ceremony?"

Brat grinned and raised her hands to quiet the crowd. "No, we've been married for quite some time and once is enough."

That left more questions unanswered and confused the hell out of everyone except Brat and Cole. Molly suddenly tugged on Brat's shirt and whispered in her ear. "Does this mean that you are Gemma?"

"No Honey, it means that Cole and I love each other so much that we're not going to worry about who I am or what's happened in the past."

"What will we call you?"

"I'm still your little Brat and will keep that name even if I suddenly remembered who I am. If I do remember, I will never tell anyone."

"Come on now, you'll tell me won't you?"

"Molly, there will be no reason to rock the boat since this is settled right now. I hope you agree with my wishes."

Molly hugged her cousin and answered, "Little sister, I just want the best for you, and of course I agree with what you just said. You and Cole are perfect for each other, and you have my support and all of my love."

Molly whispered in Cole's ear. "Well, our plan worked. You two were made for each other, and I hope you have a great life together."

Cole had been nervous about the decision to take up with Brat where he left off with Gemma. He and Molly had thoroughly discussed the pros and cons before he made up his mind. The bottom line for Cole was that whoever Brat actually was, he loved her. The bottom line for Molly in deciding to help Cole was that Cole loved Brat and not her.

While Molly and Brat were busy discussing Brat's situation, Bill walked up to Jack and Cole. "How would someone get married these days? Do you have a preacher in your group?"

Cole quickly answered before Jack could speak. "Our leader, Jack, has the power to marry people. That is unless you're religious and want to get married by a preacher."

"No, we just want to get married."

Bill and Mary's wedding was brief, and a bit rushed since they were running behind schedule. Madison drew up a marriage license while Jack conducted the wedding. Madison even gave them a ring for the ceremony. Several of the team joked about the young couple having a crappy honeymoon on the road.

☆

Chapter 11

They pulled out of Limon, just after dark, heading southwest on Highway 24 and were only about 66 miles from downtown Colorado Springs. The first few miles were awkward since Madison and Molly didn't know how to get around Brat and Cole now being married. Brat sensed the situation and started the conversation. "Bill and Mary seem like such nice kids. I just hope that going without food for as long as Mary did doesn't harm the baby."

Madison chimed into the conversation. "I think it's funny that you called them kids and I believe you're only 19 and Cole is 18. Aren't Bill and Mary 17 and 16 years old?"

Molly gave a very astute answer to the perceived difference in ages. "You know I really think that there is a big difference when you compare the two couples. While both couples have been through a lot, I think Bill and Mary just muddled through surviving while Cole and Brat have adapted to the new environment and learned what it took to fight their way to survive. You have escaped from a slave camp, killed men up close, and know more about how to kill thugs than anyone should have to learn. This maturity from living 10 years in one short year makes you seem older."

Brat reached back and punched Molly on the arm. "Are you trying to tell everyone that I'm an old lady? Darn, I just convinced Cole that I'm worth keeping and you tell him that I'm almost worn out."

Molly stuttered and was silent.

Brat chuckled. "Honey, you know I'm just pulling your leg. There is a lot to what you just said, and now I think I need a beauty salon and a facial."

They all had a good laugh and Brat had broken the tension in the truck. Several more awkward situations would occur with others in the group, but Brat and Cole used humor to defuse the tension and make everyone feel at ease.

They skipped several small villages because they only contained houses and a couple of small stores. It only took two hours to reach the suburbs of Colorado Springs. They turned west at Falcon Road and then on to Woodman Road. They stopped at a house about a mile down Woodman road on the north side of the road.

They unloaded just enough equipment and supplies from the trucks to spend a couple of nights and moved into a large house. Cole volunteered himself and Molly to scout the area around the house for any dangers. Cole asked Bill to join them on the scouting mission. "Bill, have you ever shot a gun?"

"Yes, I shot my uncle's .22 rifle and a .38 revolver several times during summer vacation. I got pretty good with the rifle but not so good with the pistol. It was one of those snub-nosed pistols."

Cole said, "You won't have a gun this time, so if the shit hits the fan you will need to hide while we deal with the problem. As time permits while we're out, Molly and I will give you some good training on what you should do when on this type of mission. Listen closely and do what we say when we say it, and you should come back alive."

They slipped out of the house just after midnight and headed west since that's where most of the survivors should be. Cole's shoulder and hip still gave him some pain but not enough to keep him from doing his job. They kept a low profile to avoid being seen due to the light from the half moon. The area around the house was flat for over a quarter mile, so they had to use a ditch beside Woodman Road to help conceal their movement west.

Bill asked, "There isn't anyone in sight. Why do we have to sneak around?"

Molly beat Cole with the answer. "Kid, you have a lot to learn. The bad guys don't wave flags and searchlights so we can see them first. We pride ourselves in being able to sneak around in the dark and see good and bad people before they see us. If you watch us and learn, you'll get good at infiltrating an area without being seen."

Cole waved at both of them to join him. "Bill, what do you see at that farmhouse up ahead?"

Bill scanned the area between the house and barn and then said. "I saw a man in the shadows just inside the barn door, and another through the window on the back left side of the house. I think the man in the barn is going to attack the people in the house."

"Good eyes Bill. You might be right about the potential for an attack, but it's too early to tell. Bill, you stay with me while Molly cuts over to the right side of the barn to see if that man is alone."

Cole and Bill moved a little closer to the house and now they could see several people asleep on the porch with one man guarding the group. It was the same man they had seen through the window. The man in the barn could now be seen with a pair of binoculars watching the people on the porch.

Cole whispered to Bill. "Bill it's hot outside thanks to this Indian summer weather, and people are sleeping on the porches again like they did in the old days. I'm beginning to think you're right about this guy being up to no good. We'll keep watching until we hear back from Molly."

It was only a few more minutes until Molly crept back to their position and gave Cole a report on what she'd seen. "Three more armed men are hiding behind the barn. They look like refugees from a grade B biker gang movie. Several have long chains hanging from their pants pocket to their back pocket and are wearing do-rags. They only have a couple of pistols and a hunting rifle with them. I think we should take them out now and then kill the man in the barn before they harm these people."

Cole pondered the situation for a minute. "If they're as ill-prepared as they are stupid looking they should be easy to capture shouldn't they?"

She smiled and chuckled under her breath. "Yeah, what's the fun in that? How will we take all three without one of them alerting the guy in the barn?"

"I'll capture him first and then come around the barn and help you with the others. That should be the safest way for the people at the house. Let's roll," Cole said.

No one was guarding the right side of the barn so Cole slipped up to the barn and worked his way in the shadows to a position just short of the door. He slowly crept up to the open door and pounced on the man knocking him to the ground. "Shut up and stay down or I'll kill you right now," Cole said with his M4 pointed at the man's chest."

The man nodded his head in agreement and then Cole bound and gagged him. Cole stuffed the man's Glock in his waistband and ran through the center of the barn to the back barn doors. The three men were on his left sitting on a hay wagon laughing and joking. Cole saw Molly and Bill behind the men with their heads barely visible in the weak moonlight. He flashed his small flashlight at them and signaled for them to attack.

Cole watched as Molly and Bill closed the gap between them and the men. Cole ambled in the shadows until he was only a few feet from the men. He saw that Molly had her rifle ready and had pushed Bill to the ground behind her. Molly caught Cole's eye, and then they both sprang into action. Cole yelled, "Drop your guns or die."

The men dropped their weapons and Cole held his M4 on them as Molly tied their hands behind them. One of the men's pants was wet, and Molly laughed at him. "This one was so scared he pissed his pants. What are you clowns doing out here trying to attack the people in this house? You should be ashamed of yourselves."

The men didn't say anything as Cole and Molly pushed them at gunpoint around to the front of the barn. Cole untied the man's feet, and they hailed the house before walking up to the front porch. "Please don't shoot; we caught these men sneaking around your barn. They looked like they were going to attack you."

Several of the people on the porch were now awake and had rifles in their hands. Several kerosene lanterns lit up the area around them. One of the men yelled back at Cole. "How do we know this isn't a trick and you are the attackers?"

Cole laughed at the problematic situation and replied. "Are these guys part of your crew? They certainly aren't our people. I guess you're right so, we will leave them with you and go back to our place. We just drove in tonight and want to hook up with the veterans who cleaned up Colorado Springs. We're looking for a safe place to stay over the winter."

Suddenly it was quiet on the porch, and Cole heard several people talking in hushed tones. Then they heard a woman's voice. "Molly is that you? I can't believe I haven't seen you since we were on that plane leaving California."

Molly shouldered her AR-15 and walked up to the porch. It was the nosy older lady from the airplane that carried the slaves from California to Kentucky. Molly couldn't remember her name but would never forget that face. "I recognize your face and remember

149

you from the plane, but I'm so sorry that I can't remember your name."

"That's good because I never gave you my name and if I had, it would've been a fake name. They dropped me off on the second stop; where did you end up?"

Molly shook the ladies hand. "My people ended up in Kentucky as slaves on a farm and in a coal mine."

"Yeah, are you still with that handsome young man that you were doctoring for the whole flight? I guess you two hooked up."

Molly cringed a bit before answering. "No, he married one of my cousins. You do remember the twins, don't you?"

"Yes I do, and they were pretty little things. Are they with you?"

"Only one made it here. A FEMA thug killed one of them with a hand grenade in a gunfight. We killed all the FEMA thugs but lost my dear cousin and another friend during the fight."

The lady gave Molly a hug. "I'm sorry I reminded you of those tragic events."

The woman finally introduced herself. "I'm Marge, and this is my band of old farts and misfits. This place is one of the Eastern outposts for the group you called the veterans. We obviously need to work on our skills and drink a little less before bedtime. You saved our bacon, and we will show you our appreciation by introducing you to our leader. Do you want to stay here until sunup?"

Molly replied, "No, we need to go back and let the others know about your invitation. There are eight of us counting that boy that is hiding in the bushes behind me. We picked him and his girlfriend up about 60 miles back, and we're going to teach them survival skills. Come on out Bill and say hello. Cole, come on up also."

Marge immediately recognized Cole. "You're that handsome young lad that had his face buried in Molly's lap for most of the plane ride. I can't believe you gave up this gorgeous woman for anyone else."

Cole laughed and answered, "I won't say anything that could later be used against me by my wife. Molly and I are best friends, and she is a wonderful person."

Molly asked, "What will you do with these four incompetent gangbangers?"

Marge made a slashing motion across her throat. "We have no patience for drug dealers, meth cookers, or gang members. They are tried, convicted, and executed quickly."

Brat remembered the woman on the plane but was surprised that the woman remembered Molly's name. "She remembered your name but didn't remember Gemma or Jenny's name. That's odd. I thought she worked for the slavers."

"That's what we thought at that time. I don't trust the woman. Her eyes darted around the room going from person-to-person, and she looks away from you from time to time while she's talking with you," Molly said.

Cole tried to remember the flight, but he had been unconscious for most of it. He did remember thinking that they couldn't trust anyone on the plane.

Molly jabbed Brat in the ribs and told her what the woman had said about Cole choosing one of the twins instead of Molly. "She also invited us back to their place in the morning, and someone will take us to visit their leader over in Colorado Springs."

Jack was excited about this turn of events and thanked everyone for a great job. Cole also noticed that Jack didn't cringe when he heard the gangbangers were to be executed. Jack told everyone to get some sleep, and he would pull guard duty until 6 AM, and they would travel over to visit with their new friends.

Cole was trying to go to sleep when he heard Bill telling Mary about their adventures. He lifted his head to hear the conversation when Brat pinched him. "Cole that's not nice. You shouldn't try to listen in on those two lovebirds. Besides, it could be embarrassing."

Cole laughed under his breath so the others wouldn't hear his reply. "Babe, you got that wrong. I was just trying to see what I could hear because that means they could hear us."

"Oh shit," Brat replied and then added, "Darn, we're just as bad as those two are. Oh my God, I can hear them... Cole, you need to talk with him in the morning about either being quieter or moving away from the rest of us."

Cole whispered in her ear, "We need to take heed of the same advice."

Cole fell asleep quickly that night without his usual tossing and turning. Before he woke up that morning, he received a visit from Grandma.

Dear Cole:

I hate to pester you so much, but I think you're walking into a dangerous situation in the morning. Neither Molly nor you trust that woman called Marge. She asked too many questions on the flight out of California and had too much freedom in the plane. Remember you saw her go into the cockpit and talk with the pilot.

Looks like shit and smells like shit, so I think you are smart enough not to have to find out if it tastes like shit.

Be careful.

Love Grandma

Molly caught Cole the next morning and made a suggestion to give Bill his own gun. "Cole we need to give him a crash course on handling a pistol. I thought taking him along unarmed was a great idea when I thought that was going to be a harmless look-see around the area. Apparently, there are no simple missions these days, and we could have used the firepower had the shit went sideways."

Molly went to get Bill while Cole checked out the Glock he had taken from one of the gangbangers. He cleaned and oiled it and then fetched two extra magazines for the 9 mm handgun. Cole gave Bill a brief training session before giving him the pistol. "Don't draw that pistol out of that holster unless I tell you to. Every time we stop and take a break, I want you to be by my side, and I'm going to give you safety and marksmanship training. Tonight we will take a break, and I'll let you shoot the pellet rifle until I feel comfortable that you understand weapon safety. In a few days, we will try to let you shoot your Glock if we can find a place where the noise won't draw in gangbangers."

Bill was just like a puppy needing attention, and this made him feel important. He shook Cole's hand and said, "Cole I want to thank you and Molly for taking the time to teach me what I need to know. I really do appreciate you helping me. I'll do anything you ask me to do."

Cole looked over at Molly and then patted Bill on the back. "Bill there is one thing you can do for yourself."

"What's that's, Cole?"

"To put it as politely as possible, you need to take Mary away from the camp when you two get amorous. The rest of us can hear everything."

Bill's face flushed and his eyes grew to twice their normal size. "Everything?"

Molly jumped into the conversation, "Everything, and I do mean everything."

Cole walked away with Molly. Before Molly could say anything, Cole said, "I know; you don't have to say anything."

☆

Chapter 12

Marge met with her old friend the leader of Colorado Springs. They had served in Iran during the last war. Marge had been a CIA operative, and Harry was the military intelligence Captain over the team working with her. Their previous assignment had been to find and eliminate a hidden Iranian weapons depot based in Ethiopia. The Iranian depot was destroyed by well-placed missiles from several U.S. Air Force F55 Super Stealth fighter-bombers. The Captain retired from the service a few months later, and Iranian AK 74s, RPG's, and plastic explosives showed up at several hotspots around the world.

The Captain was arrested along with Marge when one of the Mexican drug cartels used these weapons to try to assassinate the governor of Texas as he was inaugurating the final section of the border wall. The investigation of the cartel's assassination attempt led investigators right back to Harry and Marge. They had paid the rogue team to steal all the weapons before the bombs were dropped.

Marge looked at her old friend and said, "Damn Harry you look like something the cat dragged in. We're getting too damned old for this shit."

"Marge, speak for yourself; I'm feeling pretty damn good for a 55-year-old man. I haven't felt this good in years."

Marge laughed as she gave Harry a hug. "And I'll bet that 18-year-old girlfriend of yours has nothing to do with it. Hey, I came over to bring some new recruits but mainly wanted to discuss beefing up our Eastern security. We were caught with our pants down last night. A group of gangbangers was going to attack us but thank God, these new recruits saw them first and captured them. The new people had just arrived and were scouting around the house they were staying at when they saw these thugs about to attack us while we were sleeping. Yeah, I know our guard should've caught them first, but he didn't. I suspect we have the same problem all around Colorado Springs."

Harry was pissed at first then smiled at his old friend. "What you said pissed me off at first, but I know you're correct. All us old farts that have the experience and training tend to stay in the city and perform the cushy jobs. The youngsters that are full of pissing vinegar don't have the training but are eager to go out and shoot up gangbangers, thugs, and troublemakers. We have to improve their training, and I have to force some of the more mature men and women into our security group to help train the kids. So tell me about this new group."

Marge passed on what she knew about Cole, Molly, and the group they traveled with.

Harry was pleased with what he heard. "So most of the group were slaves in the FEMA camp and have great survival skills. I hope that translates into them being good workers in our factories, mines, and security force. I am a bit concerned that they could be troublemakers, and we don't need any more of them."

Marge responded tersely, "I'll take the men into my security group and be responsible for them. I've met two of the women, and you will know what to do with them. Of course keep them away from your little wife, because these two make her look ugly as a mud fence."

Harry's face brightened up with a big toothy grin. "So they're baby dolls."

"You always were a pervert and a letch. The third girl is about four months pregnant and won't be much help. Besides being beautiful, the other two have some good survival training and could be a handful if they catch on to your plans for them."

Jack and his team sat around a large table snacking on fruit, cheese, and iced tea. They had been waiting for over an hour and a half for the leader, Harry, to arrive. Cole knew that they should be feeling relaxed and ready to join this community; however, every warning flag and alert was going off in his head. He almost dozed off waiting for Harry when suddenly Grandma's voice came to him loud and clear.

Dear Cole:

"Cole, something doesn't smell right does it? Keep your ear to the ground and your eyes open."

Love Grandma

Cole came to attention when the door banged as the leader entered the room.

"Hello, I'm General Harold E. Smith, the commanding General of the Colorado Springs area and I'd like to welcome you. Please stand and introduce yourselves so we can get to know each other. I have to say that we have a large group and I don't meet all of our new recruits, but Marge seems to know a couple of you and spoke very highly of your group. We need good strong people to join our group if we're going to thrive and survive."

Each one of Jack's group stood up and gave their name and a few sentences about themselves. Cole was the last one to speak, and he thanked the General for allowing them to meet with him.

The General noticed that everyone but the youngest girl had their sidearm. "Marge must trust you a lot, or you wouldn't be able to bring guns into our city. Now I'll tell you a bit about..."

This raised the hair on the back of Cole's neck, and he raised his hand to speak. "General doesn't that leave you vulnerable to attack. A sizable force could cut through your outer defenses and run amok killing and plundering the city unless your citizens are armed. Also, it would be suicide for anyone to leave their guns at their homes these days."

Jack was upset with Cole speaking up. "General, please excuse my young friend's bluntness. We'd like to hear more about this community."

Molly waved her hands at Jack, "Whoa Jack. I want to hear the General's response to Cole's concerns about our weapons. Mine are staying with me, and maybe this place isn't for us."

Jack angrily responded. "Please give the General a chance to respond and please watch your manners. I hate to pull rank, but I am the leader of this group."

Harry was visibly upset with these new people's reaction about the guns. "I'm sorry that Marge didn't explain our no guns in the city policy to you before you entered. We don't allow visitors in the city at all, and usually, all guns are checked in with our police force and only reissued if we feel the threat of a large attack. Frankly, there are no large groups around that can possibly threaten us."

Cole didn't wait for Jack's permission to speak. "Harry, I'm not sure what world you live in or how good your intelligence group is, but FEMA has a strong presence a few hundred miles east of here and is moving this way. They have helicopter gunships, Humvees with machine guns, and well-trained troops. They would run through this community like a knife through butter."

The General's teeth were gritted as he answered. "Cole, I'm sure that to a young man like you the FEMA troopers can be scary and perhaps a bit overpowering. We have seasoned men with combat experience guarding our community."

Cole tersely replied, "General, we saw your experienced guards in action last night and had to save their asses. This team has met the FEMA troops in battle on several occasions, and we have defeated them every time. We also lost a few of our friends during these fights. Don't lecture me on our readiness or resolve to tackle FEMA or any group that tries to harm us. You have a nice city here and apparently, the people like the way you run it, but we are not a good fit for your city. We certainly don't want to cause you any alarm, but we will be leaving now."

Cole turned to face Jack and said, "Jack, we need to go back to our camp and discuss how to go forward. It does not appear that we are a fit for this group."

Jack tersely replied, "Cole, calm down and remember that I'm the leader and you will do what I tell you to do."

Molly stood up first with Brat, Madison, and Bill standing upright behind her. Molly placed her hands on the table. "Jack, as you know, Cole is our leader, and you were just temporary until he was back to full strength. Cole is back to full strength. Cole, please lead us back to the camp."

Cole stood up and walked to the General with his hand out to shake the General's hand. "Sir, it has been a pleasure to meet you, and I'm sure you have a fine city, but we will not surrender our guns, and it's apparent that we just need to move on and let you run your city as you see fit. Thanks for your time and the great snack. We'll be leaving now."

Jack was livid but kept his mouth shut as Cole handled the situation. The General raised his hand, and suddenly ten armed soldiers rushed into the room with rifles pointed at Cole and his team. The soldiers took the team's weapons and kept their guns trained on them. Then the General raised his hands for everyone to be quiet and spoke. "First, I need a show of hands on who is your leader. Raise your hands if Jack is your leader."

Only Carole and Jack raised their hands. The General then said, "Raise your hand if Cole is your leader."

The remaining six raised their hands signifying that Cole was their leader. The General walked over to Marge and whispered in her ear. She whispered back to him and then the General spoke again. "I'm going to ask Cole to stay with me and discuss the situation while the rest of you receive a tour of our city to make sure you make an informed decision about joining our group."

Molly interrupted, "We don't need a damn tour. We just need our guns back and let us go home."

The General pointed to the leader of the soldiers and said, "Take the outspoken young lady with Marge to our visitor quarters so Marge can educate her on the benefits of joining our team."

Molly started to resist, but two of the soldiers grabbed her by each arm and took her out of the room. The General tapped his hand on the table and said, "If you just keep an open mind I believe you too will see the benefit of joining us. We are good people but to keep control and to keep our people safe we have rules. No one violates our rules."

Brat stood up. "We don't want to live in your community. Cole made it clear that we do not want to live by your rules. Why are you keeping us here as prisoners?"

The General's face was bright red. "You are not prisoners. We feel that once you understand what we're trying to do that, you will want to stay with us."

Brat replied, "If you truly believe that, let us go and we will decide if we want to come back and listen to your story. If you don't let us go, you are holding us as prisoners and are our enemy."

The General's fists were clenched as he yelled, "Forget anything I said. Take these ungrateful assholes to the appropriate section leaders and put them on hard labor until I decide what to do with them."

Cole, Jack, and Bill found themselves shoveling horseshit into large horse-drawn wagons an hour later. A dozen men were working in the barn with half of them shoveling shit and the other half grooming and feeding horses and mules. About an hour after they arrived in the barn, a man arrived who was in charge of the operation. They could hear him talk with the man who had been directing them. They heard, "So, those three are the ones who defied the General. I'm surprised they're still alive. I guess we're short of manpower and he will hang them later. Don't take any crap off them and you're free to whip them but don't kill them."

Cole got close to one of the other workers and began a discussion. "Hey friend what gives here? We heard this was a nice and safe place to live. Why are they treating us so poorly?"

"Be careful talking. If the guard sees us, they will whip us. It's a fantastic place to live if you are ex-military or one of the General's friends. This started out with good intentions and everyone equal in the community. Then we started noticing that the older ex-military people weren't pulling their weight and doing some of the crappy jobs. People who complained were given even worse jobs. If they continued complaining, they disappeared. Several of the younger ex-military guys stood up for us but disappeared. We were told they were reassigned to outposts west of here.

The nonmilitary people tried to revolt, and the General killed them in a bloody fight. Most people here had guns, and we fought them until they started taking our wives and children as hostages.

The fighting abruptly stopped, and now we find ourselves well fed, safe, and slaves."

Cole shook his head and replied, "That's what I was afraid of when the General told us we couldn't keep our guns. Thanks and I guess we better get back to work."

Cole circulated back over to Jack and Bill and filled them in on what he just heard. Jack listened and then apologized for not listening to Cole. "Cole, I'm sorry. This was truly one of those situations where if it's too good to be true it is too good to be true. I so desperately wanted to lead us into a safe place to live that I ignored the danger signs. Forgive me, and you should remain our leader for the rest of the trip. I'll support you any way I can, but I don't want to lead again."

Cole was still mad at Jack, but he kept it to himself. "Jack let's move on and figure out how to get the hell out of here."

At 5 PM, a bell rang, and their guard came over to Cole and said, "You three will follow me to your quarters. The rest of the slackers will go to their homes. You will report back here at 7 AM and work until 5 PM every day until you can be trusted to perform other duties. Let me give you a word of advice. Don't buck the system and you and your women will be soon living in your own houses and free to go about your daily lives as long as you do your assigned jobs and don't break any rules. That doesn't sound so bad does it?"

Cole understood how this works and replied, "Yes sir, I understand now, and I'm sorry for causing alarm earlier. We were used to our freedom and were afraid to lose our guns. Now that we've seen how safe the community is we changed our mind and will do our best to fit in."

The guard laughed and shook his head. "I don't believe one damn word you said, but I do believe you'll try to fit in or get your asses kicked every single day of your lives. Follow me to your temporary quarters and just pray that one of the General's men didn't take a fancy to one of your women."

That last statement shook them to the bone. Jack told the others under his breath, "If they hurt one hair on Carole's head I will gut them like a fish."

Even though Cole felt precisely the same way as Jack did, he was surprised at Jack's choice of words. They followed the man to a row of houses that were inside of a chain-link fence that had razor ribbon on top.

The guard spoke, "These houses contain our new additions to our family. There are no guards inside the fence so expect anything. Only three of the ten houses have occupants at this time. Your people will stay in the third house on the right side of the street. I believe there is eight of you so good luck on sleeping arrangements in these three-bedroom homes. There are bunk beds in the living room for the overflow. Now get your asses over to your homes."

Bill asked, "Don't we get fed tonight?"

"Yes. There will be a horn at 5:30 AM to wake you up. At 6 AM, be here by this gate, and we will march you across the street to that large red brick building for breakfast. At 6:45AM, you will be escorted to your work assignments. Meet back here in 15 minutes to go to supper."

The men walked over to their assigned house, and Bill started to walk in. Cole grabbed him by the collar and pulled him back. "You should know better than to bust into the room with a bunch of women. Always knock first, or you might get your head knocked off."

Bill knocked on the door, they heard nothing for a minute, and then they barely heard someone tell them to come in. Cole cautiously opened the door and saw the women strewn all over the place. Molly and Brat had the couch, Mary the recliner, and Carole had a pillow on the floor.

Cole surveyed the situation and guessed that the women's jobs hadn't been a piece of cake either. He walked over to Brat and started rubbing her feet. "I would guess that your jobs might have been worse than shoveling horseshit all day. We're supposed to be heading to supper in 10 minutes. Where did y'all get cleaned up?"

Brat pointed down the hallway. "The bathroom has cold running water and the toilet flushes. I'm worn out, but I'm starving, so I'll be ready to go when you're washed up."

Bill was holding his wife's hand. "Please tell me that they didn't work you like a dog also."

Mary could barely bring her head up she was so exhausted. She wiped sweat from her brow. "No, they made the others wash clothes by hand all day, and I had to fold the clothes all day. I'm wiped out, and you might have to carry me to supper."

The men washed their faces and hands and were ready to go in a few minutes. Mary was barely able to walk, so they arrived a minute late at the gate. A different guard was there, and he said, "You are late. The next time you're late; don't bother to come up here for supper. Follow me to the cafeteria and don't get any bright ideas about escaping. There are snipers in hidden locations just watching for runners. This is like a hotel in a horror movie, you can check in, but you never check out."

The guard walked into the cafeteria and pointed in the direction of the serving line. Cole was surprised that there weren't very many people in the cafeteria, which could seat over 200 people. They joined the end of the line and only had to wait a few minutes until the first server slopped a large spoonful of Navy beans on their tray. Next, they received a large dollop of mashed potatoes, and then a big hunk of cornbread. They picked up a glass at the end of the line that was filled with water.

They sat down by themselves one row of seats away from everyone else for a little privacy. Brat was the first one to speak. "Well, at least we're not on bread and water."

Carole replied, "Maybe not, but I'm going to see if I can sleep out on the porch tonight. With this much Navy beans, it could be a dangerous night to sleep inside."

Jack nudged her in the side as the others acted as if they were laughing. Cole surveyed the room and noticed there was one guard who was fixated on them. The other three guards were laughing and joking in the far corner. Cole made sure the others knew that they were being watched closely.

They finished their meal in silence, and then a bell rang signaling time to leave the cafeteria. They saw the others jump up, take their trays to a window at the end of the serving line, and drop them off. They dropped off their trays and then followed their guard back to the entrance to their new home. The guard marched them to the gate and released them to go to their house.

As soon as they entered the house, Brat got their attention. "Ladies and gentlemen we need to get a rule in place on bathing because we all stink, and the men smell like horseshit. Now having said that, we ladies will bath first, and then the men will bathe. There is one exception, and that is that Mary will bathe first with Bill's help. Then Carole and Madison's turn and finally Molly and I will bathe, with the rest of you men bathing however you want to."

Of course, that started a debate amongst Cole and Jack with Brat on why they can't bathe with their wives. Brat had enough of it and laid down the law. "Everyone shut their pie holes. Cole as much as I'd love to have you wash my back and help me bathe, you smell like horseshit, and I can't stand to be in the room with you until you take a bath. Case closed."

Cole made a production of sniffing the air. "Babe when you stand in and shovel horse manure all day long, you no longer notice the smell. I take back my demand to bathe with my wife."

While Bill and Mary were bathing, Cole wrote a note to the others to start checking the house for hidden audio bugs and cameras. While the couple was bathing everyone searched for bugs and cameras. No one found anything in that first sweep of the house. Cole and Jack were the last ones to use the bathroom. They took turns shaving and bathing and then came out into the heat and humidity of the warm fall evening. Cole didn't see anyone in the house, so he followed Jack out to the back deck. The others were seated in lawn chairs and gathered in one corner of the deck where there was a nice breeze. Cole cleared his throat and caught their attention. He stuck his finger across his lips and then started looking for audio bugs and cameras. Then suddenly he caught their attention and nodded toward a flowerpot on the table. He mouthed the word bug.

☆

Chapter 13

Cole had Bill and Mary stay behind on the deck while the others went out on the lawn. Cole waved them to follow him to a point between the house and the garage. They all searched the area and couldn't find any bugs. Cole had them gather around him as he whispered. "I think we only have a couple of days to escape before they divide us up. Harry lusted after our women and almost drooled. I may be paranoid, but I think this is just as bad as the FEMA camp. I don't trust anyone not with us right now. Hell, even Bill and Mary could be planted in our group."

Molly asked, "Boss what's our plan?"

Cole quickly answered. "I almost hate to say it, but the plan is the same as we used to escape from the FEMA camp. Let's all look around this area for the guard's patrol patterns and weak spots in the perimeter fencing. We don't have much time before dark today, but let's make the best of it. I know we're in a hurry but don't look too desperate and draw attention to us. Brat and I will take a tour to the other end of the block, and the rest of you try to strike up conversations with some of the other captives. Expect some of the captives to be spies."

Cole and Brat walked down the middle of the street as though they were at home in Oregon without a care in the world. They laughed and joked as they watched for the other captives. They saw a family sitting out on the front porch of a house three doors down and walked up to them. Cole asked, "What's your name? We're the Biggs. I'm Cole, and this is my wife Brat."

The man on the porch replied in a low voice. "Get away from us now. The guards are always watching us. Go away and don't come back."

They continued to walk down the block until they were at the end of the houses contained by the fencing. Cole saw several cars parked around the houses just outside the fence. All of them were older vehicles that would probably run. Cole whispered to Brat. "We just need to find a way to get through the fence, and I'll bet I can get one of those cars running. Let's go on back to our house. I've seen all I need to see."

While Cole and Brat were at the other end of the compound, Molly and Madison walked to the other end close to the guard station. It was now twilight, and Madison saw movement between some houses across the field behind their fenced-in prison. She was careful not to draw attention as she pointed the movement out to Molly. Molly and Madison walked to the end of the block and pretended to talk with one of the guards while Molly watched three men sneak past the guards. The men were about 50 feet away, but Molly was sure she recognized two of them.

"Hey Madison, that was two of the FEMA guards that were guarding the convoy we escaped from. I'll never forget the big one's face. Colorado Springs is about to be attacked by FEMA. They have sent infiltration teams in to scout the area. Don't make any sudden moves, but we need to get back to Cole.

Molly filled Cole and the others in on what she and Madison had seen. Cole didn't know whether to think this was a good thing or a bad thing. "Shit, this will either foul things up for us or give us an easy way to escape in the confusion. I think we need to be ready for an attack just before sunup in the morning. If FEMA attacks, we will escape this fenced in area and head for the brush west of here. Then we can follow that creek bed back to our camp. Damn, aren't we glad now that we hid most of our supplies?"

Jack was a bit timid as he leaned toward Cole. "What if FEMA doesn't attack for several days? We will be separated, and it will be difficult to free everyone. I think we should escape in the morning even if FEMA doesn't attack."

Cole nodded as he raised his hands. "Jack is right about this. I'm not about to be separated from the rest of you. Let's take turns watching the guards for the next 3 to 4 hours and be prepared to overpower them and escape."

Madison said, "I think Molly and I can distract the guards while some of you sneak up on them. Both of them carry 9 mm Berettas and have AR-15's in the guard shack. That would give us four weapons to help with our escape."

Molly chimed in the conversation. "We really need to knock the guards out, take their weapons, and get the hell out of Dodge without anyone knowing we escaped. I suspect that the other prisoners won't wake up until morning call. That means we need to overpower the guards before about 4:30 AM. Then we shag ass out of here. "

"Molly that was so eloquently stated," Brat said.

They took turns watching the guards the rest of the night and quickly noted that the guards were very lax in their routines and lacked basic discipline. As planned, Molly and Madison left the house wearing as little clothing as possible. The nights were still relatively warm, and they walked up to the guard shack complaining about the heat. Cole, Brat, and Jack used the distraction to sneak up on the guards. Molly and Madison flirted with the guards even further to distract them.

One of the guards unlocked the gate and invited the girls to join the guards in the guard shack. Madison walked on through the gate with the first guard while Molly bent over pretending she had a rock in her shoe. The second guard moved up behind Molly and grabbed her from behind. Cole struck him on the back of the head. The man fell to the ground and Cole grabbed his pistol. Brat and Jack dragged the man behind the guard shack as Cole snuck up to the door.

Cole saw that Madison sat on the corner of the desk as the guard unstrapped his pistol belt to drop his pants. The guard was so distracted he didn't hear Cole sneak up behind him. Cole quickly wrapped an arm around his neck, grabbed his jaw, and used his other hand to snap the man's neck. The man died never knowing he had been attacked.

Cole heard a commotion behind him and turned with his pistol pointed at the two entering the shack. "Did you tie the other guard up?"

Jack responded, "No, your wife choked him to death as we dragged him behind the shack. I'd be careful pissing her off if I were you. She is one tough lady."

Brat smiled at Jack and replied, "I'm only mean to mean people. Cole is never mean to me, and you better not be mean to me."

Carole brought Bill and Mary to the front gate and joined the others. Just as they searched the shack for additional ammunition and other weapons, there was a series of explosions in the city. Cole waved at his friends to follow him. "That was our notice to get the hell out of here. If we were in doubt about FEMA attacking, those explosions were the answer."

Cole and Molly took the AR-15's; Jack and Brat took the 9 mm Berettas. They made it into the brush without being seen and then entered the creek bed to head east to their camp. Several helicopters flew past them overhead on the way into Colorado Springs. They heard heavy machine gun fire and explosions a minute after the helicopters had passed over their heads. FEMA troops were scattered all over the eastern side of the city. They had to duck and hide several times to keep from being seen.

Cole was in the lead as they walked in the shallow water of the creek. He rounded a sharp bend and ran into several FEMA troopers. Cole yelled, "Shit, shoot the bastards," and started firing immediately. The men stood there for an instant too long in disbelief that they were under attack. Cole saw them moving in slow motion as he fired his rifle. Molly joined in the battle, killed one with a shot to the chest, and another with a thrust of her knife to the man's neck. Cole was lucky that the FEMA troops were actually hiding from the fight and were taking a smoke break. The four of them were dead before they could get off a shot. Cole began searching their bodies for weapons and ammunition. "Grab their guns and bullets and let's get the hell out of here. All of this gunfire will surely attract unwanted attention."

They picked up four more AR-15's and four Berettas to add to their arms. Each dead man had four additional 30 round magazines for the AR's and three for the 9 mm pistols. Mary wouldn't take a gun, so Cole took the extra 9 mm pistol. The men also had bayonets and tactical vests. Cole, Brat, Jack, and Molly wore the tactical vests.

There was only about an hour of darkness left, and they had about two miles to go to get back to the house where their supplies were located. Cole knew that they had lost their vehicles and had to replace them to get out of FEMA's reach. Cole saw one of the Humvees parked beside the creek and motioned for the others to drop down. He waved at Molly to follow him as he checked out the Humvee.

Cole moved along the bank of the creek until he was even with the Humvee, which was about 30 feet from the stream. What Cole saw scared the shit out of him. There in front of him were three Humvees and a group of men with maps spread out on a table. Cole recognized two of the men from the FEMA prison camp in Kentucky and two more from Colorado Springs. It was Harry and Marge, the leaders of the so-called veterans who ran Colorado Springs. One of the men was the new camp commander from the FEMA camp they had escaped from earlier in the year. Molly got excited when she saw the men and Marge. She tapped Cole on the shoulder. "Cole, that's the commander of the last camp we were at and Harry and Marge. I think he's leading the attack on Colorado Springs and Harry and Marge are betraying Colorado Springs. We need to kill all of them."

Cole about choked at the suggestion. "Molly, are you crazy? There are ten heavily armed men. We wouldn't stand a chance."

"Cole, we are behind their lines. All of the soldiers are attacking Colorado Springs. Those men are the leaders of this area for FEMA and their flunky underlings. I doubt if they are real soldiers."

Cole was over the shock of seeing the commander of the slave camp meeting with Harry and Marge and agreed with Molly. "Okay, I have calmed down a bit and let's think this through. Let's spread out along the creek and ambush the bastards. You can have the commander and Marge, and I'll take Harry and the man next to him around the table. The rest of the team can shoot the other six who appear to be guards. Get the rest of the team up here now."

The others gathered around Cole as he whispered instructions to them. Mary wasn't happy that Cole ordered her to take a gun. He told her to shoot at the men until her gun was empty and then fall down to the bottom of the creek and hide. They were given their assignments and told to begin shooting when Molly fired.

What Cole's team didn't see was the convoy heading in their direction. It was only about five minutes away and had 30 FEMA

171

troopers in the back of two trucks. This was the commander's staff and the kitchen for the headquarters company.

Molly waited until all of her friends were in position and placed her sight on the commander's chest. She took a deep breath and squeezed the trigger with the pad of her finger. She shot the commander twice and then shot Marge. Cole killed Harry with a head shot and the next man with two bullets to the side and face. Gunfire erupted all around Cole, and he saw the enemy fall. Several of the FEMA soldiers started shooting but didn't have targets, so they fired at the flashes coming from the creek bank. The bullets striking the gravel around the bank resulted in a blast of rock fragments striking Cole and his team.

The fight was over quickly when the last of the enemy was dead. Molly enthusiastically used her pistol to shoot each of the men in the head to make sure the vermin were dead. Mary was shocked at the sight and got sick to her stomach. Bill helped her clean up and walked her back down into the creek bed.

Suddenly they heard the rumble of the trucks and Humvees heading their way. They quickly grabbed several of the men's M4s and AR-15's before running back down to the creek bed. Cole sprinted east along the creek bed to get as far away as possible before the trucks stopped at the massacre. Cole heard yelling behind them, and then the machine gun started strafing the area around the massacre. The FEMA troops spread out and searched for their enemy unsuccessfully. Cole and his team were now a quarter mile away and almost to their camp.

"Don't turn any lights on when we enter the house. We need to treat our wounds and get out of here quickly. I'm afraid we're going to be on foot for a while so grab all of the food, ammunition, and medical supplies that we can carry when we leave," Cole ordered.

They threw blankets over their heads and use flashlights to treat the wounds on their faces. No one had any severe injuries, but everyone had several small wounds from the rock shrapnel. Cole tended to Brat first, and when finished, she had six Band-Aids on her face. He kissed each one of her wounds and then let her take care of his wounds. They quickly finished and loaded up their backpacks and duffel bags for their trip away from Colorado Springs.

Cole fell asleep quickly when they finally holed up in a barn to get some sleep. They had all been awake for two days and were exhausted. Cole slept through the night, but just before he woke up, he saw Alice Harp standing before him. Joe's Grandma always wore a dark business suit in is dreams and had her silver hair in a tight bun.

Dear Cole:

Kid, you made me proud this week. You didn't shoot my horse's ass son, and you led your people out of that dictator's prison. Please don't go forward thinking all veterans are bad people or that every community you come across is trying to enslave you. Keep your eyes open, ask questions, and get the hell out of Dodge if things don't add up correctly.

Moving along to another topic. You seem to be okay not knowing which twin is sharing your bed. Brat must have gotten her memory back by now. That should tell you that Jenny survived.

Well, I guess that is none of my business, but I do love a good soap opera.

Love Grandma

Cole mumbled in his sleep. "Grandma, I don't care which one is with me now. I'm just happy that I have Brat."

Cole had been restless and woke Brat up several minutes before he spoke. She guessed he was talking to Joe's Grandma in his sleep and then heard what he told Grandma. The answer put a smile on Brat's face, and she woke Cole up making love to him.

The next week was a nightmare since they had to walk the first 40 miles until they found an old Chevy Blazer that would run. Even with their supplies tied onto the roof and hanging from the back of the vehicle, it was a tight squeeze to get eight people in the large SUV. As usual, they took side roads as they headed north to Wyoming where they hoped to find a place to hide and stay the winter along Highway 80.

They had dodged FEMA roadblocks and search helicopters for the first 50 miles north of Colorado Springs. Brat was in the front seat next to Cole. "Cole I think we are here. See the crossroads. I think everyone's tired and if it's okay with you, we need to go ahead and camp for the night."

"Is everybody ready to spend the night here? I think we're about 15 miles southwest of Cheyenne and according to the map, we can take Route 121 heading north so we can avoid the city. Start looking for an abandoned ranch or farmhouse where we can spend the night," Cole said as he stifled a yawn.

Jack had been silent for a long time. "Cole now that we've escaped FEMA, we need to put a plan together. The winters in Wyoming can be frigid and brutal."

Cole answered, "Jack is right, regardless of what we do the next 4 to 5 months are going to be miserable. We lost most of our food and medical supplies, and I doubt if we will be able to replace them. My guess is we're going to live day to day by hunting, fishing, and gathering what food we can find. Let's set up camp and get cleaned up a bit before we tackle our survival plan."

After they cleaned up and settled into an abandoned ranch house, Madison asked, "Wouldn't it make more sense to head south for the winter and then start over heading west again? We can go

174

straight down to the Gulf Coast for the winter and then head back up again or head to California on Highway 10 or maybe even Highway 20."

Everyone except Madison hated that idea. Molly spoke up, "Madison, that would be a great idea under normal circumstances; however, we would have to cross FEMA controlled areas twice. I'll take my chances in Wyoming."

Cole told the team. "We know that we will have to stay out of the Rockies to avoid the worst of winter. Now it's just a matter of where in Wyoming we want to spend the winter. The mildest winters are in the eastern section where we are now. We also have to factor in that we'll need to hunt and fish for food. If you look at the map, there aren't very many lakes in Wyoming. The area between Cheyenne and Laramie has several man-made reservoirs that had been stocked with trout and other game fish. I think we need to stay in this area."

Carole brought up a good point. "Let's choose one of the reservoirs not too far from Cheyenne so we can fish but also search the city for food. We just need to find a cabin or house close to a lake."

Cole said, "There's a lot of truth in what Carole says. The problem is that being close to the city means being close to people and that means being close to possible thugs and gangs. Let's try a compromise and ideas. Let's select a lake close to the city as a base camp while we searched the area for the ideal spot to spend the winter.

Molly jumped into the conversation. "I think we learned from past experience that most of the homes and businesses will have already been searched and all food, weapons, and medicines will have been taken. We need to concentrate on factories, warehouses, and rich people's homes that might have hidden doomsday bunkers. It will only take one of the bunkers full of prepper supplies to potentially feed us all winter."

Brat was looking at a map of the area. "Hey everybody, look right there on the northwest side of Cheyenne. There is a cluster of golf courses on either side of Highway 25. They have several small lakes in and around them. Golf courses also have fancy big homes. Let's scout them out as a starting point. There are always fish and turtles at golf course lakes. What do you think?"

Cole didn't notice it, but he was shaking his head the whole time Brat was talking. "I think you have some great ideas, but I'm afraid that almost anyone who has any survival skills may already be camped out at the lakes. I'm not saying we won't look at these lakes, but we need to go in with open eyes and guns ready. The people may be friendly, so we don't need itchy trigger fingers. I think we have a plan and now just need to figure out who to assign to the different teams."

Madison was very timid as she raised her hand. "I'll volunteer to stay with Mary. Bill needs the training and experience. Before you say it, I know I also need the training and experience. So Cole, if it's okay with you, Bill and I could trade up protecting Mary and our camp."

Cole thought that was an excellent idea and gave a thumbs up to Madison's suggestion. "Molly you have the most experience at scrounging through buildings for supplies. I'd like Jack and Carole to go with you to search for food in the city. I'll take Brat and Bill with me to search for a short-term place to stay close to Cheyenne. Once we find a home base, we will start rotating up searching in the city because that will be our most dangerous activity. We will drive the Blazer up to the area with the golf courses and hide it a few hours before the sun comes up. Then we will separate and start our missions. Plan to be out overnight. I don't want to drive around the area in the daytime in that big ole Blazer."

The next morning came too early for Cole. He woke up to see Brat fully dressed and sitting on the edge of the bed staring at him. His eyes fluttered open, and he smiled at her. She leaned down and

176

kissed him good morning. "Good morning my wonderful husband it's 2:30 AM and time to get up; did you sleep well last night? I'm excited about finding a place to stay this winter. It has to have a good fireplace."

Cole bolted upright in the bed, surprising Brat. "Oh shit. You just reminded me of one of our biggest issues. Smoke rising from our chimney in the winter will stand out like a sore thumb against the wide-open Wyoming sky. We will make ourselves a target. We're going to have to search for a cabin in the woods so we can use the trees to disperse the smoke."

"Honey, that's another reason you're so valuable to our team. You think of everything."

"Babe, I try my best, but we better get the team together and do a brainstorming session on how to survive without being noticed."

Brat was hesitant to say anything but gathered her courage and spoke up. "Honey, I'm glad you have me working with you today. You always seem to take Molly with you. A girl could get a little jealous even if she is my best friend and cousin."

"Babe, didn't we already have this discussion a while back."

"Honey, I don't remember it."

Cole's face turned red as he thought that perhaps it had been the conversation with Gemma. "You are correct. I tend to take Molly with me if I think we're going to be cutting throats or in a firefight. Molly has become a very efficient killer when she needs to be. She won't think twice about slicing a man's jugular vein or killing anyone that is a threat to our team. I love you dearly; however, I don't know if I want you to ever be like that."

Brat gathered her thoughts and then spoke. "I like it that you're trying to protect me from having to do things like that, but don't you think that would put me in danger if I'm confronted with a situation where I need those skills. Please treat me just like you would Molly. I hate that we have to kill people to survive, but if I'm going to do it, I want to be good at it."

Cole assured his wife that he would give her advanced training in the art of hand-to-hand combat, infiltration, and general mayhem. They finished the discussion and walked to the kitchen for breakfast as Cole thought about how similar Brat and Gemma were.

Cole and Brat were the first two in the kitchen, and Carole walked in behind them. Carole smiled and said, "I'm afraid it is smoked deer, cornbread, and water for breakfast this morning. Brat if you help me, we can put together a couple of lunch bags to take with us today."

An hour later, everyone had eaten and donned their gear for their missions. Jack drove west around the city to avoid being spotted. He took several dirt roads and a couple of old fire roads to head northwest. Brat kept checking the map and adjusting their course along the way. They had to cut some fences to cross Highway 80 west of the city. As they crossed the road, Molly exclaimed, "Hey, that sign said that there's a Walmart distribution center at the next exit. Why don't you drop us out here? It looks like it's about 3 miles from the golf course and we need to start somewhere."

Cole agreed and added, "Let's meet after midnight on the western shore of Lake Abasarraca at the complex we noted on the map. If we aren't there, go to the western shore of Lake Terry to find us. If we don't show up there, haul ass back to the camp."

Molly, Jack, and Carole took their gear and started walking the short distance to the Walmart distribution center. Cole took the driver's seat and headed north to come into the golf course area from the west.

☆

Chapter 14

Molly could see the huge warehouse from half a mile away. She cautioned the others that they would look over the place from safe locations before trying to enter the building. "Obviously this building once held a tremendous amount of product for Walmart. I'm counting three different buildings, and the largest building has three distinct sections. I just hope this isn't a home furnishing and hardware warehouse complex."

Jack tapped Molly on the shoulder. "Molly, I'm sure these buildings contain everything needed to supply all of the local Walmarts in the area for 200 to 300 miles around. It wouldn't make sense to have their dry goods and perishables spread out at different locations. We may not find food here now, but it was once here."

They spent the next hour observing the warehouse complex from all four sides. As Molly had hoped, each building had large signs indicating the contents of the building so the truckers would know which building to go to for their deliveries. Molly noted that there were also around 100 truck and trailers in the parking lot. She made a mental note to check them for food.

They moved in close to the building and walked in shadows until they arrived at the dry goods food warehouse. They came around the corner of the warehouse to the front of the building and saw several old pickup trucks and cars parked by one of the overhead doors. Molly asked the other two to stay in the shadows while she moved closer to check for any danger.

Molly crept through the middle of the cars and trucks until she was in front of the first overhead door. To the left of the overhead door was an open man door. She was discouraged when she saw the tiny glowing red dot. This told her that some asshole was smoking just inside the door. The person was obviously guarding the contents of the warehouse, which raised her hopes that there was food in the warehouse. Molly moved closer until she was beside the ramp leading from the parking lot up to the overhead door and man door. She peeked up every now and then and saw the man walk outside accompanied by a woman and another man. Both men had rifles, and the woman had a shotgun.

Molly's heart sank as it dawned on her that she would have to move on to another place to find food. Then suddenly the overhead door opened and four large straight trucks pulled out of the warehouse and went down the ramp. The two men and woman walked over to the trucks with their flashlights aimed at the back of the truck and pulled the doors down to secure the loads. Molly could see the trucks were full of canned goods and boxes that contained food. Molly then heard the following conversation.

"That will teach those bastards to rob us and hoard our food."

"Get your asses in gear. We need to get out of here before the thugs know we stole our stuff back. Get moving."

Molly went back and got the others so they could enter the warehouse and see if any food was left. They cautiously entered and immediately saw several dead bodies strewn about the place. All had been shot and their weapons and ammunition pilfered. Molly and the other two searched the area for food or any other items the team needed. They were very disappointed in the results of the search but did find two large bags of rice, a bag of cornmeal, and dozens of loose cans of food that were dropped by the crew that raided the warehouse.

Molly searched each body and found several magazines for AR-15's and a couple of Glock magazines. She then asked Jack to check the pickup trucks outside to see if any of them were in running condition. Jack was only gone for a few minutes when he came back driving an old Chevy pickup truck. They loaded their booty into the bed of the truck and drove to the other warehouses. All of the food had been taken, and only the hardware and home furnishing warehouses were full of goods. They checked the trailers, and all had been opened and looted.

They gave up the search and sped away before anyone arrived. They were very disappointed that they didn't find a cornucopia of food and medical supplies.

Molly wasn't sure who was the bad or good guys at the warehouse, but she knew damn sure she wanted to get away from there before she found out. They still had an hour before daylight, so she asked Jack to drive to Warren Air Force Base, which was only a mile and a half away from the Walmart warehouse.

They drove without headlights as they skirted around what appeared to be huge bunkers meant for storing high explosives. Molly looked on her map and thought it was odd that an Air Force Base didn't have long runways for airplanes. All they saw on the base was a collection of buildings and unusual structures.

"That sign says 90th Missile Wing USAF. Could this be an ICBM launch facility?" Molly asked.

Jack replied, "I don't know if we'll find out but they had a lot of people here, and that means they had to feed a lot of people. Let's began searching for the commissary and Post Exchange to see if anybody left some food for us."

They inspected half a dozen buildings before they found the cafeteria. What they saw shocked them. At the back of the building where the food was stored, there were several burned vehicles and over a dozen skeletons of dead soldiers. There had been a major firefight at the back of the cafeteria. There was evidence of several explosions in the vehicles, and the back of the building was riddled with bullet holes. Molly asked Jack to check out the back of the trucks while she went into the cafeteria with Carole.

The scene wasn't much better inside the cafeteria. They saw tables were overturned and chairs were thrown willy-nilly. There were hundreds of bullet holes in the walls and serving line. Molly searched the storage room while Carole searched the kitchen. Jack came into the storage room and told Molly that the trucks had been full of food when they were hit with some type of explosive and all of the food burned.

"Jack, did you dig down below the charred food? Cans won't burn, and there could be some good food deep in the piles. We will check in here and then come out and join you," Molly said sternly.

Jack was pissed at himself for not thinking of that. "Sorry I should've thought of that. The pile of rubble and burned cans is horrible looking, but there could be some usable food at the bottom of the pile. Molly, you know, most people wouldn't think of that. Good job."

Carole found a small stepladder and searched the cabinets over the cooking area. As she hoped, there were several institutional size cans of baked beans, green beans, and other vegetables. It wasn't much, but it was an excellent addition to their meager supplies. Molly and Carole hauled their discoveries out to the pickup and joined Jack as he searched through the charred remains in the truck.

Molly saw several shovels and rakes leaning against the building across the parking lot and retrieved them. She gave Jack a rake and a shovel, and then Carole and Molly dug into the second truck. As expected most of the canned goods and dry goods had been burned and were worthless; however, the bottom 2 feet of the stack had undamaged cans. They pitched the first layer of unburned cans thinking that those had been exposed to intense heat. Molly checked the sell-by dates, and most of the cans still had time left. She also knew that most canned food was good to eat for many years after the sell-by date.

"You do know that canned goods that aren't damaged nor have bulging cans can be eaten for several years after the expiration date. They do lose a little bit of nutritional value but not enough to concern us. This is a treasure, look Carole. There are some canned meat and plenty of veggies," Molly exclaimed.

Jack called out, "Hey, Molly. You're right. There are dozens of boxes of good canned goods at the bottom of this mess."

They loaded the pickup with their newfound food supply and hid it in one of the maintenance buildings. They spent the rest of the day moving from building to building searching for anything they could use without much success. They gave up searching and traded up pulling guard duty while the other two slept.

Cole parked the Blazer in a stand of trees and overgrown brush close to the Cheyenne Country Club where their first meet up location was scheduled for that night. They checked out several buildings for supplies without success. The buildings had been ransacked, and several had suffered severe fire damage.

"This won't make a good home base for us; it's too close to Highway 25 and the center of town. It looked good on a map, but let's head over to Lake Terry. It's only a quarter of a mile further west, but that could make a big difference," said Cole.

183

They had just begun walking when they heard gunfire coming from the northeast. There were only a few shots and then silence.

"That was only about half a mile from here. God, I hope we can find a peaceful place to hide out around here," said Brat.

Cole urged them to move on. "That's why we need to find our long-term hiding spot at least a few miles away from the city. These people have survived one winter and didn't do it by luck alone. I would hazard to guess that 50 percent of the survivors killed people and stole their food. The other 50 percent are very well hidden and hard to find."

It only took a few minutes to walk over to Lake Terry. Cole was disappointed when he saw there wasn't much cover around the lake. There were only two small maintenance buildings on the west side of the lake and nothing resembling a house for half a mile. The only good news was the brush and grass had grown in the last year and a half, which would help them move around without being seen. They all agreed that Lake Terry would do for a short time but didn't have enough cover for them to hide long term.

They searched two more lakes northwest of Lake Terry and found a similar situation as they found at Lake Terry. The lakes were teeming with fish and wildlife but had no cover and certainly no place to live. Cole looked at the map and saw another decent size lake northwest of their position. Cole jabbed his finger into the map. "This is the last lake of any size on the western side of Cheyenne. It's about two and a half miles from here, so let's get to walking."

They were walking on the backside of the subdivision when Bill spotted two men walking toward them waving a white flag. Cole gazed at them through his binoculars and saw it was actually a man and a woman. "They look friendly but be ready for anything. Bill this is exactly the situation where someone could be killed trying to be nice. These people could walk up on us waving their white flag in peace and suddenly shoot us down. There could also be snipers just waiting for us to get close enough."

Bill had a frown on his face as he spoke. "Do you ever run into good people? We were fortunate to find you and your group, Cole. Mary and I would probably be dead if we hadn't run into you."

"Bill, I guess it does seem that way lately, but you didn't meet some of the nice people that we met and lost along the way. Never give up on finding good people because one day it would be nice to find a nice community to live in and put down roots. I'm worn out from fighting and traveling," said an exhausted Cole.

Brat gave Bill a hug. "Bill there is plenty of good people out there; they are just afraid to show their heads thanks to a few thugs and criminals. Now let's see what these people want from us."

The man and woman walked up with their rifles slung on their shoulders and their palms extended upward. The man said, "We're not here to hurt you. We just want to know what you're doing in our area."

Cole answered, "We are on our way to our home in Oregon and need a place to stay the winter. We are exploring the area northwest of Cheyenne. We don't mean you any harm, and if we're not welcome, we'll move on."

The lady answered, "That depends on what skills you have. We have an opening in our community for a doctor or nurse. We also need to add to our security force. We are very picky about who we add to our group since there are so many bad people out there. Frankly, we saw your AR-15's and a woman in your group carrying one of the rifles. We don't see many armed women traveling through our area. The thugs and criminals tend to use and abuse women and certainly don't give them guns."

Cole laughed aloud which startled the two people. "This fearsome lady warrior is my wife, Brat. While Brat is still in training, she is a better warrior than most men are. Bill is a young lad that we found along the road and are training him in survival skills. He and his wife joined our group several weeks back. We've traveled here from Kentucky and have had our share of troubles and misfortune.

185

We have met some wonderful people and killed some horrible people. I think we have the skills, determination, and morals to benefit any group that needs us. I guess that's up to you to decide. What do you need to know?"

The man shook Cole's hand. "I'm Tom Jones, and this is my girlfriend, Betty Gant."

"This is Bill, my wife Brat, and I'm Cole Biggs. We are very glad to meet you."

Tom went on to say, "We belong to a group of people who control the western side of Cheyenne. Another friendly group like us controls the southeast part of Cheyenne. A criminal called John Smith and his gang controls the rest of Cheyenne. We have fought many battles and currently have a truce with the thugs. We know they will eventually begin their raids once more, and we are using this peaceful time to strengthen our forces and increase our arsenal to defend against them. Come with us to our headquarters, and you can meet our leadership Council to see if we are interested in you and you are interested in joining us."

"Let us have a brief discussion and then we will give you an answer."

They had a very short discussion and decided to follow the two to their headquarters.

Their headquarters was only a half a mile southwest and was located in an abandoned Best Western Hotel. Cole noticed several times that people were looking at them from inside homes and businesses. Several had rifles pointed at them. Tom stayed busy waving at them to make sure they knew everything was okay. They arrived at the headquarters, and two guards met them at the door. The guards asked for their weapons.

Cole waved the guards back. "We might as well turn around and leave now because we're not giving up our guns. The last time we gave up our guns to a nice group like you we ended up becoming slaves at their work camp. That's never going to happen again. So you have a nice day, and we will be on our way."

Tom said with urgency in his voice, "Cole, please stay and meet with us. I think we have a lot in common and you might want to become part of our group. Guards, let them pass with their weapons. I'll be responsible for them."

Cole asked, "Are your people allowed to have weapons?"

Tom answered, "Of course they can have weapons. We don't have soldiers. Our people fight our battles."

They went to the lobby of the hotel and entered one of the meeting rooms. At the back of the room was a man in a wheelchair. The man greeted them with a hearty smile. "Hi, I'm Bob Branson. I'm the leader of this motley crew. Let's get started by telling each other a little bit about ourselves. I'm from Western Idaho and was part of a survivalist group along the Oregon border. We had been preparing for years for the eventual shit hit the fan scenario. Several of my friends and I are ex-military and had enough rank to have friends that worked in the Pentagon. A few of them tipped us off about the potential for the attack that occurred.

Our main group has restored law and order to Idaho and parts of Oregon. Last I heard, we'd sent teams down into California to eliminate some slavers. I was part of the team that left Oregon almost six months ago to check out the middle of our country. We were in a damned old DC3 airplane that crashed about 30 miles north of here. That's how I got the bum legs. All of our equipment and the rest of my team perished in the wreck. I have not been in contact with the homegroup since the wreck. It also appears that someone is jamming the shortwave and other long-range radio signals. Well, that's how I got here. I'll have Tom tell you our story that starts with when I got here. Now tell us your story."

Cole was surprised the man was from the Idaho/Oregon area. "Before I start telling our story I have a question. Are you familiar with a survivalist group called the Mountain Men?"

Bob laughed and replied, "Of course I am, I'm one of the founding fathers of the group. What do you know about the Mountain Men?"

"I was born in Oregon and lived there until about a year ago. The group I was with became part of the Mountain Men. I've met Zeke and the other leaders out in Oregon. My mentor and friend, Joe Harp, became the Mountain Men leader for southwestern Oregon. The Mountain men sent a large group of us down into Northern California to wipe out a group of slavers. That's where I met my wife and several other people. We were captured by the slavers and flown east to be sold to FEMA. FEMA put us to work in mines and farms. We escaped and have been trying to get home to southern Oregon for many months."

Bob slapped his leg. "Damn it's a small world. I never met Joe Harp, but Zeke has told me about him in the past. Your group was one of our strongest groups when I left to come here. We need to get you and your family back home to Oregon."

Cole was excited and asked, "Can you contact the Mountain Men so they can get a note to my mom and Joe that I'm still alive?"

"No son, we can't. All of our equipment was destroyed in the wreck, and someone is jamming all radio signals. Our government appears to have totally disappeared. We've only seen a couple of military jets in the air since the shit hit the fan. I'm sorry that we can't help you. I am pleased to say that our little community here would like to have you join us. Now before you answer, I need to let you know that we're in a war with some thugs in Northern Cheyenne."

"Bob, I've been trained by my mentor Joe, Earl, a Marine, and my friend Wes to infiltrate the enemy and kill them in hand-to-hand or long-range tactics. I excelled at Zeke's sniper school, and I have tried my best to pass on my training to my team that's here in Wyoming. I will have to ask them to decide if we stay, but my guess is it will tickle them pink to stay here with you," answered Cole.

Bob shook Cole's hand and said, "I hope your crew decides to stay with us. I think we can be a big help to each other and I have a selfish reason for wanting you to stay. I want to get word back home to my wife and kids that I'm still alive. I would love to travel with you when you do leave but traveling these days in my condition is almost impossible, so I'm working on making the trip easier. Why don't you go round up your crew and have your meeting, and then come back here for a home-cooked meal? Even if you don't join us, we are well stocked and supplied and can help you find a place to spend the winter. Now go find your team."

☆

Chapter 15

Jack surprised everyone by being against joining the new community. "I'm just not sold on joining another community that has an ongoing fight with a large group of thugs. We deserve a break from this stuff."

Jack's pigheaded behavior pissed Molly off, and she wasn't afraid to let Jack know it. "Jack, you do know that we're stuck here a thousand miles from home with no place to live and not much food. We need some friends. There hasn't been a week gone by since we left the camp that we haven't been in a fight or had to defend ourselves. We need these people more than they need us."

Everyone but Carole had spoken to Jack trying to convince him to change his mind. They all knew that the vote would be 7 to 1 in favor of moving in with the new community but also knew what an ass Jack could be when he didn't get his way. Finally, Carole had enough and spoke her mind. "Jack, what the hell is wrong with you? We don't have food. We don't have a lot of ammunition. We don't have a warm place to stay this winter. If you have some ideas on how to fill these three needs let us know now or get off your high horse and join the rest of us with a smile on your face. That's all I've got to say about that."

Jack's face drained of all emotion and color for this was the first time that Carole had ever chewed his ass out. "But Honey...," was all he could muster.

"Don't honey me until you get your brain in gear and stop resisting what the rest of us want to do."

Jack's face had regained its color and was starting to turn a bright red. He stuttered the next time he talked. "Darling, I'll do what you want me to do. I just feel that there's too much danger in joining that group of people. I would continue to fight it if I had a better solution, but I don't. I surrender and let's move in with them. And see I'm smiling."

Molly thanked Jack for changing his mind. She then focused on Cole. "Cole, while I'm in favor of moving in with them, I do have some reservations. We need to remain low-key and not try to solve all of their problems at once. Now don't bite me, but Cole you tend to take on other people's problems too readily, and that could get us in deep trouble. Let's join them and do our fair share of the work and fighting but no more."

Cole didn't like what Molly said but knew she was right. He started to speak up when Brat interrupted. "Honey, you know she's right, and you need to agree with her and promise you won't make unnecessary sacrifices."

Cole choked down what he was going to say. "Yes dear, you and Molly are correct, and I promise to do better in the future."

Brat punched him on the arm and said, "That was too easy, you're trying to pull something on us. Just remember, if momma ain't happy, ain't nobody happy. Keep that in mind Buster."

"Yes dear."

Brat pinched him on the side and watched him try to get away. "I'll keep an eye on my husband, and I promise you that I will keep him out of trouble."

They stowed their gear in the Blazer and their new, old Chevy truck and drove the short distance to the new community's headquarters. Cole introduced the team to Bob's people and announced that they wanted to join the group. Bob and Tom were pleased with the decision, and Bob asked Tom and Betty to take them around and introduce them to the rest of the community. Since they had arrived before breakfast, Tom took them into the community cafeteria and introduced them to everyone being served breakfast that morning.

Before Tom could start the meeting one of the women raised her hand and asked why Molly and Brat had pistols strapped to their hip and their AR-15's shouldered. Cole turned to look at his wife and Molly and saw two female warriors wearing men's shirts, jeans, boots, and tactical vests. Each vest had numerous pockets for magazines for their weapons, a bayonet, and other miscellaneous gear. The women had their hair in ponytails and wore a baseball cap. Even as short as Brat was, she struck a fearsome pose.

Cole answered the lady. "I'm sorry it took me a minute to answer because I'm so used to my soldiers being dressed like this and armed for combat at all times. The short lady, Brat, is my wife and Molly is her cousin. They are equal to any of the men in our fighting unit in hand-to-hand combat and marksmanship. Molly's specialty is infiltration and elimination of enemy threats. Brat is one of our best snipers. All of our soldiers dress like this when we feel there's any threat present. We always keep our pistols on our hips. I must admit that Brat and I place our pistols under our pillows while we're sleeping."

The woman responded, "I like that and wish my husband and Bob would train us women to fight. I don't even have a gun."

There were three scheduled times for every meal so that there were always guards posted. The three schedules aided people tending to vital programs and processes throughout the day.

The people were very welcoming and glad to see the new recruits. Molly noticed it first but didn't say anything until Brat whispered in her ear. "Molly have you noticed that there are two women for every man in this group. There are also more children than one would expect for a group this size. I'm afraid to ask Tom, but I think we need to know why."

Molly replied, "Brat, I'm pretty sure that the ratio of women to men is the result of a year of fighting between these groups. I'll also bet that the women aren't pulling their weight fighting. I haven't seen any of them pulling guard duty. I'll also bet that the extra kids are from families where the parents were slaughtered or kidnapped by the gangs."

Brat wondered if they'd made a good decision joining this group. "Molly we need to get some answers quickly. Whatever they've been doing isn't working, and we're going to get caught in the middle of it."

After Tom introduced them to all three scheduled breakfast shifts, it was their turn to eat. Betty was working in the cafeteria, and Tom went to visit with her for a few minutes leaving the team alone. Brat told the group about her and Molly's discussion. "I'm not saying we need to leave here, but we really need to find out how they have been running this place and why they're losing so many people. Cole, I know I told you not to take on more than our share, but this fight needs to end now. The thugs need to be exterminated in a quick and thorough action without many losses on our side."

Cole gathered his thoughts and placed his arm around his wife's shoulders. "Honey, I've been thinking those same thoughts since the first time we heard about their fight. We need an overwhelming attack on the criminals and thugs that wipe them out quickly and efficiently. I think that we need some big assed bombs like those that Joe used to wipe out a bunch of thugs in Medford Oregon. Joe taught several of us how to make bombs from fertilizer and diesel fuel. He also taught us how to make bombs from other common household chemicals. Let's nose around and learn a lot more before we upset their applecart."

While they had their discussion, Tom found several of the leaders in the community to help him find jobs where Cole's group could best contribute to the community. Mary was assigned to their nursery so she could stay off her feet. Carole took over their small medical unit and was pleased to see that it was stocked very well. Madison joined Carole in the medical unit and was a big help to Carole in reorganizing that group. Bill was assigned a job working with their cattle ranching group.

Tom asked Brat and Molly if they wanted to work in the cafeteria, nursery, or schools. Molly took umbrage to the implied suggestion that they weren't qualified to work on a security detail or pull guard duty. "Tom, I know you didn't mean to insult us, but we planned to work on your security team and also help with any hunting or fishing that needed to be done. We also expect to fight alongside our men against those criminals over in Cheyenne."

Tom was surprised and was slow to answer, which gave Cole an opening. "Tom I can speak from experience that you're about to lose this argument if you go against what these two women are trying to tell you. In our group, everyone above the age of 12 pulls guard duty and defends our group against all attackers. The women tend to be our best snipers and are equal to most of the men in a firefight. I personally think that this could be a weakness in your group. It's easy to see that you're short on manpower and not utilizing womanpower. I hope my comments don't upset you, but I'm just talking from my experience."

Cole expected Tom to be upset with what he said. Instead, Tom was nodding in agreement, as Cole talked. Tom waited until

Cole was done talking and then answered. "Cole I agree with you 100%, but we have a very influential priest who is against the women pulling guard duty or fighting. He doesn't even want them to handle guns. So far he has a large enough base of people that support him that we haven't pushed the issue."

That gave Cole food for thought. "Do you have any men that are exempt from fighting?"

Tom looked down at his shoes as he responded. "I'm ashamed to say that we do have men that have never been in one of the battles. They always have a reason not to fight, and they are the biggest supporters of the priest."

Cole replied, "In our community up in Oregon, everyone had to fight, and everyone had to work. There were no exceptions. If anyone refused to fight, we threw them out of the community. Tom, it's evident that your community is faltering quickly. You've lost half your men and most of your fighters. Just from your words, I would guess that almost half of your remaining men don't fight."

"Cole, that's a pretty good guess. What would you do to turn the situation around?"

Cole looked over at Molly and Brat. "Ladies what would you tell Tom he needs to do to get the women sharing the load in securing this community?"

Molly stood up as she waved her hands excitedly. "I would have a town meeting to let the town know that you are approaching a dangerous situation where you could be overrun at any minute due to your lack of fighting people. Then I would say that you are taking volunteers from the men and women who currently don't fight to take combat training and guard duty training. I would guess about half of your people will come around and take the training. We will let the women know that Brat, and I will give them their basic training, and then Cole and some of your better fighters can give the women advanced training."

195

Bob and Tom were somewhat in shock as they mulled over what they'd heard from Cole and his team. Bob looked over at Cole with a glum look on his face. "Cole, you and your team have just said exactly what I've been preaching to these people ever since I arrived. After the priest pushed against me with all of his followers, I gave up thinking I would try again. I firmly believe that this community will not exist this time next year if we continue with our present effort.

With that in mind, I plan to address the community and let them know that if I am to stay the leader of this group, we will begin implementing changes that will make our community stronger and more able to resist the criminals in Northern Cheyenne.

Tom, Cole, Brat, and Molly, I will need your support and help. Cole, I'm not forgetting the rest of your team because they will be an integral part of making the improvements we need. Tom, I would like you and Cole to gather your top three people and prepare for several meetings today and tomorrow. I'm afraid those thugs are planning an attack in the near future."

Cole looked around the room and saw several new people and a man dressed as a priest. Tom introduced everyone to Cole, and his people, and then Bob took over the meeting. "I have explained to Cole and his people that this is my leadership Council and that while I make all the final decisions, I take advice from the people in this room. Now to get to the point, I firmly believe that the criminals in North Cheyenne are planning a devastating attack very soon.

I have said ever since I arrived in that broken down crashed DC3 that we need to better utilize our manpower and resources. With that in mind, I plan to ask for volunteers from our ladies and men to take training to pull guard duty and to prepare to fight to protect our community. I..."

The priest and two of the members began yelling at Bob that this was impossible and immoral. They continued yelling for a minute before Bob banged his gavel. They still didn't calm down, and Bob yelled at the top of his lungs. "Shut up, or I will remove you from the chambers."

The priest and his two supporters sat back down in their chairs and were quiet. Bob raised his hands for silence and continued. "This is something that I am not doing lightly or without forethought. Less than half of our men are prepared to go into battle to protect this community and none of our women. We are outnumbered three to one. I will ask for volunteers from the women to train for combat. I will also require that every man except Father Bryan and Pastor John began taking combat training."

Father Bryan stood up and demanded to speak. "We cannot force people to fight against their will when we should be making peace with these people. After all, we are all God's children."

Cole raised his hand to speak, and Bob gave him the floor. "Father, I totally understand where you're coming from; however, God also tells us that God helps those who help themselves. The Bible also says an eye for an eye and a tooth for a tooth. I know that I can't trade quoting Scripture with you because I will lose, but you need to realize that you personally are going to get everyone in this community killed if you don't allow the people to fight for themselves."

Father Bryan shook his fist at Cole and said, "I won't have my people killing people even if they're bad."

Cole quickly responded, "These people aren't just bad they are evil. They have kidnapped, raped, and degraded the community's women. They have killed over 70 of your men and sold young children into the sex slave market. These people must be vanquished, and you must help Bob with the mission, if not, you are supporting the evil people north of Cheyenne."

Bob thought Cole had gone a bit overboard but entirely agreed with what he said. Bob interrupted the argument and said, "The time for arguing is over. Father Bryan, I will be holding meetings with the entire community to cover the changes in our policy. Anyone who can't commit to the change will be given a week to gather their things and move out of our community. Father Bryan, that includes you. There are millions of empty homes around our country, and surely, they can find one that suits them. I cannot in good faith go forward and have a few of our people sacrifice their lives so three-fourths of the community can sit in safety while the others die. Our new motto is "Everyone works, everyone fights." Now, Father Bryan, if you can't go along with that, you are free to leave with your people that don't want to fight for our community. I have changed my mind on waiting on the meetings, and we will have our first one as soon as this meeting is over. I want to make sure our people hear what I have to say from my own mouth.

Tom, please have the evening shift and anyone from the third shift that is currently awake report to the cafeteria for a community meeting. I will cover the changes with them."

Father Bryan stood up and pounded his fist on the table. "The community voted you in, and they can vote you out as our leader."

Bob answered, "Yes they can; however, I can assure you that most of the people currently fighting for this community will then withdraw their protection from the non-fighters. You would be on your own. In the event you encourage people to vote me out, the community is doomed. If that happens, the rest of us will pull out and start a new community elsewhere. This is not a threat; it's a promise. If the others won't fight, we can't win so why stay here. Then, Father Bryan, you can walk over to the criminals and ask them to be peaceful and see how far you get."

"You wouldn't do that."

Bob smiled as he replied. "You damn tooting I will. Father, you just don't get it. Those criminals will have you hanging upside down from a cross with your guts spilling out on the ground. They will kill anyone suspected of having been a leader in our group and enslave the others. Go ahead and make good on your threat and see what happens to you personally."

Father Bryan suddenly was very quiet.

The meeting went exactly as Cole expected. About a third of the people cheered when they heard the new rules and another third booed. The others saw no change at all for them because they were already fighting and pulling guard duty. That made two-thirds of the crowd happy that they were to receive training and could protect their community. Several of the men in the crowd tried to goad the priest into fighting with Bob. The priest stayed silent.

Bob introduced Cole, then Cole gave a brief overview of the training, and skills the people would be taught. Then Molly and Brat gave an overview of the specific training the women would receive. Bob was shocked when most of the women flocked to Molly and Brat and signed up for training on the spot.

The men were an entirely different situation. About half of the men who didn't fight were either too lazy or afraid of dying. The others weren't wild about learning to fight but did understand that if they didn't fight, they could all die. Cole saw that only a little over 50% of the men were in the line to sign up for the training. He walked over to the others who were mulling around hoping the priest would say something to them. Cole waved his hands and gathered them around him. "As you all know, I'm new to the community and am learning more about your group every day. I have to say though I'm a bit confused that this many people don't think the community is worth fighting for. Please tell me why you don't think the community is worth it."

One of the priest's most ardent supporters answered, "We do think the community is worth fighting for and must be saved. We just don't believe that a man should be forced to fight if it's against his religious beliefs."

Cole shrugged and stepped up close to the man. "Let me understand what you're trying to say. Am I correct in saying that you're not willing to die to save the community, but you're okay with others dying to save your sorry ass. Do I have this right?"

The man stuttered and stumbled for an answer. "Now that's not what I mean. Many of us have led very peaceful lives and want to continue living in peace. We are not going to kill others to obtain peace."

Cole took another step into the man's face. "Did you hear anything that Bob said a while ago? The people who will be fighting will not lay their lives on the line to save your sorry ass. You and anybody that thinks like you need to move on now before you get the rest of us killed. If the other great people of this community weren't fighting the criminals, you would be a slave in the field, and that pretty wife of yours would be a sex slave for the gang. You disgust me."

Bob overheard the conversation but didn't get there in time to join in. He caught Cole off to the side. "Cole I totally agree with you, but we need to tread a little lighter until this soaks into these assholes."

"Bob, I know you're right, and I'll behave myself in the future. Now you see why I'm not the leader of a large group or will never become a politician. I can't stand mealy mouth assholes that won't stand up for themselves or fight for their beliefs."

☆

Chapter 16

Cole asked for a meeting with Bob and Tom to make some suggestions on how to help make the community safer until they could get everyone trained. Bob and Tom were very interested in hearing what Cole had to say; however, a couple of their right-hand men weren't as enthusiastic. Bob turned the meeting over to Cole and Cole covered several important points. "Please don't take offense at some of the things I'm going to bring up because these suggestions come from my experience back in Oregon.

We need to make sure that there are no spies in your group. We need to make sure that the thug's spies only hear what we want them to hear. We must quickly train snipers to enable us to decimate the thugs efficiently and quietly from a safe distance. I can teach your mechanics how to make suppressors for the rifles. We also need to make some explosives, which I can also teach you to make. We must be able to wipe this threat off the face of the earth quickly without losing any of our own people."

The group balked at first about the possibility of having spies in their group. Bob calmed them down. "Hold your horses there boys. You know darn well that we've been concerned that the enemy was always one step ahead of us. You've all met some of the captured thugs, and they aren't geniuses or military tacticians. The reasonable explanation is that there is a spy in our group."

Bob's team begrudgingly agreed to put a plan together to find the spy. Next, they worked on how to detect the enemy spies and to neutralize them or feed them with misinformation. Bob assigned Cole to train the snipers and asked one of his men to facilitate the manufacture of the suppressors.

One of Bob's men asked, "Cole what kind of explosives are you thinking of?"

Cole remembered that Earl and Joe had effectively used the combination of ammonium nitrate and diesel fuel to blow up several depots, ammunition dumps, and a gang's headquarters. "Unless you have a better idea or some Semtex or C4, I recommend we find some fertilizer, diesel fuel, and some blasting caps. If you can't find blasting caps, I know how to make some using bullets."

Bob's man replied, "We have everything you need but only have a handful of blasting caps. We just didn't have anyone with the balls to make the stuff for fear of blowing themselves to smithereens."

"Bob, please find someone that I can train to make the stuff. It's easy to make if you have the right ingredients and very safe until you add the blasting caps. Even mixed up together the mixture will burn but won't explode. I won't be around forever, and I'm afraid your people will need to know how to make the stuff for future thugs and criminals."

"Tom, find two volunteers and incentivize them to be Cole's bomb makers. Cole, I now understand why you were chosen to be the leader of your band. You have been a major asset and have helped us move forward many months in just a few days."

Cole blushed and looked up at Bob. "I'm only good at what I do because I had excellent mentors. Joe, Earl, and Wes taught me everything I know about military tactics, killing, and general mayhem. They tried to teach me how to become a man, and I can only hope they succeeded."

The days passed quickly turning into weeks. There had been several raids by the enemy on the outskirts of the community. The raiders had taken all the food, ammunition, and weapons from the homes. They also took able-bodied men and women to use as their slaves or to sell to the slavers. The community increased its security and added several more guards to its perimeter to get ahead of the raiders. Cole knew that something had to be done quickly or the loss of manpower through attrition would take them to a critical point of no return. He met with his training team and had them focus on developing a special operations team to take the fight to the enemy.

The training proceeded much better than either Bob or Cole had hoped. All except for a handful of people had now passed their basic fighter training and were well into the next phase. Cole and Brat taught sniper training and hand-to-hand combat to the men and women. Molly taught hand-to-hand combat, infiltration, and enemy elimination. Molly called it enemy elimination because the Priest and his followers balked when Molly called it throat and nut cutting. Jack and the others assisted in the training and were crucial to its success.

Cole had trained two men and one woman to be bomb makers. He instructed another dozen in the art of placing the bombs and escaping before blowing themselves up. They now had a secure building that contained over 4,000 pounds of the ammonium nitrate and over four dozen small 1-pound bombs and two dozen 10-pound bombs. They would make up anything larger for special assignments. The people handling the explosives were sworn to secrecy, and no one in the general community knew about the bomb depot or manufacturing facility. Cole took his team several miles away for each test of a bomb. His team got a kick out of blowing shit up.

Cole watched as Molly trained her infiltration team and was amazed at how professional they looked. He waved at Molly to give them a break and for her to come over to talk with him. "Molly you've got them working like a finely oiled machine. That little blonde is deadly with her knife, and the tall brunette could take down any man in this group. What do you think about us taking them on a little trip to Northern Cheyenne and creating a little bit of mayhem?"

"That sounds like a good idea. We'll never know how good our team members are until they are tested in battle. What's on your mind and how much trouble are we going to get into?"

"I thought that Brat, you, and I would lead a team up to the northern edge of town to make them think there is a new group in town that wants their territory. We will set up a longer-term situation where we have intermediate attacks on them and steal their supplies. What are your thoughts?"

Molly thought for a minute. "I think we should scare the hell out of them by killing one or two and killing them in such a fashion it scares the daylights out of them. The priest and some weak minded people won't like this, so I'll have to pick my team carefully so that I get my toughest people. What do you think?"

Cole squeezed Molly's arm. "That was a bit more than I was thinking, but I like it. I know Tom has some compound bows in the armory. How about getting half a dozen of those and let's train some of your people to use the bows. We will make some arrows that look like old Indian arrows and maybe even dress up like Indian gangbangers to scare the shit out of these people."

"I like that a lot and I think my guys will like it."

Cole asked, "When you say guys, how many of them are actually men?"

"Well, the truth is that I only have about four men who can walk across the floor without tripping on their feet and do pretty well in the training sessions. I hate to say it, but the cream of the crop was probably killed in the first few months of battle or has been promoted to leadership in the community. I'll have these four and maybe another four men ready in about a month to take on the enemy in a covert action. The girls I selected out of the larger training group are ready now to go into battle. Don't get me wrong they're not Navy SEALs, but I'll guarantee you they can whip that gang's ass up in Northern Cheyenne."

"Molly, keep this plan between you, Brat, and me. I want you to train your team hard over the next two days with the bow and arrows and be prepared to move out Thursday night. I plan to tell Bob and Tom that we're going out on a training mission. If this mission succeeds, I'd like to see how many three-man teams..."

Molly interrupted him with a scowl, "I think in this case you mean three lady teams."

"Now don't go all PC on my ass. Out in the field, everyone is going to be a guy or man, and there's not much I can do about that. The important thing is that your ladies can kill those men north of Cheyenne. After supper, I'd like to meet with you and Brat to work out some details. I want Brat to set up an overwatch with her snipers to make sure there aren't any unpleasant surprises while your ladies sneak in and slit some throats. Oh sorry, I mean slit throats and shoot some arrows up some thugs asses."

Cole caught his wife while they were cleaning up before supper and gave her a brief overview of what he planned to do. Brat was excited that her team was going to get to use their training. "Cole this is just what we need. My team is getting bored shooting at targets and needs to be challenged. You told me 100 times that there is no way to tell if a sniper will squeeze the trigger when the rifle is pointed at a living breathing human being. We need to sort these people out quickly and find the real snipers."

205

"Damn, you were listening when I was giving that training to you and Molly. Seriously, you're right, even the toughest hard case can have trouble killing someone when they're not an immediate threat. Okay, let's go to supper and then get back here to meet with Molly."

Cole filled Brat in on his plans for Molly's team to infiltrate several sections of Northern Cheyenne and quietly kill a large number of the gang. The infiltration teams would leave American Indian gang signs to confuse and strike fear into the local gang. Molly filled Brat in on her thinking about how to use fear to weaken the gang's hold on Northern Cheyenne.

Molly wanted Brat to place four sniper teams around Northern Cheyenne to kill a minimum of five thugs each after Molly's team had come back from its mission. After Brat's team completed their mission, they would all fade away and meet back up north of Cheyenne.

A short while later, Cole met with his demolition and special ops teams to cover their assignment. He only told them that they were going on a training mission that would include some live fire on the enemy. He told them to gather three times their standard load of explosives and enough food for five days. After the meeting, Cole held his team leads back and told them to load a thousand pounds of the explosives in the back of Cole's old pickup truck. They all had a perplexed look on their faces. Cole pointed to the explosives and then drew a rough map of Northern Cheyenne on a piece of paper. He labeled the Hilton Suites Hotel with the words Thugs Headquarters and then added in big letters B O O M. Cole turned to look at them. "Do you have any questions about what we're going to do? This is a strictly voluntary mission, but if you don't want to go, I'll have to place you under house arrest until we get back. Not because you've done anything wrong, but because we can't take chances on this mission leaking out to the enemy. How many volunteers do I have?"

Everyone volunteered even though they knew that some of them probably wouldn't be coming back. Molly approached Cole with a wild thought. "Cole, is it remotely possible that you plan to actually eliminate all of the Cheyenne gang in one attack?"

"Anything is possible, but I wouldn't be so bold as to tell people that was my plan."

"Cole, we are setting enough bombs to blow Northern Cheyenne off the map."

Cole took them on a circuitous route northwest of Cheyenne and then back down to the edge of town where they found a ranch just below the Highway 219 and Highway 25 junction that was suitable for their headquarters. Cole sent Brat and her snipers down to their agreed-upon locations to set up and be prepared to take out the enemy when Cole gave the signal. Cole then sent his special ops team into the northern part of the city after the sun went down to place their explosives. Molly's team was the last to leave the ranch since they waited until midnight due to having to carry the bulky compound bows and a large quantity of homemade Indian arrows. Molly had been told to use her discretion using the bow and arrows to kill any thug they caught out alone and away from the headquarters. She was to weed them out without them knowing they were under attack.

Brat had her snipers set up in four locations that were within range of the gang's headquarters and living quarters. Her snipers only had .308 caliber hunting rifles set up as sniper rifles, so 500 yards was about as far as they could stand off from their target and be sure of a kill. Waiting for Cole's signal was the toughest part of the mission for Brat's team. They had all excelled in their training and target practice, and now it was time to find out if they could actually kill the enemy.

Cole's demolition and special ops team placed 5 to 10-pound bombs made of the ammonia nitrate and diesel fuel mixture on over 50 targets. These targets were the vehicles, supply warehouses, and living quarters of the thugs. Cole's spies had informed him that there were no children in the thug's living quarters and that all females present were part of the gang. They took extra care not to place bombs near any of the slave quarters or the innocent citizens of the city. Cole's special ops team oversaw the placement of 10-25 pound bombs around the hotel that doubled as the thug's headquarters and sleeping quarters for the gang's leaders. Cole had given a great deal of thought about this project but wasn't confident that it would do anything more than disable the gang long enough for Bob's small army to attack and wipe out the thugs. Bob was in on the entire plan but wanted plausible deniability if it went sideways. Cole didn't like the politics but was so sure that his people could pull this off that he agreed to handle the situation per Bob's instructions.

All during the night, Molly's team had decimated the thugs on guard duty and attempting to travel out of the city. Dozens of the criminals had arrows sticking out of their chests or their throat slit by Molly's overachieving band of cutthroats. None of her people failed to perform their duties, and each one had numerous kills to their credit. Although Molly didn't know it, she almost single-handedly ended the Northern Cheyenne gang with one slice of her bayonet. Molly and her partner had followed a thug to a small mansion just north of the airport. The thug knocked on the door and entered. Molly and her partner snuck up to the home and looked through the windows to see a horrible scene of debauchery and depravity. Several women were chained to large columns separating the huge dining room from the living room. Another woman was being held down on the bed while she was being raped.

Molly only saw four men in the house. She sent her partner to check the other windows and report back to her. Molly checked several of the windows and saw they were open to let the cool night breeze into the home as expected. Molly's partner reported that there were no other people in the home. Molly whispered her plan to the other woman and then notched an arrow on her bowstring. She signaled her partner, and they let their arrows fly into the two men watching the woman being raped. The other two men were too busy to notice their fallen comrades. Molly pointed her friend to the man holding the woman down, and just as the arrow pierced his heart, Molly grabbed the man who was assaulting the poor girl by the hair and ripped his head back as she slid her knife across his throat. The woman on the bed was too traumatized to thank Molly for saving her. Molly found the keys to the locks and let the other women free from their chains. Molly didn't know it, but she and her partner had killed the gang's leader and his three top lieutenants.

Cole looked at his watch and saw that it was 6 o'clock and the sun was rising in the east. There was just enough daylight for Brat's snipers to select and kill their targets. He picked up his walkie-talkie and gave the signal to begin the mayhem. All of the bombs had timing devices that were set at different times depending on Cole's goals. The first bombs took out all of the gangs sleeping quarters, vehicles, and supply warehouses. Those bombs went off between 6 o'clock and 6:05. The bombs killed a large part of the gang. The next bombs went off at most of the guard shacks around the perimeter of the gang's territory. Last, but not least the massive bombs shook the area for miles as it destroyed the hotel and headquarters.

Brat's snipers had a field day shooting the survivors as they stumbled out of damaged buildings and warehouses. She only had one man who couldn't pull the trigger to shoot an unarmed woman. He did kill several of the armed and unarmed thugs. Brat thought this was a huge success and was sympathetic to the man's dilemma even though it forced her to execute the woman. Her snipers continued killing the gang members until there were no more targets. The few remaining thugs blended into the general population, or high tailed it out of town.

Cole watched as the community's troops rolled into the area unopposed. The good citizens of the city ran out to greet Cole's and the community soldiers and treated them like heroes. Cole told Brat and Molly that he was disappointed that they didn't get to terrorize the thugs with the Indian ghost attacks and maimed thugs. Brat looked a Cole in amazement. "We killed them all, and you are disappointed that you didn't get to play with their minds. Are you frigging nuts?"

Molly said, "Cole's just yanking your chain. He planned to eliminate the gang in one attack."

In one day, Cole's team had accomplished what the community had tried to do for the past year. Cole's men and women were only successful because they took the initiative to attack the entire gang and its leadership in one decisive action. The priest and a few others condemned the attacks on the thugs because a dozen innocent citizens were wounded or killed. Bob tried to tell them that the gang had killed hundreds of innocent citizens in the last year and taken several hundred as hostages. He didn't even try to tell them the number of women and children that had been raped and abused. Cole thanked God that the overwhelming majority of the community supported the action and ignored the priest and his followers. This successful action set up the community for many years of relative peace and quiet.

Cole's team now had a safe place to live with plenty of food, excellent shelter, and safety. Mary delivered a healthy baby girl and soon after Cole found out that Brat was pregnant.

☆

Chapter 17

Cheyenne, Wyoming - Eight years later.

Molly hoed the weeds from her garden that morning as the children played in the backyard. She constantly looked up and around her for threats. Her Ar-15 was propped against the fence, and her favorite Glock 17 was always on her hip. Their lives were much better now, but there were still threats from gangs passing through the area and the ever-expanding rogue FEMA empire. FEMA had spread into Western Nebraska, and their closest outpost was only 200 miles away.

The tomatoes, carrots, and lettuce covered a large part of the garden, and the weeds were trying to choke them out. Molly hated gardening but loved the fresh vegetables. She heard a squeal and saw that Jenny had thrown dirt on her twin sister Gemma. Molly yelled at Kate to keep the twins from killing each other. The twins were a handful and reminded her of her cousins that they were named after. Molly and Brat's children all looked alike, and all had red hair.

Kate was Bill's daughter and Molly's stepdaughter. Molly and Bill had married a few years after the six-year-old twins had been born. Molly needed a husband with her new babies, and Bill needed a wife and a mother for his daughter. His wife, Mary, had been killed in a battle with a drug gang a year after delivering Kate. Molly never had a husband and claimed the father of her children was killed in the same battle as Bill's wife.

At first, it was a marriage of convenience, but over the years, Molly and Bill had grown fond of each other. Bill worked in security and manned one of the southern checkpoints for Cheyenne and Molly tended to one of the large community gardens so she could watch her kids.

Bill snuck up behind Molly and said, "Hello beautiful."

Molly turned with the hoe in her hand ready to strike. "Bill, you're home early. I haven't even started supper yet."

Bill pulled her close and kissed her passionately. "Don't worry about supper. Brat and Cole invited us over for supper tonight so the kids can play together. We need to bring some tomatoes and lettuce for a salad to go with some juicy steaks."

Molly fussed at her husband. "Bill, I need to get home and give the kids and myself a bath. We've been playing in the dirt all day long."

Brat yelled at her sons to come in to get ready for supper. "Joe, Deacon, and Charlie get your butts in here right now before I have to come and get you. The boys were seven, six, and four and Brat was pregnant again. They both hoped for a girl. Cole wanted a little girl so bad he had offered to trade one of his boys to Molly for one of her girls. He told everyone he was just joking.

Brat spent her days teaching physical education and self-defense to the high school students with her kids close by in the same school. Cole was the head of security for Cheyenne and frequently employed Molly and Brat to train new recruits.

Brat saw the boys trying to outrun each other to the back door and laughed at how much they looked like their father but had red hair as she did. She made them undress in the mudroom and then sent them to the bathroom to shower.

Life changed quickly for the better after the gang in Northern Cheyenne had been exterminated. Cole and his team kept finding reasons to stay in Cheyenne, which was easy after most of the women became pregnant. Molly lived with Cole and Brat until she married Bill, so the kids were raised as brothers and sisters. Brat had tried to convince Molly not to marry Bill since Molly didn't love Bill. Brat wanted Molly to stay until she found her true love. Molly knew deep inside that she had missed her chance at true love and it was becoming weird living in the same house with Cole and her cousin.

The community had installed generators in the spillways of several of the reservoirs and found enough spare electrical parts to get several of the local wind turbines back in operation. They now had electricity, running water, a sewage system that worked, and more than enough cars, trucks, and farm equipment in service to restart modern civilization.

Bob had a team of engineers working on several prop-powered airplanes and even had a team constructing a crude refinery to make gasoline. The burned businesses and homes had been razed, and the city was thriving. There had been several attempts by gangs to attack the city, but all attacks were ineffectual against Cole's militia. The Cheyenne Militia kept the peace and doubled as the police force.

During the last few months, the community had come to grips with the fact that the rogue FEMA group would soon try to overrun them. Cole's spies brought home information daily about the buildup of troops, supplies, and heavy weapons. The community leaders had been working on contingency plans to deal with the upcoming attack by FEMA for over a year. The sad news was that no one thought that the community could prevail against FEMA.

Cole walked in the door and surprised Brat by coming home early. Cole usually stayed at work and didn't help much with preparing for company. Brat thought this was unusual as she wrapped her arms around her husband. "Honey, is this a special occasion?"

"Babe, I need to fill you in on the status of our FEMA reaction plan. Tonight I'll be telling Molly and Bill that we have implemented phase 1 of the plan and are halfway through the implementation of phase 2."

It took Brat a minute to remember what little she knew about the plans. "Honey, I thought these plans were only to be put into effect if we're in imminent danger from an attack by FEMA. Oh, shit. The volunteers who headed west to start our sister community were really part of phase 1 of bugging out of here. Tell me the truth."

"Yes dear. FEMA plans to attack in the next 30 days. We have ramped up our efforts to evacuate our community and set up new communities on the West Coast. What you haven't heard is that we secretly moved up another 500 people leaving today for Northern California. In two days, we will have a community meeting and come clean with everyone left here. A thousand people moving out of town tend to make rumors fly."

Brat had been curious about the large emergency bug out test being conducted before sunup this morning. The trucks and other vehicles rolling out of town had woken her and the boys up this morning. "So you weren't just monitoring the emergency bug out test, were you? That was the real deal."

Cole hugged his wife and said, "Babe, make sure we have our bug out bags ready to go at a moment's notice. Tom and Jack are going to stay behind and make sure the last of our group gets out safely before setting our doomsday gift to FEMA. Thank God, everyone listened to me two years ago when I told them this could happen. Staging food, supplies, and weapons along the route west will save our asses and make life much easier during the journey. Bob wants the senior leadership to leave the area tomorrow. That means we are leaving tonight to go to the airport where the trucks are staged and be ready to pull out before morning. Now, the good news. Several of us talked Bob into letting our close relatives leave early with us. That means you don't have to worry about Molly and her kids. I have added Molly and Bill to my security staff."

Brat was overwhelmed with everything she heard. "Damn, do we even have time to eat?"

Tears came to Brat's eyes since she was now leaving her home for the last seven years. All of her kids had been born in her bedroom with the help of a midwife, and they didn't know any other home. Brat clung to her husband. "I'm going to dry my tears and put a smile on my face for our boys. Please kick me in the ass if you see me crying again. Those boys need a strong mom and dad to lead them through this crisis. We need to make this appear to be a big adventure for them. Oh, Cole, we're going to get to see your mom and brother soon."

Cole squeezed his wife in his arms. "I don't think I've ever kicked your ass and I'm not about to try now. You are the strongest person I know, and I'm counting on you to help me keep my morale up as we start this new chapter in our lives. I'd be lying if I said I was unhappy about heading to the West Coast. Remember that was our plan for a long time before daily life got in the way. I must caution you that it could still take months for our journey back to Oregon."

The doorbell rang, and Cole opened the door to let Molly and her family into the house. Brat caught Molly and said, "Molly we need to catch you and Bill before supper to discuss an urgent situation. I'm going to send the kids upstairs to play, while we have the discussion."

It didn't take much urging to get the kids to go to the playroom as Molly fixed everyone a drink. Bill found his favorite whiskey in his hand and knew this must be serious. Cole had a stern look on his face as he opened the discussion. "Molly and Bill, I know that you know a little bit about our contingency plans for a potential attack by FEMA. You've taken part in the emergency drills and emergency bug outs. What you weren't told, is that these drills have been preparing our community to relocate to the West Coast where we will be out of FEMA's reach. The large group of people who left under the guise of starting a sister community was actually our first emergency bug out. Another 500 people left this morning for the West Coast. That only leaves about 300 to 400 citizens in our community. Everyone will have been moved out by the end of the week."

The color drained from Molly's face as Cole's words sank into her mind. "Oh my God, this can't be good for us to be in the last group leaving. What if FEMA catches wind of this and pulls a surprise attack?"

Cole was ready for the question. "Molly, don't worry because you and your family are leaving with us early in the morning. We're going to have supper, and then the kids will stay with us while you two go fetch anything you want to take with you beyond your bug out bags. You do have your bug out bags with you don't you?"

Molly was put off by his questioning if she was ready and prepared. "Cole, don't be a prick. You know damn well that I'm always ready and prepared to defend my family and home. Our bug out bags and extra weapons are in the truck."

Cole went on to say, "Bob has ordered his senior leadership to leave by convoy early tomorrow morning. Each of us is allowed to take close family members with us. Molly, you are our family, and I wouldn't leave without you and your family. We need to eat now and then I can fill you in on details when we get to the staging area at the airport."

They were about halfway into their meal when there was a pounding on the door. All of the adults grabbed their AR-15's and prepared for an attack. Cole cautiously answered the door and found his second in command on the doorstep. The man frantically gave Cole a message and left. Cole slammed the door shut. "This is not a drill. FEMA has armored vehicles and attack helicopters swarming towards our eastern border. You will hear the air raid alarms going off any minute, and we have to get the hell out of Dodge, now. Come on people grab your bug out bags and let's get the hell out of here."

Brat yelled for the kids. "Kids get your bug out bags out of the closet and go to Daddy's truck. I'll explain everything later."

Brat's oldest boy said, "Mom I'm tired of these drills. We always end up sleeping in the back of trucks and being bounced around. And Mom the food is no good."

Brat patted the boy on top of the head. "Boys, this is not a drill. We've been planning this new adventure for years. We're going out West to see your grandma, uncle, and a bunch of cousins. This is going to be a fun adventure for you."

It was tough getting to the airport because the entire city was evacuating and heading west. They saw several explosions and helicopter gunships strafing the downtown section of Cheyenne. Cole took several back roads and was finally at the entrance to the airport. Several soldiers were guarding the entrance and one recognized Cole. "Mr. Biggs, follow me to the airfield. Bob has given us orders to make sure you get on the flight."

This confused the hell out of Cole, but he waved back at Bill to follow them. The airfield was only a half-mile away, and the

217

soldier parked his SUV next to one of the three DC3s that had their engines warming up. Tom ran over to Cole's truck with several men who were ready to load Cole's families gear on the plane. Tom said, "Cole our plans have changed since FEMA surprised us with this attack. We have three DC3s ready to go, and you and your family will get on this one. Bob wants the senior leadership as far away from here as possible before FEMA shuts down the airway and roads. Goodbye and good luck. I hope to see you on the West Coast soon. Bye."

The first DC3 taxied to the runway and stopped. The pilot made one last check as he revved the engines. Suddenly the plane lurched forward and picked up speed. DC3s are taildraggers, and the plane was halfway down the runway before the tail came off the ground. Then the plane slowly climbed away from the runway and made a quick turn to head west. The plane that carried Cole and his family then taxied to the runway and made the turn into the wind when all hell broke loose. An Apache helicopter fired its machine guns at the DC3 that had just taken off, stitching the side of the plane with a dozen bullet holes. The Apache flew past the aircraft and made a wide turn to make another strafing run. Before he could line up on the DC3, Cole could see tracers from the community's antiaircraft battery of .50 caliber machine guns. Several of the twin .50-caliber machine guns zeroed in on the Apache with devastating accuracy. The helicopter lurched as smoke billowed from the engine and then crashed into the side of the control tower. There was an explosion, and the helicopter fell to the ground.

Little Charlie and Jenny woke up during the attack and thought it was some type of celebration like their Independence Day event. They oohed and awed at the fireworks and were disappointed the show was over when the helicopter crashed to the ground, and it was over.

The DC3 that had been attacked lumbered on into the early morning sky and was soon out of sight. The passengers on Cole's DC3 said the Lord's Prayer and sent their thoughts and prayers to the crew and passengers of the first DC3. Cole's DC3 struggled to get

218

off the ground and used every bit of the runway before its nose headed skyward. Cole looked towards the cockpit and saw several crates. He wondered how heavy the contents were because there were only about 20 people in the plane. Then he wondered what was in the crates.

All of the children were soon fast asleep as the plane's propellers droned on. The airplanes hadn't been outfitted with seats, so they all sat on the floor as they had done years ago when they were captured and flown to Kentucky. Cole looked around and even saw some 5-gallon buckets with rolls of toilet paper nearby. "Does this remind you two of anything?"

Brat laughed and poked Cole in the ribs. "Yes, that flight from Northern California to Kentucky was horrible. Having to poop and pee with just a sheet separating you from everyone else was the most embarrassing thing of my life. I do remember that you enjoyed having your head on Molly's lap for most of the trip."

Bill looked at Molly as his face turned red. Molly kicked her cousin's foot. "Cole had been hit in the head and was barely alive. If I'd wanted him, he would be the father of my children today. I'm glad I passed on him to find the man of my dreams."

Molly squeezed Bill's hand and laid her head on his shoulders. "I do remember that Cole's head was in Gemma and Jenny's lap as much as mine. So regardless of which one you are, you shared in caring for him. Seriously, this trip is so much better and different since we are flying to freedom and not slavery. Now Cole, how soon will we be in Oregon? Are we there yet?"

Cole replied, "Brat, I'm placing you in charge of your wayward cousin. Slap Molly around if you have to but get her under control. I don't know if the rest of the crew can stand much more of her antics."

219

Bill was put off that he thought Cole had indicated that Bill couldn't control his wife. "Cole, don't you think that I can control Molly?"

Cole saw the expression on Bill's face and immediately understood the situation. "Bill, please don't take offense. I assigned the duty to Brat to save you some grief and heartache. Brat doesn't have to sleep with Molly. Besides, Bill, you need to lighten up some because we're always joking and fooling around. You've been part of the family for many years and have to get over any jealousy or territorial issues. Molly is like my big sister, and I always treat her as such."

Bill moved over closer to Cole and whispered. "I'm sorry, but I can't help but feel that Molly only settled for me because you weren't available. I'm always afraid she'll leave me if another man comes along."

Cole patted Bill on the back and replied, "Look dumbass, you are married to one of the most beautiful, courageous, and wonderful women on the face of the earth. Be happy and ecstatic that she chose you to be married to and not someone else. Love her, treat her right, and get all the shit out of your head or you will lose her. Now get back over to her and give her a hug and a kiss. Wait, Molly is a strong-willed woman, and no man can handle Molly. Love her, treat her right, and hold on for the ride. Brat is the same way."

Molly woke Cole when she noticed the plane was descending. Cole woke with a start and saw Molly shaking his shoulder. "Hey, Tiger, why are you waking me? Is something happening?"

"Yes the plane is descending, and it scared me."

Cole looked out the windows and strained to see what was ahead of the plane. It was still dark, and all Cole could see were clouds in the airplanes running lights. The ride became bumpy as

220

the plane descended through the clouds. Cole got up and walked to the cockpit. "Hey, Jim are we landing?"

"Yes, we are, Cole. Due to the weight of those damn crates, we couldn't take on a full load of fuel and make it the whole 950 miles to Medford airport. We're going to land long enough to refuel, which should give you time to stretch your legs and make a pit stop at a real bathroom. I know the ladies don't like our buckets and sheets for privacy. Don't worry, everything's going to plan except I've lost communication with the other two planes. We haven't had long-range communication since the bombs dropped, but even my short-range walkie-talkie didn't raise them a couple of hours after takeoff. Don't worry they're probably just out of range because they're flying faster than us."

The pilot woke everyone up before the plane started its approach so they wouldn't be frightened or get injured. He told everyone to brace themselves the best they could in the event they had any issues. The landing turned out to be very smooth, and they taxied to the terminal and stopped by a large tanker truck to refuel. The DC3 that had been shot at by the attack helicopter was on the other side of the tanker being refueled.

The pilot came into the passenger area and said. "Ladies and gentlemen, we will be taking off for Medford, Oregon in 30 to 40 minutes. You are free to leave the plane to stretch your legs or use the bathrooms at that blue building on the left. You must be back here before the plane takes off or we will leave you here. Make sure you understand that the plane will leave without you."

Bill saw that the kids were fast asleep. "Ladies, why don't you take advantage of their bathroom while Cole and I watch the kids. I think they will sleep through our stay here and won't be a problem."

Brat and Molly hurried down the steps to the tarmac and ran over to the bathroom. Cole got Bill's attention. "Do you mind if I run over to the other DC3 and see how they are doing?"

221

Bill told Cole to hurry up and make sure he didn't miss the flight. Cole ran across the tarmac and around the tanker to the DC3. He saw the pilot and several of the other senior leaders of the community talking. Cole walked up and said hello to them. "That was one hell of a scary situation when that helicopter started shooting at you. Was anyone injured?"

Cole hadn't seen the four bodies lying on the utility cart. He saw them and shook his head. "Who did we lose?"

One of the men spoke up. "The co-pilot, George Ahearn, Charles Green, and his wife. Cole, it's much worse than that. We lost the other plane. We're not sure what happened, but they lost oil pressure in one engine climbing over the mountains. Then suddenly we heard the pilot yell that the other engine had died. We heard him screaming as they dropped from the air and then saw a tremendous explosion on the side of one of the mountains. Due to the confusion and our sudden departure, we're not sure who was on the plane. All I know is that Bob's family and Tom's family are not on these two planes. Cole that makes you our leader until we determine if Bob and Tom are alive. What are our orders?"

Tears came to Cole's eyes as he realized the two of his closest friends might be dead. "There are no changes in orders. Just get us to Oregon safely. Is there anything I can do, or anyone can do to help with the shot up plane?"

The pilot replied, "No, there's not much left to do. The bullet holes look horrible, but they did little damage to the plane. One bullet pierced our right wing tank, and we lost quite a bit of fuel. That's why we also had to stop here and refuel. One of the mechanics fixed the fuel tank and riveted some patches over the largest holes in the fuselage to cut down on the cold air and noise. We are good to go now. Better get back to your plane because we will be taking off in 10 minutes.

Oh, I forgot to tell you that the surprise for FEMA was a success. We may never know the outcome, but Bob called to tell us that thousands of the FEMA troops were destroyed along with their equipment. The radio cut out before he could finish."

Cole laughed and then said, "Two tons of explosives makes a great welcoming committee."

Cole climbed the steps into the plane and saw Bill was sleeping with his head on Molly's lap. Molly winked at Cole as he stepped over her legs to sit down beside Brat. Brat slumped down on the floor and laid her head on Cole's lap as the plane lurched away from the fuel tanker.

☆

Chapter 18

Cole daydreamed as the airplane hummed its song produced by the spinning propellers and friction of the air as it cut through the clouds like a knife. Cole thought back to the good and bad times he'd encountered since the shit hit the fan. He reminisced about Cloe, Joe, and Cobie as well as his mom, Jane, and his brother, Charlie. It amazed him that Charlie would now be a grown man and might have a wife and children. He hoped that his mom and her husband, Ben, we're doing well and couldn't wait to see them again. His mind then wondered how Cloe and Brat would get along. He desperately wanted them to be good friends and hoped that she had met and married a good man. He then laughed to himself because he knew that whoever the man was, he'd better be strong, or she would run right over him.

Cole nodded off and saw Grandma in his mind. Cole heard himself say, "Grandma, is that you?"

Dear Cole:

Cole this is Grandma speaking. You have come a long way since America suffered the Apocalypse. You listened and learned from my grandson and kept my son alive even when he tried to get all of you killed by his piss poor decisions. What I'm getting to is that you don't need me anymore and I'm a busy woman, so this is the last time that you will hear from me.

Yes, ghosts stay busy. Some haunt people in your world and others try their best to help people. I've been helping you for almost a year while helping Joe at the same time. You two have kept me busy. I'll check in from time to time, but you two are ready to be on your own.

I began helping your brother Charlie a few months ago due to his girlfriend issues interfering with his survival training. Yep, he hooked up with a very strong willed young lady and needs guidance on how to keep her in check while still advancing his skills. You had the same problems, but you were stronger than Charlie was. Cloe is a handful, but Charlie loves her. He will tame her down with my help. Yes, your brother and Cloe are thicker than fleas on a Coon Dog.

Well, goodbye, Cole. I'll miss talking with you.

Love Grandma.

Cole nodded off again and heard himself say, "Grandma don't leave me now. I still have to deal with Cloe and Brat meeting each other. They could be friends, or it could be a large explosion."

"Cole, what explosion are you talking about? You were talking in your sleep weren't you?" Brat asked.

Cole chickened out and didn't want to tell Brat his thoughts. "I must've been thinking about those large explosions back when we blew up the north Cheyenne gang. I fell asleep reminiscing about the good old bad days. Brat I love you with all of my heart, and I don't know if I'd want to live if I didn't have you by my side."

She pulled his head down and kissed him, and then whispered to him. "Even though you don't know which of the twins I

225

am, do you still love me? What if I knew who I was and had regained my memory? Would you want to know which one I am?"

"Babe I've given that a lot of thought over the years, and I'll love you regardless of who you are. I'd be lying if I didn't say that I'm a bit curious, but that's your secret to keep or share with whom you want to."

Brat kissed him again and whispered in his ear. "I've known since about six months after the explosion who I am. I was always afraid that I couldn't come to grips with one of us being dead. To help stay sane, I took on both personalities. For almost 8 years, I have had all of the traits of Gemma and Jenny. I thought at first that when we made love, took a shower together, or shared our deepest thoughts that you would think you knew who I was. I'm going to let you guess which of the twins I am, and then I will tell you the right answer."

Cole was very nervous and began sweating as he contemplated finding out the answer to the question that had bothered him for years. He pulled Brat's face down to his, smothered her in kisses, and then whispered the answer into her ear. Brat smiled at him and kissed his ear as she laughed and then whispered the answer into his ear. He quickly sat up and wrapped his arms around her. Molly had been watching and whispered to them, "You told him, didn't you?"

"Jenny, I've known all along it was you. You couldn't fool me."

Brat laughed at her cousin and said, "Molly you're just guessing and trying to trap me into responding. Only Cole and I will ever know who I am. I just told Cole a few minutes ago that I have been both of us for eight years. Deal with it, Molly. You will never know the answer. Oh you can guess, and you might be right, but you shall never know for sure."

The first DC3 landed about 20 minutes before the one carrying Cole and his family. The first plane shocked the town's people and all of the Mountain Men present at the airport. When the pilot told the crowd around the plane that Cole Biggs was on the next plane, they erupted into cheers. The control tower used their walkie-talkie to contact Joe Harp and Cole's mother to let them know that Cole was alive and landing at the airport in a few minutes.

It was early in the morning when the squelch on the walkie-talkie woke Joe and Cobie. They were in disbelief for a few minutes until it sank in and Joe immediately called Charlie and Cloe to inform them. They were all crying as they dressed and jumped into their vehicles for the 30-minute drive to Medford airport. Cole's mom, Jane, was in shock when she learned that her son was still alive. It took several minutes for her husband to console her and get her to get dressed to go meet her son. No one had told any of them that Cole had brought his family with him.

Cole's plane touched down at the Medford airport, and the passengers stumbled down the stairs on their way to the ground. They laughed and cried because they were either back home or safe at last from attack from FEMA. Cole was immediately mobbed by several of his old friends when he saw Butch's wife, Peggy. Butch had been with Cole when Molly, the twins, and Cole were abducted. The slavers killed Butch and left his body to rot. Cole hugged Peggy and told her about how Butch had given his life to save the others. Peggy had remarried and had several children but still cried as she remembered losing Butch.

Cole introduced everyone to his wife and children and Molly and her family. He had just finished the introductions when several trucks flew across the tarmac toward them. Cole saw his brother, Charlie; get out of the truck followed closely by his ex-girlfriend Cloe. They were running to him. Charlie was now larger than Cole and almost knocked Cole to the ground as he picked him up and hugged him. Just as Charlie sat his brother back on the ground, Cloe began hugging and kissing Cole on the cheek.

Cole barely recovered himself and asked, "Hey little brother, did you and my old girlfriend get out of the same truck at this time in the morning?"

Charlie put his arm around Cloe's waist. "We've been married for seven years and have a passel of kids, dogs, and cats. Did you ever find a woman that would have you?"

Brat was standing close to Cole and placed her arm around Cole's waist. "I'm Cole's wife, and we have been married for eight years. We have three little boys, and one of them is named after you, Charlie. I am so happy to be here with you and finally meet Cole's family."

Brat hugged Cloe and then Charlie just as two more vehicles pulled up. Cole hugged his brother and said to the group, "I think everyone's here and it'll be hug and kisses time for now, but let's get together up at the cabins and tell all of our war stories with a beer. Charlie, I am so happy that you and Cloe got married, and you two are so happy. Brat and I have had a wonderful life and are looking forward to our new lives here. Oh, there's my mom, Ben, and Joe."

Jane and her husband, Ben, ran up to Cole and hugged him. Jane couldn't stop crying as she hugged her son. Joe and Cobie stood there waiting for Jane to let go of her son. Then Joe gave Cole a bear hug with tears in his eyes. "Son, we're going to have to have a beer while you tell us about your adventures out East. Who is this beautiful woman next to you? Damn, she looks a lot like Cobie."

"Joe and Cobie this is my wife, Brat, and those three urchins are my sons."

"Joe is the tall one, and he is named after you. The middle one is Deacon, and Charlie is the short guy. Joe before I forget, your dad and his wife, Carole, should arrive in a couple weeks on one of our convoys. He told me to send his love and let you know that he survived. Oh, and a big surprise, Madison will arrive with them."

Cobie gave Cole an icy stare. Joe choked up and said, "I never expected to see Dad again. Honestly, I didn't think my dad had what it took to survive. So, Madison is alive. Tell me that story later."

Cole quickly answered, "We all had problems along the way, but your dad kept finding ways to survive. He has learned and grown a lot since I first met him. Oh, I want to add that I've been talking with your grandma at least once a week for the last eight years. I know people think I'm crazy, but Agnes Harp has saved my life and my family's lives many times with her wisdom and advice."

Charlie did a double take when he heard Cole's statement. "Cole we need to talk after all this celebration is done."

Cole saw Molly and her family standing out of the way. Cole walked over to Molly and Bill and brought them and the kids over to meet the rest of the people. "I want you to meet Molly who is Brat's sister cousin. Molly is a fierce warrior and has saved my butt many a time. She has been my right hand on the battlefield and a trusted and dear friend. This is her husband Bill and their three children Gemma, Jenny, and Kate. They are our family."

Everyone welcomed Molly and her family into their families. So many conversations were going on that it was hard to track what was being said. Cobie saw the dazed look in Brat's eyes and came to her rescue. Cole looked at Brat as she hugged Cobie. "Holy shit! Not only does Brat look like Cobie, but she also looks like Cloe. "

The three ladies all looked at each other and Cloe said, "Brat is very beautiful, but she doesn't look like mom and me. How did you get the name Brat?"

Cole laughed and said, "That is a long story, and we need some breakfast before we start telling you how I married twins and saved the world."

Brat laughed and punched Cole in the side. "He did marry twins; however, that stuff about saving the world is bullshit, but he did save Molly's and my world."

The End

Thanks for reading the Cole's Saga series and please don't forget to give it a great review on Amazon. Remember to read my other books on Amazon.

AJ Newman

Remember to push the **Follow** button below the author's photo on Amazon to follow AJ Newman and be notified of new books.

If you like my novel, please post a review on Amazon.

To contact or follow the Author, please leave comments @: https://www.facebook.com/newmananthonyj/

To view other books by AJ Newman, go to Amazon to my Author's page: http://www.amazon.com/-/e/B00HT84V6U

A list of my other books follows at the end.

Thanks, AJ Newman

*

Books by AJ Newman

Cole's Saga series:
Cole's Saga
FEMA WARS

American Apocalypse:
American Survivor
Descent Into Darkness
Reign of Darkness
Rising from the Apocalypse

After the Solar Flare:
Alone in the Apocalypse
Adventures in the Apocalypse

Alien Apocalypse:
The Virus
Surviving

A Family's Apocalypse Series:
Cities on Fire
Family Survival

The Day America Died:
New Beginnings
Old Enemies
Frozen Apocalypse

The Adventures of John Harris:
Surviving
Hell in the Homeland
Tyranny in the Homeland
Revenge in the Homeland

Apocalypse in the Homeland
John Returns

AJ Newman and Mack Norman:
Rogues Origin
Rogues Rising
Rogues Journey

A Samantha Jones Murder Mystery:
Where the Girls Are Buried
Who Killed the Girls?

AJ Newman and Cliff Deane:
Terror in the USA: Virus: Strain of Islam

These books are available on Amazon: AJ Newman

To contact the Author, please leave comments @
www.facebook.com/newmananthonyj

–

☆

BOOKS BY MY GOOD FRIEND CLIFF DEANE

Vigilante Series:
Into The Darkness   Into the Fray
Pale Horse   No Quarter
The Way West   Indian Territory

The OORT Chronicles:
RED ALERT: MISSILES INBOUND
The Oort Plague

Virus: Strain of Islam (with AJ Newman)

Cliff's books are available on Amazon @

https://www.amazon.com/Cliff-
Deane/e/B06XGPG7YZ/ref=sr_tc_2_0?qid=1514742671&sr=1
-2-ent

Cliff Deane's Amazon page

https://www.amazon.com/Cliff-
Deane/e/B06XGPG7YZ/ref=sr_tc_2_0?qid=1514742671&sr=1
-2-ent

About the Author

AJ Newman is the author of 27 science fiction and mystery novels and 4 audio books that have been published on Amazon. He was born and raised in a small town in the western part of Kentucky. His Dad taught him how to handle guns very early in life, and he and his best friend Mike spent summers shooting .22 rifles and fishing.

Reading is his passion, and he read every book he could get his hands on and fell in love with science fiction. He graduated from USI with a degree in Chemistry and made a career working in manufacturing and logistics, but always fancied himself as an author.

He served six years in the Army National Guard in an armored unit and spent six years performing every function on M48 and M60 army tanks. This gave him great respect for our veterans who lay their lives on the line to protect our country and freedoms.

He currently resides in a small town just outside of Owensboro, Kentucky with his wife Patsy and their four tiny Shih Tzu's, Sammy, Cotton, Callie, and Benny. All except Benny are rescue dogs.

Made in the USA
Middletown, DE
16 July 2023

35218584R00139